Murder in the Charlestown Bricks

By Tom MacDonald

Other Dermot Sparhawk Novels by Tom MacDonald

The Charlestown Connection

Beyond the Bridge

The Revenge of Liam McGrew

ISBN-13: 978-0-9967332-3-6

ISBN-10: 0-9967332-3-X

For
Cheryl Bliss Waxman

1

THE FIRST TIME I saw her was at an AA meeting in Powder House Square in Somerville, not far from Tufts University. She was accompanied by a man with a silver ponytail and a craggy face, who wore tan Dickies and work boots. She was wearing blue jeans and a red button-down shirt, with the shirttail untucked and falling freely around her backside. Her face was tanned, her cheekbones were full, and her nose was somewhat prominent, but by no means unattractive.

She sat in front and crossed her long legs. I studied the back of her head, the slender neckline and level shoulders. Her chestnut hair shined with highlights, and the highlights looked natural, not from a bottle. Everything about her looked natural, the way she talked and gestured, the way she listened and waited, it all seemed unaffected. The ponytailed man handed her a cup of coffee and sat next to her. She raised the cup and grinned. I don't know if that was the moment I fell in love with her, but it might have been. I know my heart jumped, and it hadn't jumped in quite a long time.

After the Lord's Prayer she left through a side door.

The next time I saw her was at the Sparrow Group in the South End, near Titus Sparrow Park. She was wearing white pants and a black pullover with the words Carlisle Indian School written in red. The Sparrow Group attracted Native American alcoholics, mostly working men and women—house painters, window washers, restaurant people, ironworkers. The meeting's founder was Ike Fivekiller, a full-blooded Cherokee from Memphis who drank with my father. How Ike ended up in Boston, nobody knew, and he wasn't saying. She whispered something to him, and Ike tilted his head back and laughed. I found myself smiling, as if her magnetism reached across the room and put joy in my heart.

The building had oversized windows that allowed the sun to brighten the room, most notably the gold in her hair. She raised her face and she pushed up her sleeves and let her arms dangle at her sides. Did she look my way? The man with the silver ponytail came in and gave her a hug, the type of hug a girl gets from a devoted father. Seeing the chaste embrace elated me. When I looked for her after the meeting she was gone.

The next time I'd see her would be in a jailhouse.

2

JUST BEFORE MIDNIGHT on a mild May evening, just moments after the Red Sox beat the Tigers in Detroit to break a four-game losing streak, I heard a police siren racing by the front of the house. I folded the newspaper and looked out the window to the street below. A cruiser sped into the projects and stopped on O'Reilly Way, followed by an ambulance. Probably an overdose. I didn't pay much attention. Hearing a siren in the Charlestown bricks is like hearing bells in a church steeple. You expect it at regular intervals. I was about to go back to the newspaper when I saw an unmarked car drive to the scene, and it was moving.

This was no overdose.

I laced up my sneakers and left the house, and when I got to O'Reilly Way a crowd of tenants was gathering on the sidewalks. They lit cigarettes and spoke in hushed tones, the gossip already starting. I saw Officer Partridge, wearing a jacket and tie, standing next to the unmarked car, busy on his cell phone. The man next to him also wore a jacket and tie. I went up to them.

"Officer Partridge," I said.

"It's Detective Partridge now," he said, hanging up. "I was promoted last month."

"Congratulations," I said. "Who's your rabbi?"

"Superintendent Hanson, of course, but you knew that. He's my guy. For some reason he likes me." Partridge, a tall man with sandy hair and a trim mustache, motioned to the cop next to him and said, "This is Detective Scott McClellan, my senior partner. He's showing me the ropes."

I extended my hand, but McClellan ignored it and walked away.

"What happened in the building?" I asked Partridge.

"Robbery-homicide," he answered. "A junky beat an old lady to death. Did a nasty job on her, really busted her up."

"What's her name? I grew up in that building."

"One second." Partridge looked at his notepad. "Gertrude Murray."

"My God, not Gert." I had known Mrs. Murray my whole life. "I loved that lady."

"I'm sorry for your loss, Sparhawk."

Partridge walked back to McClellan, while I thought about Gertrude Murray. She cared for me when I lost my mother. I was seven at the time. And when my father went on a toot, as in toot aloo Dermot, hello Jim Beam bourbon, Gert was there for me, shielding me from state authorities. How she did it I'll never know. A single mother with three boys, all of them Charlestown crazy, she treated me like one of her own. In the projects, we looked out for each other back then.

The two detectives went into the building, accompanied by the forensics team. I waited outside. I wouldn't leave until they carried her out. At sunrise two morgue men rolled out a gurney carrying the body and brought it to the ambulance, with Partridge and McClellan escorting.

I went up to them and said, "Can I see her?"

"It's ugly," Partridge said.

"Please."

Partridge looked at McClellan, who nodded.

Partridge unzipped the bag and exposed Gert Murray from the shoulders up. Her head was dented, a round dent that could have been made by a flying shot put. Scratches and welts marred her face and throat. The jaw was lopsided. When I was a kid I'd tear baseball cards in half and match the top half of one card with

4

the bottom half of the other, creating a Picasso effect. That was Gert's face, a grotesque distortion.

"What the hell did he hit her with?" I said.

"A bowling ball," McClellan answered, speaking to me for the first time. "To be specific, a candlepin ball. I was about to say at least it wasn't a tenpin ball, but what's the difference? She's dead."

Was McClellan dissing Gert as a way of dissing me? Some cops will do that. They'll taunt you, hoping you'll take the bait.

"Gert kept the ball on a shelf," I said. "She bowled when she was younger."

The thought of a man crushing Gert's head with a bowling ball sickened me, and my stomach started to churn. I walked into the street and with my hands on my hips, shaking my head, pissed. Partridge came over to me.

"Don't do anything stupid, Sparhawk," he said. "We've got the guy, a doper with a long criminal record, and he's going away for life." He paused for a moment, as if reflecting on the scene. "I don't get the drugs. Killing an old lady just to get high? I don't get it."

I couldn't sit in judgment, being a recovering alcoholic myself, so I said nothing. Poor Gertrude Murray, dead in the bricks, all because of a man's addiction. At least they caught the son of a bitch. I was about to leave when Detective McClellan came up to me and extended his hand and said, "Sorry about the tenpin remark, Sparhawk. It was callous of me. I understand you knew the old lady."

"I did. She lived next door to me—"

"Ehhh!" he mocked. "You're too easy." He started back to the unmarked car. I took a step toward him, but Partridge intercepted me and said, "McClellan is nuts, as in PTSD nuts. He saw too much action in the Kandahar region, too damn much. Noggin shrapnel, too. He can't go through a metal detector without triggering the alarm."

"He triggered my alarm, Detective," I said. "Ridiculing Gert like that, I'll put him in the hospital."

"I didn't hear that remark," Partridge said. "Go home."

3

THE NEXT DAY I was eating lunch in Chinatown when I got a call from Buck Louis, my downstairs tenant and business partner. Buckley Louis III, or Buck as he likes to be called, is a practicing attorney who had recently passed the state bar exam, after collecting a sheepskin from Boston College Law School. I poked my chopsticks into a platter of pan-fried noodles and answered the phone. We exchanged hellos and Buck got to the matter at hand.

"We have our first case," he said.

"Shit, that was fast."

"There might be a slight problem." Buck hesitated. "I'm not sure you'll want to take it."

"Why not?"

"The client's name is Victor Diaz."

"Is that supposed to mean something to me?"

"It will in a second. Last night the police charged Diaz with the murder of Gert Murray."

Diaz killed Gert?

"No fuckin' way, Buck. We're not taking it."

"I understand your reluctance." His voice gathered momentum to present his case, to build an argument to get me on board. "Victor's mother is sitting across the desk from me."

"Tell her to sit in the visiting area at Cedar Junction, because that's where Victor will be living for the rest of his life."

"Dermot—"

"I'm not touching it, Buck."

"There are extenuating circumstances. It's not what it seems."

"Give me a break," I said. "Diaz broke into Gert's apartment and killed her. The cops found him standing over her body."

"That's not what happened, not exactly, and exactitude is central to this case. Details, Dermot, this case hinges on details. All I'm asking is that you hear me out before you make a decision. Will you do that for me?"

I hated to be coerced, but when Buck did it, it didn't bother me too much.

"I'll give you ten minutes, no more," I said. "I'm on my way."

I took a cab to the Charlestown Navy Yard, where Buck and I leased space in a warehouse on Pier 3, overlooking Dry Dock 2. We had formed an alliance of sorts, a two-man team that played to our strengths—that's what we told ourselves anyway. Buck handled the lawyering, while I handled the investigating. Our office is located on the ground floor, which suits us fine, because Buck is a paraplegic.

I went into the office.

Buck was sitting in his wheelchair behind a big oak desk, whistling a song I didn't know. His handsome brown face glowed with health, and his nearly shaved head painted a five-o'clock shadow on his scalp. I sat in the client's chair and stared at the exposed ceiling rafters. The whistling stopped.

"Thanks for hearing me out," Buck said. "I know this isn't easy."

"You said something about extenuating circumstances."

"The evidence, Dermot, all I'm asking is that you look at the evidence. If you still think Diaz is guilty, I won't take the case. Deal?"

"Why do I feel like I'm getting conned?"

"The DA's office sent the preliminary discovery package. Read it and tell me what you think." He handed me the report. "You'll see what I mean about details."

I went through the discovery, page by page, studying the pictures and reading the text. The first photo showed Gert's apartment torn apart—framed pictures smashed, cushions cut open, drawers emptied on the floor—the place was a mess, but a methodical mess.

"Diaz was looking for something specific," I said. "You don't dump drawers and slice cushions unless you're looking for something specific."

I continued to read. One photo showed a bloody footprint next to Gert's body. A yardstick indicated it was twelve inches long. The footprint wasn't just long, it was wide, too, the print of a big-boned man. According to the report, Diaz's shoes were free of blood, and so were his socks and pant cuffs. The police found blood on the tiles leading out the rear of the building. Diaz was arrested coming out the front. I stopped reading.

"He didn't do it," I said. "The lack of blood on him proves it."

"The police disagree."

"Do they think Diaz changed his socks and shoes after the murder? His clothes would have been spattered, too. He didn't kill Mrs. Murray."

"And a twelve-inch footprint translates to a size fourteen shoe," Buck said. "Diaz wears size eight. The print was made by a waffle sole, like a work boot. Diaz was wearing running shoes, and the soles were bald."

"Why do they think he's guilty?"

"Keep reading," Buck said.

On the next page I saw a picture of Gertrude Murray sprawled on the floor. Her pockets were slashed open, and, of course, her head was smashed hollow. I looked away and said, "The killer hit her with a bowling ball."

"Broken cheekbone, broken jaw, fractured skull," Buck said. "In my opinion the crime scene is contradictory. The murder looks like a crime of passion, the result of an enraged man who went berserk. But the room looks like it was carefully dissected, the work of a criminal in search of a particular item."

"Fuckin' bastard, I'll dissect *him*." Then I read something that would be a big problem for Victor Diaz. "When the police arrested Diaz, they saw another man running out the back of the building."

"And therein lies the problem."

"Diaz had an accomplice," I said.

"The police think the accomplice committed the actual murder."

I read further.

"Diaz admits there was an accomplice, but he won't name him." I stood and paced the room, a luxury Buck would never enjoy. "He will go away for this, Buck. Diaz was in on the crime that led to Gert's death. He has to pay."

"If that's the case, he should pay," Buck said.

"What do you mean, if? Diaz broke in with another guy, and now Gert is dead. If you think Diaz is getting railroaded because of the accomplice, get him to plea."

"Diaz refuses to plea. He insists he didn't kill her. He also insists his accomplice didn't kill her. Diaz swears that Gert Murray was already dead when they broke in." Buck grabbed the wheels but didn't move. "How's that for an opening statement? Ladies and gentlemen of the jury, Gertrude Murray was already dead when my client broke in to rob her."

Buck was right. It would be a tough sell to a jury.

"You said Diaz has a sheet."

"A long one, but nothing violent." Buck opened a manila folder and began to read. "Car thefts, muggings, B&Es, selling hot merchandise, and then there's the drug stuff. Possession with intent, sale in a school zone."

"I don't like the school zone charge." I took the sheet from Buck and I glanced at it. "But murder seems out of step for him."

"Diaz is hooked on scat, Dermot. He steals for drug money. He just got out of yet another rehab, according to his heartsick mother."

"It's not an excuse."

"The DA is charging him with felony murder. An eighty-year-old woman got her head bashed, and he's the fall guy. Diaz will take the hit on this."

"Where are they holding him?"

"Nashua Street," Buck said. "They booked him in this morning."

"I'll talk to him," I said. "If I sense that he or his accomplice murdered Gert, I'm out."

"Thanks, Dermot," Buck gestured to the door. "I won't hold you up."

In other words, get moving.

4

THE NASHUA STREET Jail is located in Boston's West End, a short distance from the Charlestown waterfront. As I was walking there, sweating in the afternoon mugginess, I thought about the unlikely friendship that developed between Buck Louis and me. Buck is African American, a country boy from rural Kentucky. I'm a half-breed, a city kid from Charlestown. We met at Boston College as freshmen on the football team. Buck played running back, I played linebacker, and somehow we hit it off.

A coach's dream, Buck outclassed the competition with speed, balance, and power. Even if you caught him, you couldn't knock him down. After two days of contact, Buck was first on the depth chart—as a freshman. This was unheard of at Boston College. Doug Flutie didn't see the field until he was a sophomore.

Buck was participating in an Oklahoma drill, a violent endeavor that pitted an offensive lineman against a defensive lineman between two orange cones, with a running back trying to break through. And that's when it happened, the paralyzing injury. Buck landed on his head the wrong way. Soon after the crippling blow, Buck dropped out of school, despite the Jesuits' pleas for him to stay. After that I lost touch with him.

We ran into each other years later in Thompson Square. I didn't recognize him, but he recognized me. We had coffee, got to talking, and Buck told me of his plight. He ended up homeless, living in shelters when he was lucky enough to find a bed, or in alleys when he wasn't so lucky. He told me that he didn't drink or do drugs. He wasn't a charity case, he said, just a guy down on his luck.

Buck came home with me and stayed the night, and then he accepted my offer to move into the first floor of my two-family house. The stability of a permanent address agreed with him. He went back to school and earned a bachelor's degree followed by a law degree, with Jesuits at his side. He also became something of a computer whiz, a skill he used to help me solve two complex murder cases.

Buck and I would sit on the porch and talk about starting a business that would help our neighbors in need, both of us wanting to serve the underserved. The idea seemed like a fantasy at the time, until fate intervened. I came into a boatload of money from an international case I worked on—actually, shipload might be more a more accurate term, shipload as in millions. I live the same way I did before I got the money. Nobody knows. I keep it in a trust, giving to charities and people in need. I used part of it to launch our business, a law practice to ensure justice for the poor. And now we have our first client, a man charged with murdering my de facto mother, Gertrude Murray, a case I wanted nothing to do with.

I walked down Lomasney Way to the Nashua Street Jail, Victor Diaz's current address. I submitted to the rigmarole required of visitors and went through the gate to the netherworld of the incarcerated. I sat in a chair and became one with the gloom. Gray hues dulled the area. Gray walls and gray floors, gray complexions on sullen faces. Barred windows filtered the sunlight, casting vertical shadows across the visiting room, which hammered home the grimness of imprisonment. The place reminded me of the projects, except the locks worked.

Victor Diaz, a wiry man with darting eyes, came in wearing tattered jeans and a white T shirt. Blue tattoos covered his forearms and more tattoos crawled up his neck. A crooked smirk turned his mouth into a defiant sneer, a mime's fuck you. He strutted to the table like an important man, sat in a chair and stared at me. I thought about Gertrude Murray, dead in a city morgue with her skull smashed to pieces, and I almost got up and left. I leaned forward instead.

"My name is Dermot Sparhawk, and I work for your lawyer, Buckley Louis. The attorney-client privilege extends to us. Everything you say to me is confidential and protected under the law. I cannot be compelled to reveal any information you disclose. It would be illegal for me to do so. Do you understand?"

"I know you," Victor said, with no discernible accent. "You run the food pantry. How the fuck can you help me?"

I had relinquished most of my duties in the food pantry when Buck and I opened our law office, but most people in Charlestown still see me as the pantry man, the schmuck who hands out rice.

"Afraid you won't get your money's worth?" I said.

"Fuck you, I don't need this shit."

"Show me your hands."

"Huh?"

"Show me your fuckin' hands, or I'm out of here."

Diaz held them out. There wasn't a mark on them. I got a better look at him under the fluorescent lighting and saw a boxer's face, the tiny scars edging the eyes, the strong nose beginning to flatten. He was in shape, too. His hands were small but strong, and his arms were toned and muscled.

"What gym do you fight out of?" I asked.

"What are you talking about?" He pointed at me and said, "I didn't kill that old lady."

"That old lady had a name, Diaz. And it was Gertrude Murray, Mrs. Murray to you. Did you break into her apartment?"

"Yeah, I broke in."

"Why her apartment?"

"What do you mean?"

"Was it random? Did you target her? Maybe you figured a frail woman like Gert wouldn't put up a fight," I said. "Nothing's easier than busting up an old lady, right Diaz?"

"I never touched her." He feigned indifference. "She was dead before I got in there."

"Did you follow her home?"

"No." He looked at his hands as he spoke. "I knocked on her door but she didn't answer, so I broke in. I was looking for stuff. I checked the freezer. Sometimes old people hide money in the freezer. I went to the bedroom and saw her on the floor. She was already dead."

"Sure she was."

"Are you on my side or not?" he said. "I'm innocent."

"You trashed the place."

"No I didn't, I swear," he said. "The room was trashed when I broke in. Stupid, I should've got out of there when I saw the mess. Stupid, stupid, stupid!"

For the first time he sounded genuine.

"Who was your accomplice?"

"He didn't kill her, either," Diaz said. "Why should I get him in trouble?"

"He's already in trouble for felony-murder, just like you. If you testify together, it could help your case."

"No one's gonna believe us. You work for my lawyer, and you don't believe me. I wish my mother never fuckin' hired you."

I half-respected Diaz's loyalty to his partner, and I was taken by his devotion to the code of silence, which is a highly held Charlestown custom. But he wasn't dummying up on principle. He was protecting somebody. But who? A family member? A close friend? A gang affiliate? I decided it didn't matter who.

"So you stalked Mrs. Murray."

"I didn't stalk her and didn't kill her. I robbed her, that's all." Diaz crossed his arms, and the tattoos merged into a jumble of Spanish graffiti. "Let me ask you something. You liked Mrs. Murray. If you think I killed her, why are you helping me?"

I'd been asking myself the same question.

"Your mother hired us to defend you, and that's what we're going to do."

"You don't give a shit about me."

"Not if you murdered Mrs. Murray, I don't." I got up from the table. "I'll presume you're innocent for now, but if I find out that you or your accomplice killed her, I'm out."

"We didn't do it," he shouted, as I walked out of the room. "We're innocent."

I couldn't get a solid read on Diaz, but there was something about him that felt right— enough that my gut was telling me he was not guilty. I signaled for the guard.

5

I WENT THROUGH security and into the lobby and that's where I saw her, the woman I had seen at the AA meetings. She was leaning against the wall and talking on the phone, fully engrossed in conversation. Tall, lean, angular, she was all legs and arms. Her body was athletic and fit, not curvy. She wore a black pencil skirt with a white silk blouse. On her feet she wore black pumps. Her professional attire contrasted with the casual style I had seen her in before.

Both worked.

I walked up to her after she hung up and said, "I saw you at a couple of meetings this week. Friend of Bill W's?"

"Ah, not really."

Though she hesitated, her body language remained poised. Shoulders back, chin up. Did I violate her anonymity? I looked around. No one was within earshot of us.

"Sorry, I didn't mean to embarrass you," I said. "I'm Dermot. I saw you at the Powder House Square meeting." I waited, no reply. "I saw you at the Sparrow Group, too." It sounded like I was following her. "You were talking to Ike the Indian."

She smiled. "You know Ike?"

"Sure, I know him," I said. "I'm not a stalker. I just sound like one." I laughed nervously. "I was at the same meetings. That's all."

"Okay." She laughed too, thank God. "What did you say your name was?"

"Dermot Sparhawk."

"I'm Cheyenne Starr." Her eyes smiled, crinkling at the corners. We shook hands and she asked, "Are you Native American?"

"Half Irish, half Micmac."

"I'm a Cherokee, from way down in Georgia," she said with an exaggerated southern accent. Now it was my turn to laugh. Without any accent, she said, "Isn't Micmac an Algonquin tribe?"

"Yes, it is. My father was the Micmac. He came from Nova Scotia. The ironworkers called him Chief Sparhawk. I thought they were riding him because he was an Indian, but he turned out to be an authentic chief. I didn't find out until after he died. The booze did him in." *Why was I telling her this?* "I'm sober. I don't drink anymore, not in a long time." *Stop talking, dummy.*

"Of course," she said, touching my arm. "I understand all about alcoholism and recovery."

"Who's the ponytailed man?" I asked.

Her smile brightened and her eyes twinkled again. "My father, I support him by going to meetings."

"You're not an alcoholic yourself?"

"I've never taken a drink," she said. "Growing up with an alcoholic father turned me away from it."

"Wow, good for you," I said. "It didn't work that way for me."

"What do you mean?" She leaned closer and looked me in the eyes.

"I followed in my father's tippling ways," I said, "until I tipped over from an alcoholic seizure in a Martha's Vineyard bar." *Keep it up, Dermot. You're really winning her over.*

She chuckled. "Sorry, I didn't mean to laugh. You are quite funny. But seriously, I'm sorry to hear that."

"Don't be, it saved my life." *Time to change the subject, fuckhead.* "What are you doing here at the jail?"

"I'm out on bail on an electronic bracelet," she said. Now it was my turn to laugh, and she continued. "I'm a student intern.

17

I go to the Tufts grad school for social work." She brushed back her chestnut hair with an open hand. "I'm starting a prison ministry for Native American Indians when I graduate next year. I'm laying the groundwork for it now."

"I'm impressed."

"I've seen the miracle of recovery firsthand, and I want to help others. I'm proud of my Indian heritage." She handed me a card. "I have to run. Give me a call if you'd like."

If I'd like? Was she kidding?

6

FROM THE JAIL I walked back to Charlestown over the Gridley Dam, but I could have leaped over the river I was so excited. When I reached the middle, still giddy about Cheyenne Starr, my cell phone rang. Buck Louis was panting on the other end. His words came in a rush, barely understandable. I asked him to slow down, but he couldn't.

"Some crazy bastard stormed the office waving a gun looking for you."

"What? Are you okay?"

"Yeah, I'm okay. I thought he was going to shoot me."

"You're not hurt." I waited a couple of seconds before I spoke again, in an effort to slow him down. "What did he look like?"

"Oh my God, he is a complete lunatic." Buck rattled off a damn good description, considering his agitated state. "Mid-sixties, buzz cut, crazy blue eyes, huge ears, a squeaky voice. He's after you, Dermot. I had to tell him where you were or he'd have shot me. I am so sorry."

His words clicked faster than a dead battery. I told Buck not to worry, that I'd handle it, and I hung up.

As if on cue, a man in his sixties with buzzed gray hair marched toward me from the opposite end of the locks. When he got closer he picked up speed and threw a wild punch at my head. I parried it past my jaw, but it brushed my cheek. He fired another

19

one and missed. I didn't have the heart to blast him on the chin, so I tapped him in the ribs with a light jab. He buckled like I had hit him with a pickax, doubling over with his hands on his knees. What happened? I barely touched him. He eventually stood up, his face glaring red and snot running from his nose. He looked familiar, definitely a Charlestown guy, but I couldn't place him.

"You're supposed to be a Townie," he said, gasping. "Why are you helping the prick that killed my mother?"

Shit, it was Bo Murray, Gert's felon son.

"When did you get out, Bo?"

"Fuck you, Sparhawk," he said, regaining his wind. "My last day in the can and I find out my mother is murdered. And then I find out you're defending her killer. What the fuck's wrong with you?"

"I won't help Diaz if he killed Gert."

"You won't help him at all, fucknut. If you talk to him again, I'll put a hole in your brain." He raised his shirt, showing a gun. "The same goes for your crippled pal."

"If you go near Buck, I'll shove that gun up your ass and empty it."

"You'll what?"

"You heard me."

"You're gonna regret saying that." He pointed at me. "Another thing, if you ever put a hand on me again I'll crush your skull, fuckin' punching me like that."

"It was a love tap, Bo. You're supposed to be a Townie."

"You're gonna regret saying that, too."

He turned and left the lock.

I hustled down Chelsea Street to the Navy Yard and when I got back to the office, a shaken Buck Louis said to me, "I thought he was going to kill me."

"Are you doing okay?"

"Yeah, I'm fine. Who the hell was he?"

"His name is Bo Murray, Gertrude's son." I went to the cupboard and prepped the coffeemaker. "He just got out of federal prison."

"I didn't tell him where you were until he cocked the hammer. I feel like a rat."

"Don't, he would have found me sooner or later." I started the coffee brewing. "Better to get it over with. You don't want a guy like Bo Murray festering."

"Is he a threat?"

"Hell, yeah, he's a threat. He's soft as shit." The coffee plunked into the pot. "Bo solves problems the old Townie way, with violence. He's been charged twice with murder, but never convicted, which shows he's smart, too."

"What was he in for?"

"An armored car robbery," I said. "Bo's gun jammed. The Loomis guard's didn't. After Bo recovered from the gunshot wounds, he went away."

"My hands are still trembling." Buck held them out. "He aimed at my head. Shouldn't we call the police or something?"

"We don't do that in Charlestown."

"You people are mad," Buck said. "What are we going to do about him?"

"I don't know yet." I thought about it. "We'll stay off his radar for now."

"Pretty passive approach."

"True, but it's best to stay away from a rabid dog, especially when he's frothing. Bo is a killer, Buck, a heartless killer. He is not a man to be taken lightly."

The coffeemaker hissed and beeped, letting us know it was done. I poured two cups, added cream and sugar to both, and gave one to Buck. I saw a folder on his desk with the DA's logo on it.

"More evidence came in." He handed me the legal-size folder. "You probably knew this already, since you grew up in the building with her. Gertrude Murray collected silver coins."

"What are you talking about?"

"Just what I said, she collected silver coins." He sipped his coffee. "She started when she was working at the T in a token booth. After she retired, she kept it going."

"Kept it going how?"

"The stores in Charlestown set aside coins for her, dimes and quarters minted before 1965. Apparently they were silver back then. The police said she's been collecting them for sixty years if you include her time at the T."

"I didn't know she collected coins." Why didn't I know? Gert told me everything.

"The police found silver coins in Diaz's pocket." Buck seemed to be calming down. "They didn't put much stock in it until they found coin-collector folders on Gert's dresser. They were empty, probably for future use. The police are now saying that Diaz demolished the place looking for coins."

"Why didn't I know about the coins?"

"Excuse me?"

"Nothing," I said. "Diaz told me the place was already trashed when he broke in."

"Did you buy it?"

"I thought he was telling the truth."

"When they arrested Diaz, he had a mercury dime, five silver Roosevelt dimes, circa mid-1940s, two buffalo nickels, a wheat-leaf penny, and something called a standing-liberty quarter."

I glanced at the report again.

"He had ninety-six cents when they arrested him?" I shook my head. "Busted for murder while stealing pennies, what a dumb bastard."

"No one said he was smart."

"No wonder he's our client." The idea of stealing coins began to sink in, and I didn't buy it as a motive. Junkies look for quick scores, TVs and computers and phones, things they can sell fast. Coins? I couldn't picture Diaz going into a coin dealership, unless it was to rob the place. "I don't know, Buck. Stealing coins?"

"I thought the same thing, until I did some research." Buck showed me a computer printout. "The payoff is good."

"What do you mean?"

"I looked up the coins Diaz stole. On Ebay I found a 1931 mercury dime that goes for $30. Silver Roosevelt dimes go for $10 apiece, and he had four of them. That's $70 right there. The standing-liberty quarter can fetch as much as $100. That's big dough for a doper."

"Selling coins takes patience, Buck. Diaz is fidgety, itching for a score." Was I assuming too much? "Maybe I'm wrong. Maybe Diaz knows about coins."

"Or maybe he was using them at face value. A bag of dope is cheap these days."

"A drug dealer accepting coins as payment? I don't think so."

"Maybe his drug dealer is a coin collector, or maybe his brother-in-law owns a coin shop." Buck paused. "We can speculate about Diaz all day. What's our next move?"

I finished my coffee and rinsed the cup in the sink.

"I'll canvass the stores in Charlestown and find out where Gert got the coins."

"I'll call Mrs. Diaz and bring her up-to-date," Buck said.

I walked out of the office to Dry Dock 2 and called Cheyenne Starr, but she didn't answer. I left a message and began to canvass on Chelsea Street, starting at the river and working my way to City Square. Most of the businesses were yuppified, or franchised, or corporatized. The cashiers, programmed like cyborgs, robotically processed orders. They were devoid of personalities, barely looking at the customers, let alone making eye contact with them. Were they even human? Would they recognize a silver dime if you handed them one?

I stopped myself and thought: alcoholism. I had slipped into a dry drunk, painting the world in a negative light. The canvassing had gone lousy, and I was feeling sorry for myself, pouting and kvetching, wallowing in self-pity. Poor me, pour me another drink—make it a double. Selfish and angry, I walked away with my head up my ass, holding in my hand a fistful of gimme. It didn't help that Cheyenne hadn't called back. I went into St. Jude Thaddeus Church and sat in the first pew in front of the tabernacle and meditated.

7

BO MURRAY PRESENTED a serious threat. If he came at me I could handle it — maybe — but if he went after Buck, he'd eat him up. Buck was vulnerable, and guys like Bo prey on the vulnerable. I needed to protect him, and with that in mind I made two phone calls, one to my uncle Glooscap, and one to his son and my cousin Harraseeket Kid. Glooscap is my father's half-brother, a full-blooded Micmac Indian originally from Antigonish, Nova Scotia. He is my advisor and my confidant, a trusted elder who shares his wisdom with me.

We set a time to meet at the auto-body shop in Andrew Square. They were waiting for me in Glooscap's office when I got there. Glooscap's pipe, which was an appendage to his mouth, glowed orange with fiery embers. His copper face was stoic and still, as if posing for an Indianhead penny. Kid, on the other hand, was animated. He too had a coppery complexion, but instead of stoic and still, his was expressive, agitated, and chomping for action.

I sat down and said, "I'm worried about Buck Louis." I gave them a thumbnail of Gertrude Murray's murder case. I told them about Victor Diaz, the accused, and Buck's role in defending him. I told them about Bo Murray's threat against Buck. "Buck needs protection."

"Buck is good with a gun," Kid said, "as we well know."

"That shooting shook him," I said. "I don't think he's over it yet, and I don't think he's comfortable carrying a gun. It took a lot out of him, killing that cop."

"It was self-defense," Kid said. "The cop was crooked."

Glooscap blew a plume from his mouth, a smoke signal announcing he had something to say. "What does Buck think about the threat?"

"I haven't told him, yet," I said. "I wanted to talk to you two first."

"His life may be in danger, Dermot," Glooscap said. "You have a responsibility to tell him what is going on."

"I know I do."

We were quiet for a time, Glooscap smoking his pipe, Kid fidgeting with a ratchet, while I sat waiting to hear what they had to say.

"I'll talk to him about a gun," Kid said. "I'll convince him to keep one in his desk drawer as a precaution. Then I'll take a few days off and watch him. If he's in any danger, I'll see it."

"Thanks, Kid," I said.

"I shall call Vic Lennox in Nova Scotia." Glooscap puffed away. "Vic enjoyed the last trip he made to Boston, and he is a good scout. Vic can help Kid defend Buck."

"We'll do shifts. Vic can live with me in the cellar."

Kid lives in my basement, by choice. He loves the sound of sump pumps gushing and boilers clicking on and water draining through pipes. He has turned the place into a subterranean hunter's lodge, with oak paneling, deer antler mounts, a rifle cabinet, terrazzo flooring, and track lighting. He installed dehumidifiers and ventilation fans and an alarm system. It's probably the best space in the house.

"On another subject," I said, thinking about Cheyenne. "I met a woman recently, a Cherokee Indian from Georgia. Her name is Cheyenne Starr."

"The Cherokee are good people," Glooscap said. "And you like her?"

I couldn't answer, because my throat dried and closed. I lowered my head and stared at the floor. I finally managed to say yes. "Oh, Jesus," Kid said. "You have it bad."

8

I HAD A hunch about the scar tissue around Victor Diaz's eyes, so I called the local boxing clubs and asked them if they knew him. Boxing is a dying sport, at least in Boston, and it took only three calls to find him. He trained in Lowell at a gym called D'Amico's Boxing Club. The owner of the club, an ex-pug named Barney D'Amico, answered the phone on the first ring.

I asked D'Amico about Victor Diaz, but he wanted to talk about himself instead. He crowed about his storied boxing career, "a dazzlin' pugilistic odyssey." He talked about his big bouts, "I had Bobby Chacon beat, 'til he knocked me out in the third." He lamented his lost dream of a title shot, "I was slated to fight Arguello in Vegas, but I broke my hand in training, and things went sour gradually all at once. After that I was a spent shell."

It was only after I pressed him on Diaz that he grudgingly switched topics. He said that he'd been training Diaz for three years, and that he liked the kid and thought he had a promising future. I asked D'Amico if I could visit him. He said sure, come on up. I hopped onto I-93 and headed for Lowell.

When I got there, he invited me into his office, a shabby hatch that smelled like old socks and Bengay. He wore crooked glasses held together with athletic tape, and his white hair was tightly cropped and retreating. Yellowing newspaper clippings were tacked on the walls, providing a chronology of D'Amico's career in the ring, which dated back to the 1970s. On his desk were boxing magazines, handgrips, and a parched, dog-eared book written by A.J. Liebling.

He lit a twig of a cigar and dropped the dead match into an ashtray. He seemed pleased to have company, and who could blame him? The gym was empty, except for the cockroaches rolling dice in the corner. I asked D'Amico about Victor Diaz. He tilted his head back and snorted smoke through a nostril—only one nostril allowed passage—and contemplated the question like an emeritus professor who had spent a lifetime teaching the Sweet Science.

"Diaz has been AWOL for a week now, which ain't like him. The boy's not afraid to work." D'Amico nodded as if something came to him. "He's in trouble."

"Big trouble," I said.

"I'm sorry to hear that. He's a respectful kid in his own way, not a punk." D'Amico puffed up a cloud. "Diaz has a tremendous right hand, like a lead pipe. He can take a punch, too, and he ain't scared of getting hit. And blood don't bother him none, his or the other guy's."

"He's in jail for murder."

"What, murder?" He sat up. "No fuckin' way. Diaz is a tough kid, but there's no way he's a murderer?"

"Just so you know, I don't think he did it," I said. "What kind of fighter is he?"

"Talented, tough, ready to learn." D'Amico smoked. "Diaz was hungry for money, so he fought all the time, and he wasn't picky, either. He'd fight anyone I put in front of him."

I thought back to my visit with Diaz at the Nahua Street Jail.

"He seemed secretive about his boxing," I said. "When I asked him about it, he changed topics. I got the feeling he didn't want me to know about."

"A lot of guys are like that," D'Amico said. "But he was in the right profession, I can you that. He's strong as hell and his ring smarts was gettin' honed. He showed promise, so much promise

I thought he was ready to move up in class. Maybe I rushed him too fast."

"Too fast?"

"I put him in with an animal from Bridgeport, a Golden Glover with a good pro record, and the fight was down there in Connecticut. I thought Diaz could hang in there with him, you know, give him a go. And as it turned out he *did* hang in with him, hanged with him real good, but it was a brutal fight, a six-rounder that went to the cards."

"A decision."

"The Bridgeport guy tagged Diaz in the last round. Whammo, a straight right to the chin. Diaz got froze by that punch."

"Did he go down?"

"Nope, he took it standing. The fight ended in a draw, but a draw in the other guy's place is like a win in a neutral setting. Hometown judges, it's the same everywhere. You practically gotta put a guy in the emergency room to get a win. I got jobbed myself five or six times. One night at the Felt Forum I fought a guy from Jersey, Newark I think, and—"

"So the fight ended in a draw," I said, bringing him back.

"Yeah, a draw. It was a major step for Diaz, taking on that Bridgeport guy, but I think it shook his confidence. If anything it should have boosted it, fighting a quality opponent like that."

I love the language of the fight game—"lead-pipe right" "went to the cards" "got froze by that punch" "moving up in class"—it's a language privy to few, too few.

"Was Diaz friendly with anyone up here?" I asked. "A sparring partner? A trainer?"

D'Amico took off his glasses and massaged his scarred eyelids.

"I'm his trainer, his manager, and his sparring partner," D'Amico said, with a modicum of pride. "And to answer your question, Diaz drove up here with an itty bitty flyweight named Juan, who couldn't box for shit, but he had a car if that's what you wanna call it."

"What's Juan's last name?"

"Don't remember."

"Do you have a photo of him?"

"A photo of Juan?" he said. "Of course not."

"Can you describe him?"

"Scrawny, black hair, prison tats." D'Amico relit his petering cigar. "He drove a shit box. I had to jump start it once."

"What kind of car?"

"One with a dead battery," he said.

In the projects, a dead battery doesn't narrow the field. If D'Amico said the car had a good battery, I'd know who Juan was immediately.

"Anything else about Victor Diaz?"

"I can't believe Diaz got pinched for murder, but he done it to himself, no one else." He blew a perfect smoke ring and admired it until it vanished. "You look like a pretty rugged guy. Did you fight?"

"I played football."

"Well, football ain't fighting, friend. When a fighter scores, he don't give the ball back."

We talked a little longer, mostly about boxing, and when I saw an opening, I thanked him for his time and started for the door. Before I opened it, D'Amico said, "Diaz is basically a good kid. Did I tell ya he's got a crucifix tattooed on his back. He's no killer, get him off."

"I'll do my best."

Now I had to find a flyweight named Juan.

9

THAT NIGHT I canvassed in Hayes Square, starting at Uncle Joe's Diner, a Worcester dining car that looked like it once rolled the rails. A blue neon sign glowed in the steamy window, and the smell of fried food wafted from the ventilators. By the time I stepped inside I was hungry.

A young couple drinking milkshakes occupied one of the booths, and a man who looked like a workhand sat at the counter with a newspaper. Sitting in another booth, counting the day's receipts, was the owner, Joe Lally. A lean man with wispy white hair and gold-rim glasses, Joe was a daily communicant at St. Jude Thaddeus Parish. I sat across from him. Without looking up, he said, "Hey, Dermot. The meatloaf was baked fresh today."

"Meatloaf sounds good to me," I said. "Coffee, too."

"Betsy." Joe signaled the waitress. "Dermot wants—"

"I heard him," she yelled back.

"Ladle on the gravy, Betsy." Joe looked at me. "I made the gravy stock from veal bones this morning. We had a veal special yesterday."

Betsy wrote on her pad and went to the kitchen.

"Did you hear about Gert Murray?" I asked.

"Of course I heard." He set aside the receipts. "It's a shame, isn't it, an old lady like Gert getting killed in her own home. Sometimes I wonder about the projects. The drugs, the crime,

32

the violence, nobody looks out for anyone anymore, not like when we lived there."

"Those days are gone."

"Long gone," Joe said. "In the old days you had to get to Mass early to get a seat. Now you have a row to yourself."

"Everything changes."

"It sure does." He looked across Hayes Square to the bricks. "I heard she was killed for a dollar in change."

"Ninety-six cents, to be exact."

Betsy served the coffee and went back to the kitchen. When she got to the swinging doors, a large man clomped through and bumped into her, almost knocking her to the floor.

"Sorry, Betsy," the man said, reaching out to steady her. "Are you okay?"

"I'm fine, Donald."

"You're always so nice to me, Betsy." Donald walked toward us and said, "Hi Uncle Joe."

"Hello, Donald." Joe turned to me and said, "I love Donald, but one of these days he's going to kill somebody he's so clumsy."

"You're awfully good to him, Joe."

"Even though he's got issues, Donald is practically part of the family." He removed his glasses and wiped the lenses with a handkerchief. "This Diaz character, do you know him?"

"Not really. Diaz's mother asked Buck Louis to defend him. Buck and I are partners, so I'm looking into the case. I don't think Diaz killed her." The meatloaf came and I ate a forkful. "The evidence against him is weak. In fact the evidence almost proves his innocence. I want to nail the real killer, Joe. Maybe you can help me." I showed him a photo of the stolen coins. "Gertrude Murray collected coins."

"I know she did." He looked at the photo. "I saved them for her. We get a lot of coins in here, because we don't take credit cards." Joe pointed to the photo. "This coin here, the 1916 stand-ing-liberty quarter, I gave it to her."

"Are you sure it's the same one?"

"Sure I'm sure, the date matches, and it's not every day you see one of these. I saw it in a coin shop downtown. It was marked down to $40, so I bought it for her and let her find it."

"How did she find it?"

"We have a routine—I should say *had* a routine. When Gert came in I would dump the coins on the counter, you know, the coins from the cash register, and she would sift through them. One by one she inspected each coin, and when she found the standing-liberty quarter she gasped with joy. That's my last memory of Gert, finding the silver quarter. Can you believe she wanted me to keep it? She thought it was too valuable."

"Did everyone know she collected coins?"

"I didn't tell anyone, not in this neighborhood," Joe said. "You might as well write 'mug me' on her back."

"You're right about that."

I thanked Joe and got up to leave, dropping a twenty on the table for Betsy.

"Find the killer, Dermot. Find the bastard and drown him in the harbor."

10

THE NEXT MORNING began dark and foggy, with the empty feeling of predawn in the air, except it wasn't predawn. It was nine o'clock. The nightlight stayed on even after I opened the blinds, the drabness winning the day. I started a pot of coffee and the smell of it stimulated my energy. I ate toast, drank a cup black, and read both Boston dailies, filling in the crosswords and Sudoku puzzles, and reading the comics. By noontime the front had lifted and so had my frame of mind. I showered, shaved, dressed, and went to the Navy Yard to talk to Buck.

I passed through Gate 4 at the ropewalk and kept walking toward the harbor. I spotted Vic Lennox on Pier 3, keeping an eye on our office, poised to help Buck if he needed it. Vic was doing his best to look inconspicuous, but he was clad head to toe in faded denim with brass studs and he was wearing scuffed cowboy boots, which would make him inconspicuous in Laramie, Wyoming, not Boston, Massachusetts.

I feigned a nod to Vic, crossed First Avenue to Dry Dock 2, and went to the office. Buck, looking sharp in a tan suit and a pale blue oxford shirt, rolled out from his desk to greet me.

"An eyewitness came forward," Buck said. "Her name is Santa Reyes. She lives in Gertrude Murray's building, down the hall from Gert's apartment."

"I know Santa." I sat at the table and rubbed my eyes with the heels of my hands, hoping to clear the cobwebs. "She's a regular at the food pantry. I'm surprised she talked."

"There's more," Buck said. "New evidence came in from the forensics team. They raised a partial print in the dried blood."

"Was it Diaz's?" I asked.

"No, it wasn't," Buck answered. "The print isn't on file."

"That's interesting," I said, more to myself.

"The police believe the print belongs to the killer, and they are strongly speculating the accomplice is the killer."

"The killer doesn't have a record," I said. I remembered something that Barney D'Amico said about the yet-to-be-identified flyweight Juan, that he was covered with prison tattoos. "This bodes well for our case."

11

I WALKED TO the Navy Yard Bistro, a popular restaurant on the corner of Third Street and Second Avenue, to question the staff. Before I went in I called Cheyenne Starr. Her answering service kicked in and I left another message.

The bistro is a brick-granite-slate structure that dates back to the early 1800s, when the Navy Yard was built. The bistro's owner is John Moore, a lean man with a ready smile and a generous spirit. John is a big Bruins fan, and it is not unusual to see a bruised defenseman or a stitched-up winger sitting at the bar after a tough game. He was standing in the open kitchen area talking to the chef when I came in. He saw me and came out.

"Dermot, how are you." He clapped me on the back. "You're a bit early for dinner, but the guys can throw something together for you if you're hungry."

"Thanks, but I'm here on another matter. I'm investigating Gertrude Murray's murder."

"Ah, Gert. I still can't believe it." He looked down at the floor and said, "I loved that lady, everyone did. I just saw her Monday evening. She came in for dinner."

"Was anyone with her?"

"No, she was alone."

Gertrude was murdered Monday night.

"Did you see anyone hanging around outside," I said, "anyone who might have followed her home when she left?"

"Nobody I noticed. Hey, wait here a second, Mandy might know something." John went to the kitchen and returned a minute later, accompanied by a young woman with black spiky hair. He said, "Dermot, this is Mandy, the night manager. She worked Monday. Mandy, tell Dermot what you told me."

Her eyelashes fluttered as she talked. "I gave Gertrude a ride home after she ate. It looked like it might rain."

"What time was that roughly?" I asked.

"Around six-thirty," Mandy said. "I remember because the metered spaces were opening up. That happens at six-thirty, when people are leaving for home."

"And you dropped her at her building?" I said.

"Yes, on O'Reilly Way."

"Did anyone go into the building after you dropped her off?" I asked.

"Nobody followed her in, I'm sure of that," Mandy said. "I waited until she got inside before I drove away."

"Was anyone hanging outside the building?"

"I don't think so." She looked at John. "I wasn't really paying attention. God, I wish I had been paying attention. I can't believe someone killed her, I just can't believe it."

"Neither can I, Mandy." John patted her arm. "I know this is hard to talk about it, but Dermot needs information. The more information he has, the quicker he'll find the killer. Can you tell him anything else?"

"I, ah, I'm not sure." Her lips trembled.

"Not sure about what, Mandy?" John asked. "What's wrong?"

"Raoul came along for the ride," she said, swallowing hard. "I always get nervous in the projects, so I asked Raoul to come with me."

"Who's Raoul?" I asked.

"He works here," John said.

"Is he a big guy?" I asked.

"He's about six-five, six-six." John answered. "He played basketball in college."

"That's why I asked Raoul to go with me," Mandy said, "because he's big and strong and protective, too."

"Did Raoul come back with you?" I asked Mandy.

"Yes, he did."

I turned to John. "What time did Raoul leave work Monday night?"

"He must have been here until closing," John said. "We were busy Monday, in the weeds all night."

"Can I talk to him?"

"Sure, but he's off today."

"What's his full name?" I said.

"Raoul Naulls."

I asked for Raoul's address. Mandy went to the office to get it. I thanked them for their time and left the bistro.

12

I CONTINUED TO canvass. I went to the 7-Eleven in Thompson Square, Jenny's Pizza on Medford Street, the Grasshopper Café on Bunker Hill Street, McCarthy's Liquors in Hayes Square, Zume's Coffee House on Main, and Speedy Chen's, formally Speedy Wong's. I went to every business in Charlestown that had a cash register, and they all said the same thing, that they liked Gertrude Murray, that they set aside coins for her, and that they hoped I'd find her killer.

At Old Sully's, an original Charlestown taproom where real Townies drink, the patrons, all men, told me that if they found the bastard who killed Mrs. Murray, they'd hang him from the Zakim Bridge—no courtroom needed. From Old Sully's I walked home. When I reached my front stairs, a car skidded to a stop and Bo Murray got out. He wasn't happy.

"Sparhawk! I told you to back off."

"Diaz didn't kill her, Bo, but I'm going to find out who did."

"You're not listening." His face was gray and his arms were slack, as if the muscles had been drained out of them. "Back the fuck off!"

"Don't you want the truth?"

"I know the truth, and so do you. Diaz broke into my mother's house and robbed her. Whether he killed her, I don't care." Bo paused for air. "There's something you don't understand. I could kill you and Diaz and Louis, and it wouldn't matter a damn to me. Prison don't matter to me, understand?"

"I understand this much," I stepped closer to Bo. "If *my* mother got murdered, I'd want to know who did it."

"Watch your mouth, fuck brain." Bo jammed a gun into my ribs. I never saw it in his hand. He put it away and walked back to his car, saying, "You've been warned, Sparhawk. Back the fuck off."

I went inside and rested on the couch. At seven o'clock my cell phone rang. It was Cheyenne Starr, and my attitude went from aloof to alert. We talked for a couple of minutes, mostly small talk, feeling each other out, and when I sensed an opening I asked her if she'd like to go out for coffee. She said yes and asked me to pick her up. Tonight? I asked. Yes, tonight, she said to my delight. After a rinse-off shower and quick shave, I drove to her apartment in Somerville.

She answered the door wearing a sleeveless tie-dyed maxi dress, blotched with oblong patterns in navy blue and white. As we walked along Holland Street, I noticed young men gawking at her. I felt like I was escorting a movie star. In Davis Square we went into a hip café crowded with university students. They were loud and energetic and friendly, and they wore college garb from their respective schools. Tufts, Boston University, Harvard, MIT. They were the cream of a handpicked crop, the best and the brightest culled from the finest.

Cheyenne ordered chai tea, I ordered coffee, and we sat at a small round table. I felt like a square, wearing a collared shirt and matching socks. Cheyenne's tie-dyed attire was more in keeping with the student setting, while I felt like a professor.

"How was your day?" she asked.

"Busy," I said, stirring sugar into my coffee. "Yours?"

"I spent most of it in class, cognitive behavior therapy in the morning, adult psychological trauma in the afternoon. Then I had a study group in psychosocial pathology. I like the classes, and the study group is awesome, so I had a good day. What can

I say? I'm a nerd." She laughed with her whole body. "What did you do?"

I told her that I spent the day investigating a murder, not exactly first-date material, but I wanted to get it out there, and I didn't want to sugarcoat it. As soon as I said it I thought: Was I trying to impress her or test her? I apparently accomplished neither. Her expression never changed. She remained seated, which was a good sign. I figured she'd run for the door.

"So, *you* are *not* a nerd. How did you become a private investigator?" she asked.

I rocked back in my seat. "Is there anything worse than a guy talking about himself?"

"No, I'm fascinated, I really am. Tell me about the murder case you're working on."

Damn, I liked her.

"Okay, but tell me if you get bored. We're representing a young man charged with felony murder. His name is Victor Diaz. He is accused of killing a woman named Gertrude Murray. I knew Gert growing up."

"That's terrible. You knew her? Do you think he's guilty?"

"Yes, Gert was a great lady. And no, I don't think Diaz killed her. He broke into Mrs. Murray's apartment to rob her, and Diaz admitted to robbing her, but he insists he didn't kill her."

"Do you believe him?"

"I believe the evidence, and the evidence says he didn't do it."

Cheyenne drank more tea and studied my face. "It must be hard for you to be objective, since you knew Mrs. Murray."

"It is hard at times, but my objective is to find Gert's killer." An image of Gert buying me an ice-cream cone came to me. We were at the Ice Creamsmith in Lower Mills. The sun was shining and Gert was smiling. And then an image of her dented head pushed away her smile. "I'm gonna nail the son of a bitch. I'm gonna put him in a goddamn cage." My voice got loud, and I was getting intense. "Sorry, let's talk about something else."

"Yes, let's," she said. She reached out and touched my hand. "Are you okay?"

I told her I was fine, and the conversation took on a lighter note. We finished our drinks, and I walked her home. When we reached her building I said goodnight, but I didn't try to kiss her. The murder talk had quashed the romantic mood. I drove home wondering if I blew it.

13

THE NEXT MORNING I kept at it, visiting retail stores, coffee shops, eateries, and pubs, all of which proved to be a waste of time. Needing a break from the tedium, I walked to Kormann & Schuhwerk's Deli in the Navy Yard and ordered an egg bagel with Nova Scotia sturgeon and cream cheese. I felt as if I had finally accomplished something when I finished it. I sat at a harbor window at the end of the counter and mulled my next move, wondering how to proceed. I drank three more cups of coffee, mulled, mulled, mulled, and then got off my ass and headed to Terminal Street.

The first place I went to was Avakian's Market, a small grocery store that sold cigarettes, liquor, and other sundry items. I picked up a few things and took them to the cash register. The cashier, a young Hispanic woman with a tremendous build, rang in the order. I paid in cash, and she bagged the purchase. I told her that my name was Dermot Sparhawk, but she didn't reply. With her looks, she was probably fed up with men introducing themselves to her. I showed her a picture of Gertrude Murray and asked, "Have you seen this woman?"

"That's Mrs. Murray, the poor lady. She came in almost every day."

"Was she in here last Monday?"

"The day she was murdered?"

"Yes, that day."

44

"She might have been." She slid the bag across the counter to me. "I work sixty hours a week. The days run together after a while."

"Did you work the Monday she was murdered?"

"That's my scheduled day, so yes, I was working."

She sounded defensive. I asked, "What's your name?"

"How come you want to know?"

"Just curious."

"Not a good enough reason," she said.

A man with thinning black hair, probably the owner judging by the way he comported himself, came out of the back room and walked toward us. He said to the cashier, "Bianca, can you work late today? Larry called in sick yet again. The guy is always sick—sick of working is what I think."

Bianca said that she could stay as long as he wanted, and then she said to him, "Will you get me two liters of Stolichnaya, Mr. Avakian? I can't reach that high."

"No problem," he said, and grabbed two liters by the neck with one hand and put them on the countertop. "Big order, Bianca?"

"Pretty big, it's the weekly delivery to the Halligan Club. Nick asked me to prep the package for him."

"Good job, Bianca," he said, and started for the back room.

"Excuse me," I said to him.

He looked at me. "Yes?"

"I am investigating Gertrude Murray's murder."

"Is that so?" Avakian wore chunky glasses with thick lenses. A milky film clouded one of his eyes. "I've seen you around the neighborhood. Did you know Gertrude Murray?"

"I grew up in the same building," I said. "We've never met." I extended my right hand. "My name is Dermot Sparhawk."

"I'm Aram Avakian, and this is my store." He crossed his long arms. "Avakian's Market has been in Charlestown for sixty years, and Mrs. Murray has been coming here since my father opened the place in the late fifties."

"Avakian's has a good name in the neighborhood," I said.

"What can you tell me bout Gertrude Murray? I heard she collected coins."

"You're right," Avakian answered. "I saved coins for her, just like my father did. Silver dimes, silver quarters, I set them aside for her, right Bianca?"

"That's right, Mr. Avakian," Bianca said, as she organized lottery paraphernalia. "We put them in an ashtray."

"Because you can't use ashtrays for ashes anymore, not in a public place," he said. "I also gave her Indian Head pennies and buffalo nickels, at face value, no markup. These days you don't see many silver coins. And she'd buy her lottery tickets and chewing gum and root beer. She was a nice person, Gertrude Murray, first class all the way. It pains me she's gone. Tell me, what kind of an animal kills an old lady like that?"

"That's what I'm trying to find out."

A young man came out of the back room rolling a two-wheeler loaded with cases of wine. He said to Mr. Avakian, "I have a delivery in the Navy Yard, Pop. Then I'll go from there to the Halligan Club." He continued to a van out front.

"That's my son, Nick," Mr. Avakian said. "He finished college three years ago and got a good job in finance, which shows he's smart. But he didn't like it. He decided to take the reins here when I retire. He'll do right by the Avakian name."

"I'm sure he will," I said. "Back to Mrs. Murray, did she come in last Monday?"

"I can't say for sure. Gert came here three or four times a week, sometimes more." He turned to Bianca and asked, "Did Gert Murray come in on Monday?"

"I don't remember," she said.

"How could you? We're open sixteen hours a day." Avakian turned to me. "It's hard to keep track of everyone. Sorry I can't be of more help."

"I understand." I handed Avakian my card. "If you remember anything, please call."

I also gave Bianca a card on my way out.

14

FROM AVAKIAN'S MARKET I walked to the projects, found Mrs. Diaz's building in Carney Court, and went inside. The hall windows were made of opaque glass that obscured the outside world from view. Strong smells of dead mice and urine pervaded the corridors, but the stench was sweetened by the aroma of marijuana, the project's air freshener. The soles of my shoes stuck to linoleum like Velcro as I climbed the stairs to the second story. In the brick gulags of Charlestown, carpe diem translates to crappy day.

I knocked on Mrs. Diaz's door. A woman's voice from inside asked who I was. I told her that I was Dermot Sparhawk, Buckley Louis's investigator, and that I had visited her son Victor in jail. The lock clicked. A Latina woman with a proud posture let me in and invited me to sit on a wooden chair. She sat in a chair next to me.

"Victor is innocent," she said in broken English. "He never hurt nobody."

"He might be innocent of murder, but he's not innocent," I said. "He robbed an old lady."

"But he no kill her." Mrs. Diaz teared up. "He never hurt nobody. I tell you, he is not a murderer, not my boy."

"I don't think he killed Mrs. Murray," I said, "but I think he knows who did. He was there when it happened."

"He is innocent." She slammed her fist on the table. "Innocent!"

"I hope to prove it." I tried to placate her with a smile, but it didn't seem to work. "If Victor cooperates with the police, they might go easier on him."

"But he still go to jail?"

I saw terror in her eyes, a look I've seen far too often from mothers in the projects, especially when the oldest child gets in trouble. When the trouble works its way down to the third or fourth child, the look of terror becomes a look of resignation. The mothers expect the worst, and more often than not, their expectations are realized.

"I'll work to get Victor the best deal possible."

"But he go to jail?"

"Yeah, he'll go to jail."

She mumbled in Spanish and prayed to Jesus, kissing the cross on her rosary beads and blessing herself over and over. When she settled down, I said, "Does Victor have a girlfriend?"

"Nada, no girlfriend."

"Does he have friends, anyone he hung around with?"

"Si, a boy named Juan, but he no live here."

I asked her where Juan lived, and she said Dorchester or Roxbury, maybe Mattapan. I asked her if she knew Juan's last name but she didn't.

"What kind of guy is Juan?" I asked.

"No good," she answered.

"Does Victor have any brothers or sisters?" The question sounded weird, so I recast it. "Do you have other children?"

"Si, my daughter in Jamaica Plain. She a good girl."

"I'd like to talk to her," I said. "Do you have her phone number?"

"Si." Her face changed. "Her boyfriend is jealous. He check her calls."

"Where does she work?" I asked. "I can talk to her there."

"She have a good job." Her face changed again, this time showing pride. "Ester cuts hair at Keldara Salon and Spa. It is in Dedham." She touched my arm. "It is a good job she has. I no want her to lose it."

"I'll be careful," I said.

I walked to Gertrude Murray's building on O'Reilly Way and found the apartment of Santa Reyes, the woman who witnessed the accomplice fleeing the night of the murder. She answered the door with a smile, but when Santa saw it was me, she looked down the hall in both directions and rushed me inside, not wanting her neighbors to see me. A round woman with silver hair and fat cheeks, Santa could barely speak English, but that didn't stop her from trying.

I asked her about the man she saw leaving the building the night Mrs. Murray was killed. She struggled to tell me. He was "veinte" which meant twenty, "Spanish" self-explanatory, "muy poco" meaning very little, "el adicto" she pretended to put a needle in her arm. I asked her if the man was walking or running. He was walking "rapido" and she pumped her arms. Did she recognize him? "Nada," she said. Santa went on to tell me he had black hair and a beard. She then pushed me out of the apartment and into the hall. A picture of the accomplice formed in my mind, a picture of a small Hispanic man, likely an addict, and more importantly, a man who probably had small feet. He couldn't be the killer if he had small feet.

Somebody else must have been in Gert's apartment before Victor and his accomplice broke in, and whoever he was had killed Mrs. Murray. A thought came to me. What if there was a third person involved? Suppose that in addition to Diaz and the accomplice, there was another accomplice, one with big feet. And then another thought came to me. What if the man Santa saw wasn't an accomplice at all, but a man leaving the building, a man who had nothing to do with crime?

I needed more information, a lot more.

15

I WALKED DOWN the hall to the apartment of Craig Gruskowski, the man who called 911 the night that Gertrude Murray was murdered. I knocked on his door, and a big man with a dockworker's build answered. He gazed up at me and didn't say anything. I looked inside. His place was immaculate. Music played in the background, an Eagles song from the seventies.

"Mr. Gruskowski?" I said to break the silence.

"I already talked to you guys."

"I'm not a cop," I said. "My name is Dermot Sparhawk. My family lived next door to Mrs. Murray when I was a kid. We lived in this very apartment."

"You're shitting me, this apartment?"

"I'd like to ask you a few questions about Gertrude, Mr. Gruskowski."

"Sure, but call me Skeeter—it's the ski in Gruskowski. My friends made it up." He let me in. "I've been living in Charlestown my whole life, born up there on Bartlett Street where it crosses Sullivan. Know where I'm talking about, by the steep hill?"

"It's a nice block."

"I hit some hard times, my own fault, and I ended up here in the projects five years ago." He sat down in a stuffed chair. "I have to sit a lot these days. The old heart ain't what it used to be. I know the name Sparhawk. Your father was that big Indian, right?"

"That's him."

"He was an ironworker, Local 7, a tough son of a bitch and a little crazy, too. He didn't mind having a drink now and then. Didn't you play football at Boston College?"

"Right on all the above," I said to him. "About Mrs. Murray—"

"Hold on, I love this one." Skeeter cranked the CD player. "My favorite Eagles song of all time, Take It Easy." He sang along with it, moving his hands like a conductor. "'Well, I'm a standing on a corner in Winslow, Arizona, such a fine sight to see. It's a girl, my Lord, in a flatbed Ford, slowing down to take a look at me.' What a story, what lyrics!"

"Skeeter, about the night Mrs. Murray was killed—"

"One of these days I'm gonna see Winslow, Arizona, gonna see the whole Southwest. Route 66, Albuquerque, St. Looey, the Grand Canyon, everything. I got this book on Route 66, read it five times already."

"That's great, but I'd like to ask you about—"

"I get mailings from the Route 66 Association, the Arizona chapter in the town of Kingman. That's where Flagstaff is, in Arizona. I watched a YouTube video of Billy Connolly, that funny bastard from Glasgow. He toured Route 66 on a three-wheel motorcycle."

"Skeeter—"

"Billy loved the desert. He's Scottish, so he never saw a desert before, never saw cactus or cinder cones, either. That's what he said." He paused for a second, which probably seemed like an eternity to him. "Sorry, you wanted to talk about Gert."

"I work for the lawyer representing Victor Diaz. I'm trying to find out if Diaz really killed Gert Murray. I don't think he did."

"I heard about Victor Diaz," Skeeter said. "News travels fast in the bricks, like an echo chamber in here."

"We used to say that if someone sneezed, ten people said God bless you."

"And another ten yelled keep it down. I forgot you grew up here."

I looked out to the courtyard. When I was a kid I'd wrestled my father out there, practicing half-nelsons and headlocks and toeholds. He'd make me do pull-ups on the clothesline pole and pushups on the tar, eventually graduating to handstand pushups. He taught me not to blink. He did this by flicking jabs to within a whisker of my nose, and when I got used to the blur knuckles coming at me, I stopped blinking. Once he flicked a jab so violently that it broke the second hand on his Timex, snapping it off the post.

"Tell me about the night of the murder," I said.

"I heard loud thumps coming from Gert's apartment, and I mean loud," he said. "That's when I called the cops."

"What else did you hear?"

"I heard footsteps running down the hall."

"Running, not walking?"

"Definitely running," Skeeter said. "You can tell the difference."

"You heard the footsteps after the thumps?"

"Yes, right after the thumps, so it must've been the other guy Diaz was with, because Diaz was too stupid to scram. He hung around too long and the cops grabbed him."

"They grabbed him, all right."

Something about his story didn't add up—not the story itself, but the way Skeeter reacted to the thumping sounds. In Charlestown we don't call the cops. We intervene directly and without thought, leading with our chin, and we usually get clipped on the chin when we do this, but it's our culture, our Townie pride.

"When you heard the thumping, why didn't you help her? How could you just listen and do nothing?"

He looked down.

"I've had three heart attacks. My doctor told me I hadda watch myself, don't overdo it. When I heard the thumps I grabbed my baseball bat, ready to bust heads. I took a couple of warm-up swings, full cuts, and I got dizzy and fell on the floor. I popped a nitro and tried to give it another go, but I couldn't breathe. My heart was pounding out of my chest. So I did the next best thing, I dialed 911 to get Gert help."

"I forgot about your heart."

"I had to leave the longshoremen because of it, and I've been out of work ever since. And I was no scallawag, either. I operated a crane, which pays big money. Five years without work, how's that for a working-class guy?"

"I'm sorry to hear it."

"As humiliating as it is to admit, I did what I could for Gert. In the old days I'd have kicked ass. Believe me when I tell you that."

"I was out of line."

"You didn't know." Skeeter stood up, holding the arms of the chair. "How the fuck do you think I feel, not being a man anymore? If I was my old self, I might have saved her life."

"I believe you might have."

"Look, I'm gonna lie down for a while and listen to the Eagles. One of these days I'm gonna get to Winslow, Arizona. I'm gonna go to Route 66 and find that girl on a flat-bed Ford."

"I hope you make it out there, Skeeter," I said.

"Come back if you have more questions."

I told him I would and left his apartment, feeling like an asshole for giving him such a hard time.

16

I TALKED TO a few more residents in Skeeter's building and learned nothing of note. Then I thought of a man who might be able to help me, and I was pretty sure I knew where to find him. He'd be fishing at Little Mystic Channel, locally known as Montego Bay, a saltwater inlet that flowed into Charlestown under the Tobin Bridge.

His name is Rod Liveliner, a retired tugboat pilot who spends his summers angling for blues and stripers. In Little Mystic Channel, Rod had a better chance of hooking a car bumper than a fish. He had been friends with my father. Both were Vietnam vets, both combat Marines, and both came back from Southeast Asia haunted. Rod kept his demons at bay by fishing. My father did it with booze. As for which worked better, Rod is still alive. I walked to the channel and saw Rod casting a line.

"Any bites?" I said, approaching him from behind.

A smile broke across Rod's sunburnt face. He was wearing a canvas sailor hat with the brim turned down and salt-stained aviator sunglasses with green lenses. His arms were flaking, and his hands were blotched with liver spots that looked like a map of the harbor islands.

"Dermot, what brings you here?"

"Neighborhood crime." I leaned on the railing next to him. "You probably heard about Gertrude Murray."

"Everyone's heard about it." He reeled in his line and cast it again. "Gert was a nice lady. Her sons are nuts, but she was nice."

"I'm investigating her homicide."

"I heard about that, too. Bo Murray isn't too pleased about it." He lightly tugged the line. "Bo isn't the most balanced arrow in the quiver."

"Tell me about it."

"He's sick, too. I heard the doctors gave him six months." He pointed to the tackle box. "Grab a drop line. The chubs are in the bucket."

"Sounds good." I grabbed a spool of line, baited the hook, and unwound it into the water. "I talked to Gert's neighbor, Skeeter Gruskowski. Do you know him?"

"Sure do." Rod's smile broadened. "Skeeter is a classic."

"Skeeter called 911 the night Gert got killed." I felt the line. Nothing. "He said he has a bad heart."

"Skeeter was a crane operator, doing quite well for himself, and then he had a heart attack unloading a container ship." Rod reeled in the line, checked the bait, and hooked a fresh chub. "He went back to work three months later and the same thing happened, another heart attack."

"It must have been dangerous. Those containers are enormous."

"It ended his career," Rod said. "He's been on the dole ever since."

"Is he married?"

"He was married." Rod flicked his wrist and the sinker plunked thirty yards out. "He's divorced now."

"What happened?"

"Gambling," Rod said. "A few of us waterfront workers, including Skeeter, played poker years ago, small stakes." Rod gently pulled the line. "I guess he caught the gambling bug, and it got out of control. Horses, greyhounds, football, hockey, he bet the lot. He started hitting Foxwoods and that other casino down there."

"Does he still gamble?"

"He doesn't have the money," Rod said. "It cost him every-thing—house, car, credit, marriage—and now he's stuck in the projects."

I hear the same stories at AA meetings, addiction taking away every material thing you own, and then it goes for your soul.

"Do you know anything about Victor Diaz?" I asked.

"The man accused of killing Gert?" he said. "Don't know him."

"His family lives in the bricks."

"I know," Rod said. "The scuttlebutt says his accomplice killed Gert, which makes Diaz guilty, too. You have your work cut out for you."

"I know." I wound the line and threw the limp chub in the water. "I have to go, Rod. If you hear anything, let me know."

"Sure," he said. "Glooscap and I go deep-sea fishing every month. It's peaceful out there, out beyond the horizon, the perfect setting to talk about the war. We never stop processing it, Dermot, the Vietnam years. And Vietnam vets are getting harder to find."

"Like codfish."

"We're as rare as codfish, but not as protected. You should join us next time. Glooscap and I go out past the brink."

"I might take you up on that." I looked at Little Mystic Channel. A film of motor oil rippled on the surface, and scum floated east on its way to the harbor. "Do you catch anything here?"

"Once in a while, but the real fishing is out deep. Glooscap and I hauled in some lunkers this last month, stripers as long as your arm. Last year Glooscap snagged a 300-pound halibut, big as the one in the Winslow Homer painting."

"I saw the photo on his wall," I said. "It was a proud moment for Glooscap." *Not so proud for the halibut.* "He framed it."

"Way out there by George's Bank, that's where he caught it," Rod said. "We were eating halibut steaks and halibut stew for six months."

I handed Rod my card. He handed me his phone number and told me to call him. Before I left, Rod said, "Be careful of Bo

Murray. He's buried two people that I know of and got away with it. One of them was a teenage girl."

"Fuckin' asshole, killing a young girl. I'll keep my eyes open."

I stood at the railing and watched the cars crossing the Tobin Bridge. The tollbooths were gone now, replaced by automated scanners that tally the fees, but the upgrade hasn't improved the traffic flow, which is still a molasses trickle from Chelsea to Charlestown.

"You remind me of your father." Rod said, putting an end to my musing. He removed his sunglasses and swallowed hard, his Adam's apple bobbing up and down. "He was the best man I ever met, and as you well know, I owe my life to him. I am in his debt."

I had heard this story many times before, but out of respect I listened with interest.

"He saved my life in Vietnam." Tears welled in Rod's eyes. "I was what they called a one-digit midget, less than ten days left in my hitch. It's the scariest time for a Marine, when you're about to be discharged. You get superstitious."

"I can see why."

"Your father saved my life two days before I got my honorable. We were fighting in Da Nang, Military Region 5, when it happened. I won't go into the details because it's still too painful to talk about, but I can tell you this much: Your father should have got a Silver Star for his actions. I'm alive today because of Chief. You now hold his debt, my debt to your father. If you ask me for anything, I will honor your request."

His eye sockets overflowed and tears spilled down his cheeks. The debt was important to Rod, and I wanted to respond in a respectful way, but I wasn't sure what to say. So I said something I hoped would ease his mind. "My old man loved you. There is no debt to pay."

"I fulfill my obligations," he said. "And watch out for Bo Murray."

Rod turned to the channel and cast his line.

Night had fallen and my energy had ebbed. I sat in the parlor, looking at the stream of white headlights coming into the city and the stripe of red taillights going to the suburbs. A humming transformer on a telephone pole lulled me into a rhythmic trance, chasing away the noise in my head. In Alcoholics Anonymous, Step Eleven suggests that we pray and meditate to get closer to our Higher Power. This is the only way I can pray and meditate—staring at cityscapes and listening to city sounds. The sight of distant traffic calms me, probably because I'm not in it, and the hum of the transformer brings me back to my childhood, to the scratchy static from my father's transistor radio.

I had just reached a contemplative state when a spray of bullets shattered the windows. I dropped to the floor and rolled to the wall. No sound accompanied the volley—they must have used a silencer. I got out my phone to dial 911 but stopped. I didn't want to deal with the police. A car sped away. I shook off the glass and peeked out the window and saw nothing threatening below. Judging by the angle of the bullet holes in the ceiling, the shooter fired from street level, probably from a car, most likely the car I heard speeding away.

In Tibet, a meditation is ended by the peaceful gong of a resonant bell, in Charlestown it's ended by a hail of gunfire. In the past I considered moving to an elevator condo, an upscale place with lobby security and underground parking and surveillance cameras, but that seemed like cheating. A man should handle his own problems, not farm them out to others. Why should I put a security guard at risk because someone is after me?

So instead of moving, I took amateurish measures, but at least it was something. I placed a length-long mirror on the front landing and angled it so I could see who was coming up the stairs. I added a Fox police lock to the door, making it tougher to break down. I installed a deadbolt on the outside of the rear door. If an intruder came up the front stairs, I could engage the Fox police lock, go to the rear stairwell and deadbolt the door from the outside, thus preventing the intruder from getting through and giving me time to escape.

A Jesuit priest once told me that material security is an illusion, at best a hoax, and that genuine security came from God. Tell that to a cop whose Kevlar vest just stopped a bullet. It's not that I'm paranoid, thinking they're out to get me, although sometimes I think they are. It's that I'm a skeptic, anticipating the worst. I'm like a football coach who takes every precaution possible to prevent a turnover that'll cost him a game—or in this case, my life.

I thought about the gun attack. It had to be Bo Murray. I called Harraseeket Kid and left a message about the barrage of bullets and the shot-up windows.

17

SKEETER GRUSKOWSKI DROVE his red Corvette convertible with alloy mags over the Broadway Bridge into South Boston and parked in front of the Aces & Eights, a tired-looking place with graying shingles and sagging gutters. He went inside and nodded to the bartender, Gage Lauria, who was wearing a black sweat suit with white piping, classy by Aces & Eights standards. Skeeter removed his Ray-Ban sunglasses and tossed them on the bar, making sure they landed with a clunk.

"What's with the fancy shades?" Gage asked.

"Like 'em?" Skeeter said.

Gage scoffed and served a customer. Skeeter looked out the back window. An inbound commuter train crawled along the tracks, and beyond the tracks, a cluster of traffic choked the expressway, but the skies were blue and the trees were greening.

"Hey, Gage." Skeeter held out his wrist. "Like my new Rolex?"

"Rolodex?" Gage laughed.

"Not Rolodex, you dickhead, Rolex, it's imported from Geneva, Switzerland, cost me thirty-five hundred."

"Is that what the guy in the trench coat told you, that it came from Switzerland?"

"Fuck you, asshole. It's real, the oyster dial and everything."

"Sure, sure, whatever you say, Skeeter." Gage chuckled and loaded the dishwasher. "The Rembrandt on my calendar is real, too."

On the flat-screen TV the Red Sox were playing the White Sox in Chicago. The Chicago skies were blue, too. Skeeter ate a handful of pretzels and ordered a beer. Gage, a trim man of forty, with thick brown hair and an athlete's build, poured a mug of draft and rested it on the bar.

"Not that piss." Skeeter pushed it away. "Give me a Heineken, ice cold with a glass."

"Did you hit the lottery or something?"

"Sort of," Skeeter said, as he put a prescription bottle on the bar. "Nitroglycerin, in case my heart flairs up again."

"It's a good thing you have imported beer to wash it down."

"You don't swallow it. It dissolves under your tongue." Skeeter drank some Heineken, burped, and then startled Gage when he asked, "Are you up for a road trip?"

"A road trip? What are you talking about?"

"I'm talkin' Route 66, the Mother Road. I love that song 'I Get My Kicks on Route 66' Remember the lyrics? Flagstaff, Arizona. Don't forget Winona?" Skeeter hummed and sang out, "And Oklahoma City is mighty pretty."

"Quit singing. You sound like an idiot." Gage dried his hands on a bar towel. "What the fuck are you on today, a batch of bad acid?"

"A natural high, a Highway 66 high! We can see it all, Gage, Saint Looey, the Texas Panhandle, Santa Monica Pier. Wanna join me?"

"Yeah sure, Skeeter, sign me up, crazy man."

"I'm serious," Skeeter said. "I'm going to Route 66, gonna drive it from beginning to end, and I want you to come with me."

Gage folded the bar towel the long way and draped it over the faucet. "I can barely swing the rent. It's not like the old days with the longshoremen."

"Those were good days, weren't they? We raked it in back then."

"Yeah, back then. Now I'm pouring foam for pocket change."

"At least you're not making license plates anymore," Skeeter said. "What if I paid your rent for a couple of months, you know, advanced it to you? That way you can go on the trip."

"Cut the shit." Gage propped his hands on the bar and leaned forward. "You've lost it. You went over the edge."

"I haven't lost it, I came into some money," Skeeter said. "I can lend it to you, no sweat."

"Sure you can." Gage picked up his tip jar and gave it a shake. The coins jingled freely, with no bills to get in the way. "And just how am I'm supposed to pay you back?"

"Hmm, an apt question." Skeeter peeled the Heineken label with his thumbnail. "Forget about paying it back. My treat, the whole shebang, I'll cover everything."

"You can't afford that."

"Sure I can." Skeeter laid a $100 bill on the bar. "Keep the change."

"A hundred?"

"Follow me." Skeeter opened the barroom door and pointed to the red Corvette convertible. "Ain't she a beauty?"

"You can't be serious." Gage shouldered the door to keep it open. "No way it's yours."

"Wanna bet?" Skeeter pressed the fob and the car tweeted. "I bought it on the Auto Mile, out there in Norwood. I told the suit I wanted the best 'vette on the lot."

"What the fuck's going on?" The expression on Gage's face changed from skeptical to baffled. "Where did you get it?"

"I told you, the Auto Mile."

"Not the car, knucklehead, the money. You live in the projects, for Christ's sake."

"I'm taking a break from the bricks." Skeeter opened a checkbook. "What's your rent?"

"A checkbook?" Gage stared at it. "In a leather case?"

"How much?"

"Nine hundred a month."

"I'll pay four months ahead." Skeeter filled in $3,600. "Who do I make it out to?"

Gage Lauria's mouth hung open in disbelief. "Better make it out to me," he said. "The landlord likes cash."

"Got it." Skeeter handed him the check. "Don't worry, the funds are in there. Now you can go on the trip"

"Not so fast." Gage tucked he check into his pocket. "Where did you get it, Skeeter? I don't wanna be in the middle of Flagstaff when a bunch of Feds close in on us. I've had my fill of the Feds."

"I know you have. You stood up on that one."

"Stood up, my ass. I was a patsy for the union." Gage's voice grew louder with each word. "The money?"

"Okay, okay, I'll tell you. I came into a small fortune, ten grand to be exact, and I took it to Foxwoods and turned it into a big fortune, six hundred grand."

"Fuck off, Skeeter."

"Look at this." Skeeter took a document from his pocket. "Here's the title to the car. There's my name, Craig Gruskowski. And here's the receipt. The car is paid in full."

"Gimme those." Gage studied them. "Jesus, it *is* paid in full."

"I'm not conning you." Skeeter slapped him on the shoulder. "Are you in or not?"

"What about your heart?"

"My heart'll be fine. I cut back on the cigars, started drinking light beer."

"You're a regular health nut."

"So what do you say, Gage?" Skeeter urged. "Where's your Sicilian sense of adventure? You can do it, I know you can."

"Maybe." Gage looked inside the Aces & Eights. One of the patrons was slumped on a barstool, muttering about his sainted Irish mother. Another was passed out in a booth, his face in a pool of beer. Across the street a construction crew was busy erecting a new building, and next to the building a trendy bar had just opened. A man wearing a suit went into the new bar. Gage said, "Okay, I'm in. I'll go on the trip."

"Yes!" Skeeter yelled. "I'll buy you a Swiss watch, just like the one I got."

"I don't want a watch," Gage said, and then quickly added, "but I'll take an iPhone."

"You got it."

The deal was done. Skeeter and Gage would be taking a road trip across America. Gage went into the Aces & Eights, returning to the stink of defeat, where the highpoint of the day was punching out. Skeeter drove back to the Charlestown projects, where he ended up after he gambled away everything.

Three days later, after the check had cleared, Skeeter Gruskowski picked up Gage Lauria in front of the Aces & Eights, handed him a coffee, and said, "First stop Chicago, Illinois, the headwaters of Route 66."

"I've never been to Chicago before, even when I was playing college ball," Gage said. "We played Marquette once, but that was in Milwaukee."

"Tomorrow it's Wrigley Field for the Cubs and Cardinals. I got us two primo seats right behind the Cubs dugout." Skeeter tossed Gage a box. "Your new iPhone, ready to go."

Gage said thanks and tore it open. They drove up Dorchester Avenue to the Broadway Bridge and ramped onto the Mass Pike west, heading for Chicago and Route 66.

18

I CALLED CHEYENNE Starr and I asked her if she'd like to join me for dinner. She said yes and asked where we were going. I told her about a place in Randolph, a classy trattoria called Caffe Bella. She asked what she should wear, and I drew a blank. She might as well have asked me who won the 1907 Kentucky Derby. I answered the question by not answering it. I told her that I'd be wearing a shirt with a collar, and shoes, not sneakers. She laughed and told me she'd be ready at six o'clock.

We arrived at Caffe Bella at seven and the place was packed. The bar was three deep with patrons vying for libation. The wait time for a table was forty minutes, but the awaiting customers wouldn't have cared if it was four hours, once they got a drink. The maître d', a man with an Irish face and a booming voice, came up to us and said our table was ready. Had he made a mistake? He led us to the rear of the dining area and sat us under a tapestry of a winemaking scene in an Italian vineyard. We were secluded in a semi-alcove, almost like a private room, but with the energy of being out on the town. I palmed him twenty, and he said, "Angel told me to take care of you. I'll split it with her."

I glanced at the bar and sure enough Angel the beautiful bartender was on duty, pouring beer and mixing drinks. I caught her eye and nodded a thank you. I had been to Caffe Bella once before when I met a key witness here, and the witness's information busted open a case I was working on. The witness happened to be Angel's friend.

A fortyish waitress with a taut, curvaceous build came to the table to take our order. She didn't walk so much as shift, her hips swaying with power. I didn't stare, but she was impossible to miss. Cheyenne, who didn't seem to notice her, ordered a Caesar's Salad with shaved grana pandano and grilled salmon. I asked for the sauté pan, a hearty meal served in a saucepan loaded with Cape Cod little necks, PEI mussels, and Italian sausages, cooked in a marinara that couldn't be topped. We both ordered Cokes, mine without ice.

When the waitress left, I asked Cheyenne about her day. She told me she spent most of it inside the Nashua Street Jail, working with the inmates. Her eyes lit up when she talked about her work.

"I just love what I'm doing." She smiled and touched my arm. "I feel like I found my purpose in life. Does that sound corny?"

"No, not all. You're lucky you love what you do."

"I agree."

She held my hand until the waitress returned with a wicker basket of homemade breads and dipping oil. Cheyenne asked me about my day and I gave her the abridged version, telling her about the people I interviewed while canvassing the neighborhood.

"You really got around. I can't believe you talked to all those people. So, what's next, Dermot?"

I loved it when she called me Dermot.

"Victor Diaz's sister, Ester, is next," I said. "She has an insanely jealous boyfriend who lives with her, so I have to talk to her at work."

"Where does she work?"

"Keldara Salon and Spa in Dedham," I said.

Cheyenne dipped the bread in the oil and popped it in her mouth. "Mmm, this is so good. Did you book an appointment at Keldara?"

"No, I don't need a haircut."

"A haircut? You don't go to a place called Keldara Spa and Salon for a haircut. You go for shampoo and styling, or a facial."

"The last time I got a facial the man was wearing boxing gloves."

"Glad I missed that one. Hang on." She punched up her cell phone and put it to her ear.

"Who are you calling?" I asked.

"Dedham, Massachusetts," she said into the phone. "Keldara Salon and Spa."

"They're probably closed."

"Got the number, let's see." A second later she said. "Keldara?" Cheyenne smiled and winked. "I'd like to make an appointment with Ester. Two, actually." She paused. "Tomorrow at four o'clock is fine. The name is Sparhawk." She ended the call and looked at me. "Maybe I can be your assistant P.I."

"You're hired." I leaned across the table and kissed her, and she kissed me back. I almost levitated out of my chair.

The waitress was back again. She handed me another napkin and said, "Use it as a bib or you'll ruin your shirt. The sauté pan is a hands-on meal, not for the delicate eater."

I tucked it into my collar and started to eat, but my eyes kept going to Cheyenne, with her big brown eyes and full cheeks, all a blend of symmetry. After the meal, the waitress served coffee and pointed to my bib. "See what I mean?" The cloth was dotted with so much red it looked like I needed a cut man. I thanked her and she went away smiling.

"What will you ask Ester?" Cheyenne said.

"I'll ask her about Victor's accomplice." I drank some coffee. "He's the key to the case, at least that's my theory. I'll ask her if Victor has a girlfriend, and if he does, I'll want to talk to her. Women in love tend to spill."

"Tend to spill?" Cheyenne laughed and tipped her head back.

"What? What did I say?"

"You sound like a detective from a 1950s P.I. movie." She looked at me. "My father and I watch those old films. He has all the DVDs."

"I love the film-noir genre, too, especially the old black-and-whites with Robert Mitchum and Joseph Cotten."

"My father is a big Mitchum fan," Cheyenne said. "He loved the movie with Deborah Kerr as a nun, *Heaven Knows, Mr. Allison*."

"Not to one-up you, but my father chauffeured Mitchum during the filming of *The Friends of Eddie Coyle*. He just got back from Vietnam and needed work, and the Teamsters put him on as a temp limo driver. Mitchum and Chief got hammered a few times with the Winter Hill Gang. I have a great photo of them."

"Was your father a member of the Winter Hill Gang?"

"No, my father was a loner for the most part." I thought about my father's life. "He committed some petty crimes." *One of them wasn't so petty.* "But mostly he worked. I think the crimes gave him a break from the boredom, a challenge."

"He never went to prison?"

"No, but he might have if he met you," I said. She looked at me confused. I said, "Your prison program for Indians."

"Oh." She laughed and put her hand in mine. "I see."

"I'd rob a bank myself if it was the only way to meet you."

She let loose a full-throated laugh and her big eyes sparkled. I kissed her again, this time a little bit longer. As I paid the bill I thought: *Man, I'm in trouble. I'm falling for her.* I left the restaurant walking on air.

19

I'D NEVER BEEN to a salon—a saloon yes, but not a salon—and
I wasn't looking forward to it. But with Cheyenne sitting next to
me in the car, quietly giving directions, there was nowhere else
I'd rather be. She guided me to a shopping mall on Route 1A in
Dedham, and we parked in front of Keldara Salon and Spa, where
Ester Diaz worked. I opened the car door for Cheyenne.

"Where's the barber pole?" I said.

"Funny boy, follow me." She reached for my hand and led
me inside. The polished floors gleamed in the ambient lighting. Leather chairs and shampoo sinks and arched mirrors were
arranged around the room, bringing to mind a Roman bath. I
walked past an area called the quiet zone. Quiet zone? Cheyenne
and I checked in at the front desk, and seconds later Ester Diaz
came out to greet us. Her hair was coifed and her makeup was
flawless. Unlike her mother, Ester was petite and cheery, but the
cheeriness vanished when she asked who'd recommended her.

"Your mother," I said.

"My mother?" She inhaled through her mouth. "You know
my mother?"

"I talked to her in Carney Court yesterday." I saw fear set into
her eyes. "My name is Dermot Sparhawk and I work with Buckley
Louis, Victor's attorney. This is Cheyenne Starr. I am investigating Gertrude Murray's murder."

"An investigator?" She looked around. "Is that why you're here?"

"I just want to pick your brain a little, just a talk."

"Sure, just a talk. Come this way." I followed Ester to her station. She draped a smock around me and snapped it tightly behind my neck, probably fantasizing strangling me. So far it felt like a typical barbering experience, except I didn't see any Barbasol shaving cream or bay rum aftershave. Ester went to work, shampooing my hair and massaging my scalp. My eyes began to close.

"I'd like to ask you some questions before I fall asleep," I said. "Victor had an accomplice the night of the murder."

"Robbery, not murder," she said in a low voice. "Victor didn't kill Gertrude Murray."

"Do you know the accomplice? His name might be Juan."

She shook her head no. I peeked at the mirror and looked at her face. Her brow was creased and her lips were tensed. I continued the questioning. "Does Victor have any close friends, anyone he hangs around with?"

"Victor has lots of friends if that's what you want to call them." She cut my hair with steel scissors. "He is very popular."

"Who's his best friend?"

"I don't know his friends anymore," she said. "I moved away from Charlestown. I live in Jamaica Plain now, not in the projects."

"You must remember some of them."

"I never paid attention. They were trouble."

Ester wasn't going to tell me a thing, but I pressed ahead anyway. "Back to his friend Juan, he might live in Dorchester or Roxbury. Juan boxed with Victor in Lowell."

"Juan who?"

"I don't know his last name," I said.

"Don't know him."

"How about a girlfriend? Was Victor seeing anyone?"

"Victor always has girlfriends, usually more than one." Ester brushed my hair with a tortoiseshell comb and assessed her work.

She then flipped open a straight razor and stared at my throat. "He doesn't take girls seriously. He doesn't appreciate them."

"Can you remember any of their names or where they lived or worked? I'm trying to save Victor's life, Ester."

She applied shaving gel to the back of my neck and went to work with the razor, tickling my skin with each swipe of the blade.

"I don't remember their names." She stepped back and looked at my hair again. "Victor probably doesn't remember their names, either. He uses them."

She simultaneously defended him and attacked him—like a typical sister.

"What else can you tell me about Victor?"

"Nothing," she said. "I don't hang around with him anymore."

I asked her a few more questions, and in true Townie fashion she dodged them. I didn't learn a damn thing, but at least my hair looked good. I handed her two hundred dollars for a tip and met Cheyenne in the waiting area.

"How did it go?" she asked.

"Lousy," I growled.

"That's too bad. Wait for me in the car, and I'll see what I can do." She kissed me on the cheek.

I went to the car and listened to the experts on sports radio. Nothing changes in Boston, not when it comes to sports. We build up our heroes to tear them down, and the harder they fall the happier we are. Today the Red Sox were on the chopping block, primed to be dissected by the Hub's baseball gurus. Everyone knew what was wrong with the team, and everyone knew how to fix it. The hosts knew, and the callers knew. All of them could do a better job running the club, given the chance, but of course they'd never get the chance, so they managed from cell phones and broadcasting booths instead of dugouts. The game was simple, they said, and they cited lessons learned in little league or softball, real inside baseball. They offered advice to hitters, strategies to pitchers, and can't-miss prospects to scouts.

Some thought the manager should be fired, while others thought he should be extended.

It would be easy to laugh at Red Sox Nation, but I can't because I'm one of them. I knew how to fix the Red Sox, too. An hour later Cheyenne came out to the car and looked at me.

"Well, what do you think?"

"What do you mean?"

"My hair, how does it look?"

Oops... "Oh, tremendous," I said. "You always look tremendous."

She punched my arm. "It doesn't count if I had to ask." She grinned, and her cell phone rang. "Sorry, Dermot, I have to take this."

As she talked on the phone I meandered back to Boston, wanting the ride to last a long time. I drove down the VFW Parkway and the Jamaicaway and Brookline Avenue. If I came to a yellow light, I stopped instead of pushing through, a mortal sin in Boston. My punishment for the offense was the blasting of car horns, but it was worth it to be with Cheyenne a little longer. When we got to Teele Square, Cheyenne hung up the phone and said, "Sorry about that. School stuff, prison stuff."

"No problem."

"So, I had an interesting conversation with Ester. I can't wait to tell you about it."

It never occurred to me that Ester might have told Cheyenne things that she didn't tell me. Hell, she didn't tell me anything. "You questioned her?"

"I didn't *question* her. We just talked."

I parked in front of her building.

"Come on up," she said. "I'll make coffee."

We went up to her apartment, which was a small studio on the second floor with two small windows and a galley kitchen. A tan couch centered the room and a wing chair sat in a corner. I saw no TV or desktop computer. A painting of a man with intense eyes hung on the wall. A tin plaque on the frame read 'Henry

Starr, The Cherokee Bad Man.' Cheyenne must have seen me looking at it, because she said, "That's my grandfather."

"He looks like a tough guy."

"He was. Look him up on the Internet. Henry Starr was a legend."

She came out of the galley holding two mugs of coffee and placed them on the end table, took one of them and sat on the couch. I took the other and sat next to her. Cheyenne said, "I asked Ester about Victor's friends. She told me he has only one friend, Juan Rico. Rico lives in Grove Hall. Rico was the accomplice."

"Ester told you that?"

"Yes, she did."

"Wow, I'm impressed. How did you get her to talk?"

"We spoke Spanish," she said. "I think it made her feel more comfortable, because everyone else in the spa speaks English. No one could understand us."

"I didn't know you spoke Spanish?"

"I also speak Portuguese and little Italian, and I'm trying to learn various Wampanoag dialects, too," she said.

"Smart and beautiful."

Cheyenne blushed. "You rattled Ester a little when you said you talked to her mother. She doesn't want anyone to know that she grew up in the Charlestown projects. I think she felt relieved to speak in Spanish, and she became more relaxed as the conversation went on. By the end of it we were talking freely, like friends."

"I didn't mean to rattle her," I said. "Did she say if Victor has a girlfriend?"

"He had a girlfriend, but she died of an overdose—heroin laced with fentanyl. She never had a chance." Cheyenne's voice softened. "Another opioid death in the city, what else is new?"

"It's a plague."

"Mmm." She sipped her coffee. "So, how did I do?"

"You did great work. I think I need to hire you." I kissed her. "Thank you."

"It was fun, very exciting, actually. What's your plan now?"

"I need to find Juan Rico," I said.

"Ester thinks she can track him down. There's more." Cheyenne stopped talking and leaned on me, wedging into my side. "Ester is terrified of her boyfriend. She wants to break it off, but she's afraid of what he'll do."

"Do you want me to help?" I asked. "I'll come down on him like—"

"I knew you would say that. I love that you want to defend her." She leaned over and kissed my cheek and then my ear. "Ester wants to get away from him, but she can't afford it. Motels add up fast. I offered to find her a safe house for abused women, but she'd have to quit her job."

"Why?"

"Safe houses don't allow the residents to work, because their boyfriends could follow them there and put everyone in jeopardy."

I took a sip of my coffee, and an idea came to me.

"My friend Al Barese owns a hotel called Casa Abruzzi in the Ink Block. I'll tell him about Ester's predicament. If you think I'm protective, wait 'til you meet Al. He'll insist that Ester stay at Casa Abruzzi until she straightens things out with her boyfriend."

"He will?" she said. "How do you know Al?"

"He coached me at Boston College." I chuckled, thinking back. "Al Barese was the most demanding man I have ever met—anywhere, not just football—and the best motivator, too." *I won the Butkus Award for best college linebacker in the nation because of him.* "When his father retired from Hotel Abruzzi, Al took over the operation."

"It sounds too good to be true," she said. "What if Ester's boyfriend follows her there?"

"He'll wish he hadn't." I thought about the situation. "Talk to Ester. Convince her to take a week off from work. That will give me time to fix the mess she's in."

"How much will it cost?"

"Don't worry about it. Tell Ester to pack, and I'll call Al and fill him in."

"Are you always this good at fixing problems?"

Cheyenne kissed me and I kissed her back. Prickling electricity shocked my insides, as if my heart had touched a bare wire. My head went woozy, so woozy I thought I might faint. But I didn't faint, which was a good thing, because if I had, I would have missed the rest.

20

EARLY THE NEXT morning I heard Cheyenne stirring in the kitchen. She came into the room and handed me a cup of coffee and sat on the edge of the bed.

"Good morning," she said.

"You ain't kidding." I pulled her to me.

She snuggled into my chest. "Last night was perfect. I feel like we've been together forever."

"I agree," I said. "Let's go for a perfect morning."

"Now now." She sat up. "I think we have a lead."

"A lead?"

"I'm trying to sound like a P.I." She handed me a glass of water. "Ester called while you were asleep. She set up a meeting with Juan Rico."

"You're kidding me. You already found him?"

"Ester found him," Cheyenne said. "The meeting is at five o'clock in Grove Hall. Ester insisted on coming with us. She's moving out today."

"You work fast, that's good news."

"I told her we'd pick her up."

At four o'clock we went to Keldara Spa and Salon and picked up Ester, who came out carrying two suitcases. The three of us drove to Grove Hall, with Cheyenne's cellphone GPS dictating the best route. We turned onto Blue Hill Avenue near Franklin Park and pulled over at the corner of Geneva Avenue, one of the most dangerous intersections in the city, not because of the traffic, but because of the gangs. At least it was daytime.

"He said he'd be down there." Ester pointed at an alley. "That's what he told me."

We got out of the car and went down an alley that was paved with broken bottles and crushed butts. The path doglegged to the left, bending behind a brick building that secluded us from the streets. A tall chain-link fence topped with razor wire blocked the end of it, offering no escape. I felt like a desperado trapped in a canyon, but instead the threat coming from a band of Mexican marauders like in an old Western, it'd come from a team of MS-13 gangsters. I looked at Ester.

"This is where he said to meet," she said.

"Hey," a man's voice said, "over here."

I turned around and saw a diminutive Hispanic man, wearing baggy beige shorts and a drab-green tank top, standing in the shade. His hair was longish, and he hadn't shaved.

"Juan Rico?" I asked, feeling like a dummy. *Who else would it be?*

"Yes, I'm Juan." He was smartly on the other side of the fence, the fence serving as a barrier. "Victor didn't kill the old lady. She was dead when we broke in."

"Are you willing to testify to that in court?" I asked, hoping.

"If I do, I'll go away for murder." He stood a yard away from the fence, out of reach, ready to run if he had to. "All I can tell you is Victor didn't kill her. And I didn't, either. She was already dead."

"Victor said the same thing." I looked at his small feet. "I believe you."

"That doesn't mean a court will believe me."

I wasn't prepared for this. If I had taken an affidavit form with me, I could have documented his testimony. But I didn't, and that angered me. It meant I was distracted.

"Victor will do a lot of time, Juan."

"If I testify, we'll both do a lot of time."

"Not if she was already dead," I said.

"Who's going to believe us?"

I didn't debate him, because he was probably right.

"Tell me about the coins," I said.

"Victor knew about the coins. He heard that the old lady had jars of them inside her apartment. We knocked a couple of times, but no one answered."

"So you broke in."

"We thought no one was home. Victor took the coins on the table. We started looking for the jars, and that's when we saw her on the floor. I got out of there. Victor stayed too long."

"Does he have a girlfriend?"

"He did, she died."

I thought about the crime scene and asked, "Was there a third man in on the break-in, or was it just you and Victor?"

"Just us two," he said. "Why?"

I told him about the bloody footprint made by a large shoe. Juan said he didn't notice it. He didn't notice anything, except the dead woman on the floor. Juan didn't look like a killer to me, which was wonderful for him, but it wouldn't help Victor Diaz much.

"Are you sure you won't testify?" I asked again.

"Juan," Ester pleaded. "Please help Victor. He's your friend."

"I can't," he said, and then he was gone, vanishing in the other direction.

I looked at Cheyenne and Ester and said, "Now what?"

"We got what we came for, a meeting with Juan Rico," Cheyenne said. "He told us the same story that Victor told you. That must count for something."

"It does," I said. "And we know he's not the killer, because of his feet."

I wanted more from Juan Rico, but the meeting was still successful. He corroborated Victor's version of events.

"Let's go to the Casa Abruzzi," I said. "You'll be safe there, Ester."

21

WE DROVE UP Harrison Avenue and parked in front of Casa Abruzzi, a brick structure with keystone windows framed in granite. Casa Abruzzi contrasted with the luxury hotels and condos sprouting up around it, refreshingly so. I grabbed Ester's suitcases from the trunk. A redcap held the door as we went inside, stepping from rough concrete to luxurious carpeting. The lobby exemplified Old World elegance, with its dark woods and center staircase, its rococo balusters and mahogany banisters. To the right was a coffee bar with a copper espresso machine that looked like a deep-sea diving helmet. To the left was a barbershop enclosed in glass walls. The gold-leaf lettering on the glass read Andy the Clipper.

Al Barese, a muscular man with dark brown eyes and a strong nose, greeted us wordlessly, his eyes showing concern. His brother Andy, a modern-day Luca Brasi, took Ester's suitcases from me. They looked like lunchboxes in his hands. No one spoke, unless you counted Al Barese's body language, which communicated alarm. I wondered if I had overstated Ester's quandary to him.

Al and Andy escorted us to a suite in the rear of the building, and it was commodious, a square room with high ceilings and tall wainscoting. I introduced Ester to Al, just to get people talking, and Ester told Al her story. Al listened with intent, asking Ester questions as she talked, especially when she talked about her boyfriend.

"Does he carry a gun?" Al asked.

"He always carries a gun, and so do his friends." She started to say something else and stopped, and then her eyes widened. "He wears a wrist knife, too. He straps the sheath to his forearm and the blade clicks out the end."

"A spring-loaded assassin's stiletto," Al said. He looked at Andy, who nodded and left the room. Al continued. "I'm told he deals drugs."

"I didn't know that when I met him. He moved in with me, and then his friends—they're mostly Cape Verdean—they started hanging around my apartment. I overheard some phone calls, and I figured out they were dealing."

"He's dangerous," Al affirmed.

"He's extremely dangerous, but I didn't know that when I met him. I thought he was a nice guy."

"A charmer." Al folded his hands and lowered his head, and while looking at the floor he said, "You'll be safe here. You can stay as long as you want."

"Thank you," Ester said.

"Yes, thank you for this, Al," Cheyenne said. "You are doing a wonderful thing. Now why don't you gentlemen catch up in the lobby, while Ester and I talk?"

We went to the lobby and sat in leather chairs. Out on Harrison Avenue, pedestrians paced by while texting messages, walking into the street oblivious to traffic. Instead of the pedestrians looking both ways before they crossed, drivers looked both ways to avoid hitting them. It was ass backwards.

"She's a knockout," Al said. "Are you seeing her?"

"We're just starting out."

"I like an assertive woman." Al must have noticed me looking at the barbershop, because he said, "Andy has a select clientele, old goombahs from East Boston and the North End. Each client keeps a straightedge razor in the shop."

Andy joined us, and in a deep voice he said. "I give the closest shave in the city. If you want to join the club, buy a razor. Carbon steel is the best. I'll strop it sharp."

I looked at Andy's banana fingers and gorilla wrists. A straight-razor shave? If he twitched, he'd cut my head off.

"Let me think about it, Andy."

A redcap opened the brass-framed doors and two Italian men entered the lobby wearing European-style suits, one in a charcoal chalk-stripe, the other in an indigo sharkskin. The man in the sharkskin glanced at Al, but just barely, and went to the coffee bar with his pal.

"Help has arrived," Al said. "My version of going to the mattresses, my good friends from Eastie. They'll hang around for a couple of days, just in case there's trouble. The Cape Verdeans are tough sons of bitches."

"Nice suits," I said. "Are the holsters sewn into the linings?"

"Always a joker," Al said. "The fabric is imported from Italy, the finest wool in the world." He pointed down the hallway. "Our tailor, Don DeRosa, is from Sicily. Let me know if you want one and I'll have him custom tailor it for you. A navy herringbone with thin lapels would look good on you. Don will fix you up."

I wondered if Don was his name or a title. I decided not to ask.

"I'm not really a suit guy, Al." *A suit?* My clothes have never felt the heat of an iron. "Thanks anyway."

"You have a first-class lady, so you might want a first-class suit to bring her out." Al paused. "I guess you're not an opera fan, either."

"Nope."

"Too bad, I have opera seats that Cheyenne might enjoy. Me, I love the opera." Al pulled a cigar from his breast pocket, ran it under his nose and sniffed it so hard I thought he'd unravel the tobacco wrapper. "You look good, Dermot, very good. I heard you, ah..."

"You heard right. I stopped drinking."

"Well done." He squeezed my arm. "Good man."

I watched the men in the suits as they slowly sipped their coffee. They were all business, but they sure as hell weren't businessmen.

"Al, I have a cousin who's a Micmac Indian." I opened a photo of Kid on my cell phone and showed it him. "His name is Harraseeket Kid, and he'll be checking in on Ester from time to time. Your friends at the coffee bar might get a little jumpy when he comes in. Kid has a formidable presence, if you know what I mean."

"Send me the photo, I'll show it to them."

Cheyenne and I left the Casa Abruzzi and drove to Somerville to her place. As I navigated the rotary at Tufts University, I said, "What about Ester's job? Won't he stalk her there?"

"He already stalks her there. Ester asked for time off to deal with the problem. The owners, Eileen and Jean, are cool people. They told her to take as much time as she needed. Her job will be waiting for her."

"Good." I parked at Cheyenne's building and walked her to the door. "I'll call you later." We kissed and she went inside.

22

ON THE SUNNIEST of summer mornings I walked to the Navy Yard and went to the office and told Buck Louis about my conversation with Juan Rico in the alley.

"Juan won't testify," I said. "I tried to convince him, but he's afraid. He knows he'll go away. If I were Rico, I wouldn't testify, either."

"His testimony wouldn't have helped anyway," Buck said. "A jury wouldn't believe him."

I didn't agree with Buck on Juan Rico. I think his testimony would help Victor. But there was no sense arguing with Buck on it, because Rico refused to testify, so what's the difference.

"I wasted my time, hunting him down," I said.

"It wasn't a waste of time. The meeting with Juan Rico was important. We now know with certainty that neither Diaz nor Rico killed Gertrude Murray. Diaz clean cuffs and shoes prove it, and Rico's shoe size proves it. They are innocent of murder."

"But *we* can't prove it."

"Not yet, but we will, because the truth is on our side." Buck rubbed his jawline. "All we have to do now is get the evidence. It's out there somewhere, and we have to find it."

"I'll re-canvass the neighborhood, focusing on the people I missed the first time around."

"And I'll call the prosecutor's office and tell them what we know. I'll try to get them to issue an arrest warrant for Juan Rico. If we get Rico into court, he'll have to testify."

"You said his testimony wouldn't help the case."

"I was wrong on that. I was looking at Juan Rico the witness, not Juan Rico the man with small feet. Rico's small feet gives us physical evidence. He couldn't have left the bloody footprint. Okay, Dermot, let's get to it."

I went back to Gert Murray's building to question the residents I missed the last time, talked to three of them, and learned nothing. I was about to leave when I thought about Skeeter Gruskowski and decided to have another go at him. I knocked on his door, but he didn't answer. Where was he? With his bad heart and empty wallet he couldn't have gone far.

A bearded city worker known as Harry from Housing, who was also a longtime member of Alcoholics Anonymous, walked down the hall toward me. "Hey, Harry." I said, getting his attention. "I'm looking for Skeeter Gruskowski."

Harry leaned his broom against the wall and scratched his bushy brown beard. "Skeeter's gone. He left yesterday in a fancy Corvette. He won't be back for a while."

"Where did he go?"

"Don't know."

"Where did he get the Corvette?"

"Don't know, didn't ask," Harry said. "Skeeter said he'd be gone a month or two. He gave me two stamped envelopes, one for each month's rent. And then he gave me three hundred dollars to mail them at the appropriate time."

I told Harry that I was investigating Gertrude Murray's murder, and that I wanted to ask Skeeter a few more questions.

"A few *more* questions?" Harry sounded surprised. "You already talked to him?"

"Yes, earlier in the week," I said. "Skeeter told me he called 911 for Gert. He told me about his bad heart, too."

"He told you about his heart? Skeeter is usually mum about his heart. He doesn't want people to know about it, figures it makes him an easy target in the bricks."

"Makes sense," I said. "He would be an easy target."

"I heard you think Diaz is innocent."

"I do, based on the evidence I've seen."

"You're the only one who thinks that, but I have to agree with you. Diaz might be a thief and a junky, but he's not a killer." Harry's face flushed. "Wait a minute, do you think Skeeter had something to do with the killing?"

"I'm still gathering information," I said. "How well do you know Skeeter?"

"Pretty well, I guess. Skeeter and I watch sports together, the Red Sox and Patriots, sometimes the Bruins. He has cable. Once in a while his buddy joins us."

"What's his buddy's name?"

"Gage Lauria," Harry said. "They were longshoremen together in Southie, over there at the Conley Terminal. Gage got in trouble for embezzling union funds. The poor bastard lost his job and went away, federal time. Talk to Gage if you want to find Skeeter. He should be able to help you."

Finally, some progress.

"Where can I find him?"

"He tends bar at the Aces & Eights in Andrew Square, been doing it since he got out."

"The Aces & Eights, I'll go there." I thought about the Corvette and the two months' rent and the three hundred dollars for Harry. "Skeeter laid out a lot of money for a guy who's supposedly broke. Did he say where he got it?"

"He didn't say, and I didn't ask."

Of course he didn't, Harry's a Townie.

"Thanks for the help, Harry."

23

I GOT INTO my car and banged the steering wheel. Where the hell did Skeeter get the money? Nobody has money in the projects. Gert did. Gert had a coin collection. Son of a bitch! That bastard killed Gert for her coin collection. I had him. I never suspected him, and now he was gone. He played me, the bastard. I took a deep breath and exhaled slowly, drove to the Aces & Eights and parked in front. I had a feeling there would always be parking in front of the Aces & Eights, unless an ambulance pulled in to resuscitate a patron. The building tilted to the side like an old man on a rickety cane, and the drainpipes looked like they belonged on the Leaning Tower of Pisa.

I went in.

A group of men gathered at the bar, honing their skills as gin-joint athletes, alternating reps between shots and beers. The noncompetitive drinkers sipped wine from juice glasses, content to pace themselves for the long haul. Their faces were blank and their clothes were tattered. It was the first time in my life I felt overdressed.

Each year on my sobriety date I get together with my sponsor, Mickey Pappas, and we watch *On the Bowery*, and on Mick's anniversary we watch *Fat City*. Mickey tells me the movies are a good remember-when, as if I needed reminding. The Aces & Eights could have been in either film.

I stepped up to the rail and cleared my throat. A drowsy barman shuffled over and leaned on the chrome tap dispenser. Ribbons of flesh flapped under his chin, pennants to a hard-lived life, or maybe they were flags of surrender. He opened his mouth, fighting a yawn. Crooked gray teeth jutted from ulcerated gums like tombstones—an oral history of a roadhouse cemetery. I put a twenty on the bar and said, "I'd like to talk to Gage Lauria."

He rubbed his bulbous nose with a shaky hand, never taking his eyes off the bill. "I know Gage Lauria, know him well. As a matter of fact I'm working his shift today." He scooped up the twenty. "I heard he left town."

"Do you know where he went?"

"My memory is a little foggy on that one." He looked at the twenty in his hand and then he looked at me. "He told me where he was going but I can't seem to recall. My memory ain't what it used to be and keeps getting worse. It could be early onset Alzheimer's"

More like early onset Budweiser. I put another twenty on the bar and kept my finger on it. "Where is Gage Lauria?"

He hesitated, but only for a brief second. "Chicago, I think."

I removed my finger. "Can you be more specific?"

"He said Chicago, that's all." His hand flicked out and snagged the twenty. It was the quickest he'd moved since I came into the place. "He was excited to go, no question about it. Who wouldn't be excited to get out of this dump?"

"Yeah, who wouldn't," I said.

The drone of the television provided the only sound, except for the snorts, sniffles, and grunts—I glimpsed to see if Belichick was on the tube. A stooped man ordered a glass of port wine, using the same juice glass he'd been drinking from, and he took to a booth, cupping it with both hands like a priest carrying a chalice. I asked the barman for a Coke, no ice, and paid with a crisp ten, telling him to keep the change. I drank some and enjoyed the thick syrupy sweetness. Nothing beats a barroom Coke from the tap.

"You said you were filling in for Gage." I waved the glass for a refill. "Who makes out the schedule?"

"That'd be Dick Murphy, the owner."

"Is he in?"

"No sir, I don't believe he's in at the moment."

I waited for him to elaborate, but of course he didn't. Talking to this man defined the tired cliché of pulling teeth. No wonder he had so few left in his mouth.

"When will Dick Murphy be in?"

"Let's see, when will Murphy be in?" He kept looking at the bar for another twenty to appear. "Sometimes he comes in early, sometimes he comes in late, sometimes he—"

"Quit screwing around and tell me when Murphy will be in." I slammed my palms on the bar. "When will Murphy be here."

"Whoa, easy." He stepped back. "He'll be in at three."

I had a couple of hours to kill, so I drove to the L Street Bathhouse for a swim. I got my gym bag from the trunk, changed in the locker room, and inched into the icy salt water. After twenty minutes my body began to numb and shrivel, and my fingertips wrinkled to fleshy prunes. I showered off the salt and drove to Castle Island, where I ate a couple of hotdogs, drank another Coke, and walked around the fort three times, listening to cawing seagulls.

I drove back to the Aces & Eights at three o'clock. I went in and saw a well-dressed man sitting at a table, writing on a yellow legal pad with an Adirondack pencil. I assumed he was Murphy, either that or the place was being audited.

"Mr. Murphy?" I said.

He looked up.

"I'm Dick Murphy." He had short white hair parted on the side, and stylish horn-rimmed glasses over his bright blue eyes. He placed the pencil on the pad and gestured for me to sit. "Can I help you with something?"

"I'd like to talk to you about Gage Lauria."

"Gage?" He studied me more closely. "Why?"

"He bartends here, right?"

"Gage works here." Murphy put his hands on the table as if readying for a debate. "He's on the books. All my workers are on the books."

"I don't care about your books," I said. "I heard Gage went to Chicago, and I was wondering if you knew anything about it."

"I might." His eyes fixated on me. "Who are you?"

I was surprised he hadn't asked earlier.

"My name is Dermot Sparhawk," I said. "I'm investigating a murder in Charlestown, and I'd like to ask Gage a few questions about it. I work for a lawyer named Buckley Louis, who represents Victor Diaz. Diaz is charged with the murder. I'm investigating it."

"I heard about the murder." Murphy adjusted his glasses. "I grew up in those projects, in McNulty Court."

Common ground. "I lived on O'Reilly Way."

"I moved out decades ago." He picked up the pencil and tapped the eraser on the table. "What does Gage have to do with a murder in Charlestown?"

"He's friends with a man named Skeeter Gruskowski," I said. "I've been looking for Gruskowski, and my search led me here."

"Skeeter, Gage's pal from the longshoremen. He comes in once in a while, has a few drinks, tells a few jokes."

"I heard that Skeeter left town and Gage went with him."

"They left for Chicago yesterday. Gage asked for time off and I told him to take as much time as he needed. He's too good for this shit hole. He never should have worked here in the first place, but he couldn't find a job."

"Because he's an ex-con."

"You know about that," he said. "Gage Lauria is a good man. I'm friends with his father, his whole family actually."

"How long has he worked here?"

"Year, year and a half. I can look it up if it's important."

I shook my head. "And now he's in Chicago."

"That's what Gage told me. To be frank, I hope he never comes back. I hope he meets a nice Italian girl in Chicago, maybe in Cicero, that's Italian. I hope he stays there and has a big family."

Shit, maybe they aren't coming back.

"He left yesterday, you said."

"He did," Murphy said. "He paid me two months' rent before he left."

"Gage rents from you?"

"He does, he lives upstairs." Murphy looked up toward the ceiling. "He paid me a thousand for the next two months. I don't know where he got the money and I don't care. He wasn't dipping into the till, because I have cameras."

Cameras in this dump?

"The rent is only five hundred a month?"

"It's not exactly the Ritz," Murphy said. "And I know he doesn't make much bartending, so I give him a break on the rent."

"Where is up there, exactly?"

"Above the bar, on the second floor," he answered. "When Gage got sprung from the hoosegow he needed a place to live, so I took care of him."

"How much time did he do?"

"Five, six years, something like that. He stole from a pension fund, that's what I heard. Then I heard he was a fall guy for the union. Who's to say? He did federal time, though, did it out there in Fort Devens, so at least he was close to his family."

"And Skeeter was in the same union."

"Yup, same union, the I.L.A."

"Where did they get the money?" I said, thinking out loud. "Skeeter lives in the projects. Gage lives in a rooming house. Where did they get the money for Chicago?"

"Supposedly Skeeter hit it big at Foxwoods." Murphy thought for a second. "He must have hit it big, because he picked Gage up in a new Corvette."

Harry was right. about the Corvette. I felt my blood pressure rise.

Murphy continued. "Gage said that Skeeter got a stake, I think he said ten grand, and then he gambled it into a bigger stake at Foxwoods, six hundred grand."

Ten grand to six hundred grand? No way possible. Murphy must have read my mind, because he said, "I'm just telling you what Gage told me."

"Can I look at Gage's room?"

"I don't see why not." Murphy got up from the table. "This way."

We went up a slanting stairwell to the second floor, which was also slanting. Balancing on the floorboards, I felt like a surfer riding a wave. Murphy took out his keys and led me into Gage's apartment, which consisted of a single room with a window and no air conditioner. The heat was stifling. A metal cot abutted one wall. Next to the cot was a nightstand with a glossy pamphlet of Route 66 on it. The pamphlet showed an arcing red line that went from Chicago to Los Angeles, presumably the path of the famous highway.

"The tenants share a bathroom down the hall," Murphy said. "They share a payphone, too. Like I said, it's not the Ritz."

"It's not bad, either." I picked up the pamphlet. "Did Gage say anything about Route 66?"

"He didn't." Murphy looked at the pamphlet. "He said he was going to Chicago."

"Gruskowski read books about Route 66. He watched a video of Billy Connolly riding a motorcycle down Route 66."

"Billy Connolly, the Scottish comedian?" Murphy took off his glasses. "Why would Billy Connolly care about Route 66?"

"Maybe he likes deserts."

I saw trophies, a pair of high-top Converse sneakers, a leather basketball, a whistle on a cord, an Adidas gym bag. Murphy must have noticed me looking, because he said, "Gage was the best schoolboy basketball player in city in his day, all-scholastic two years running. I never saw a better white ballplayer."

"Did he get any offers?"

"A full scholarship to Villanova," he said.

"He must have been damn good if he got a ride to Villanova."

"Good enough to play as a freshman." Murphy picked up the ball. "Gage didn't like college much. It wasn't the academics— he's a smart kid—it was the culture, the money, the rich kids, the fancy clothes. Gage wears T-shirts and shorts. He only lasted a year, but he passed all his courses. Too bad, he could have been a great high school coach."

"And then he went away."

"For a felony, so teaching and coaching are out."

Gage Lauria, the name came back to me. He was all everything when I was a boy. Murphy asked me if I wanted to see anything else and I said no. He locked the door and we went down to the bar. When we got there he took my arm.

"It's not easy running a rooming house," he said. "It wears on you after a while. But I keep my place neat and bug-free. The rents are low and I've never evicted a man. I just wish I had the means to make the rooms nicer."

"I grew up in the projects eating government cheese," I said. "If I have a roof over my head, I'm happy."

"Let me know if you ever need a room," he joked.

"You never know." I then asked him, "Does Gage have a cell phone?"

"I don't think so. I assumed he used the payphone at the end of the hall."

I thanked Murphy and left the Aces & Eights, leaving behind the stench of booze and the pain of defeat. Only I didn't leave it behind. I took it with me. The aura of liquor clung to me like 90-proof glue, filling my nostrils and consuming my mind. I suddenly missed the drinking days, the alluring debauchery of a whiskey spree, the excuses, the lapses, the fuck-ups. The losing side of life didn't repulse me, but rather enticed me.

I was in trouble.

The fresh air didn't help. The craving for alcohol intensified. I could feel the booze warming my gullet and easing my worries and infecting my soul. One drink couldn't hurt. What harm could a single beer do? The desire became an obsession, and the obsession became a con. I told myself I had a right to drink, that I wasn't that bad when I drank. In fact I was pretty damned sociable when I had a buzz on.

But I was that bad.

Social drinkers don't end up bound by restraints in hospital beds. They don't get banned from barrooms, fitted for straitjackets, prescribed Antabuse, rushed to emergency rooms. And they sure don't think One Bourbon, One Scotch, One Beer should be the National Anthem. I dug out my cell phone and found a four-o'clock meeting in East Boston on Liverpool Street called the Fab Four.

I drove to Eastie straightaway, snaking through the Ted Williams Tunnel and Maverick Square. I parked on Liverpool Street and hustled in. The speaker, an old Pisano from Orient Heights wearing a felt fedora, talked about the flaw of perfectionism, a character defect common to many alcoholics. He talked about how perfectionism leads to procrastination, and how procrastination leads to paralysis, and nothing gets done. He finished his story saying, "When I was panhandling on Dover Street, bloody, smelly, and drunk, nobody looked at me and said, 'There stands a perfectionist.'"

The meeting worked, I didn't drink.

24

CHICAGO, ILLINOIS, THE City of the Broad Shoulders, home to Roger Ebert, Buddy Guy, Michael Jordan, and my father's hero, Dick Butkus. I was going to need help in Chicago, and I was going to need it from someone plugged in, so I called Kenny Bowen. Kenny and I had worked together on a case a couple of years ago, a case that netted me a fortune in reward money.

Kenny and I would meet at a South End jazz club called Greenburg's Nightspot, the coolest club in the Hub, and that's where were meeting tonight. I wanted to invite Cheyenne Starr along, because the place is so hip, but I didn't want to insult her by asking her at the last minute. Still, I knew she'd love it.

At eight o'clock I got in my car to meet Kenny at Greenburg's, and as soon as I started the engine my cellphone rang. It was Cheyenne. She asked me what I was doing and I told her about my meeting with Kenny Bowen, giving her the Cliffs Notes version of the history between us. Her voice filled with energy.

"I'd love to join you if that's okay." She hesitated. "Is it okay?"

"Of course it's okay." *Yes!* "How soon can you be ready?"

"I'm ready now," she said.

"I'm on my way."

She was waiting on the sidewalk when I pulled up, and we drove from Somerville to the South End. I said, "I'm glad you called. Greenburg's Nightspot is tremendous. The jazz pianist is tops." I inhaled deeply as we drove in trifling traffic. "Last night was special."

"For me, too."

"I'm glad you said that." I parked on Columbus Avenue at Southampton Street. "Very glad."

The South End is quiet on this block, where it overlaps with Lower Roxbury. If you listen closely you can hear the sodium street lamps purring on the poles and the pneumatic bus doors whooshing open. Cheyenne broke my thoughts when she said, "Ester Diaz is glad to be out of her apartment, but she is still scared. She changed cellphones, because she's afraid he might track her down using GPS."

"She was smart to change cell phones."

"She is terrified. He has some nasty friends."

"Don't worry, Cheyenne." I took her hand. "Al Barese will handle everything. Ester is safe inside Hotel Abruzzi."

"I know she's safe there. There's one more problem. The apartment is in Ester's name. She wants to break the lease but she's afraid of what he'll do to her if she does."

"We'll get Ester out of this jam. I'll think of something."

"Thanks, Dermot. I really like Ester."

We went into Greenburg's. The place hadn't changed since my last visit. The décor was still Art Nouveau, the lighting was still pale blue, and Zack Sanders, the African American pianist, was still wearing a black tuxedo with satin lapels and tapping out jazz on his Steinway grand. Tonight he was accompanied by a tenor saxophonist, who was also African American and also in a black tux.

Kenny Bowen was sitting at a table near the piano. I escorted Cheyenne across the room and introduced her to him, and Kenny, ever the gentleman, stood to greet her. Ruth Greenburg, the club's owner, came to say hello. I introduced Ruth to Cheyenne, and although it wasn't Ruth's custom, she took our order. We asked for coffee, and Ruth went to the bar.

"Dermot, it's been too long. How are you doing?"

"Plugging away."

We shook hands like lost brothers. Kenny is a Lakota-Cherokee Indian and a big man, as in Olympic shot-putter big. To enhance his imposing presence, he sports a shaved head, which sits atop his tree-trunk neck like a totem. He is an Ivy League graduate and a Rhodes Scholar. That is to say, Kenny can outsmart you as well as outmuscle you.

"How's the consulting business?" I asked.

"Busy," he said. "Still investigating questionable insurance claims, still thwarting crooks, still making sure my clients aren't getting bilked by frauds."

"And the recovery part?" I asked.

"Nothing as big as the case we worked on."

Kenny's biggest clients are insurance companies, who hire him to recover stolen items that are insured by the company. That's when we first met. We worked together to recover $100,000 bills that were stolen from a money show in Boston. That's when I hit the jackpot, working with him in recovery. Kenny made out equally on the deal.

"So," Kenny said, cutting out the small talk, "bring me up to date."

I told him about Gertrude Murray and Victor Diaz. I told him about Skeeter Gruskowski and Gage Lauria, two men with no money who left for Chicago in a Corvette. I recounted Skeeter's Foxwood story, a tale that sounded absurd to me. When I finished, Kenny asked me what I wanted from him.

"I am almost certain that Skeeter killed Gert Murray for her coin collection," I said. "If he didn't murder her, I think he knows who did. I'm going after him, and I'm going to need help tracking him down."

"I see." Kenny pushed aside his drink. "I'd be glad to help you, but shouldn't the police be handling this? They can track down Gruskowski and Lauria much faster than I can."

Ruth Greenburg delivered the coffee and left the table.

"The police aren't interested in Gruskowski and Lauria," I said. "The police have their man, Victor Diaz. They are convinced that

Diaz and his accomplice murdered Gert Murray. As far as the police are concerned, the job is done."

"So the police don't know about Skeeter and Gage."

"They know about Skeeter because he called 911 the night Gert got murdered, but they don't see him as a suspect."

"He called 911, interesting." Kenny sat back. "That's a nice piece of misdirection on his part if he's involved in the killing."

Kenny caught the eye of a cocktail waitress and tapped his empty glass with a fingernail the size of a guitar pick. She went to the bar.

"I need help finding Skeeter and Gage," I said. "They went to Chicago, and that's where I'll start looking."

Kenny swirled the melting ice cubes on the bottom of his glass. "So, you think Skeeter could be the killer." He paused and stopped swirling. "Look, Dermot, I'd like to help you, but sometimes you can be reckless."

"I'm not reckless. What are you talking about?"

"Come on, man. The last case we worked on, you flew to Belfast to confront the IRA."

"Hey, I helped you get the insurance money. You didn't complain then." I was feeling embarrassed that he said this in front of Cheyenne.

"That's not the point, Dermot. You could have been killed. You were a wildcard over there. If O'Byrne hadn't befriended you, McGrew would have murdered you. You must know that." The waitress delivered Kenny's drink, an amber blend topped with a cherry, probably a Rob Roy or a Manhattan, or perhaps a bourbon Manhattan, a drink my father favored, not that I'm obsessed with booze. She placed it on a napkin and gave Kenny's arm a squeeze. He sipped it and said, "I like you, Dermot, and I don't want to see you get hurt—or worse."

I was taken aback by Kenny's comments. Reckless? Wildcard? Cheyenne was looking down at the table. I calmed myself by listening to Zack Sanders on the piano playing A Kiss is Just a Kiss. The saxophonist blew a solo, producing a windy sound, soft and smooth and sometimes discordant. My defensive nature got the better of me, and I said, "I am not reckless, Kenny. I might be impulsive, and maybe a little soft at times, but I'm not reckless."

"I didn't mean to offend you." He stirred his drink a couple of times. "Are we okay?"

"We're fine." I thought about my conversation with Skeeter Gruskowski. "If it makes you feel any better, I didn't think Skeeter was a killer when I met him."

"Then why are you chasing him?" Kenny asked.

"Because he's on the run. Because he knows something. I think he robbed her, and I don't think he's coming back. I need to find out what he knows."

Cheyenne finally looked at me and said, "So you think Skeeter stole Gertrude's coin collection. That makes sense."

I told Kenny about Gertrude's coin collection, a sixty-year amassment of silver, and I ventured, "According to Murphy, Gage's boss, Skeeter took ten thousand to Foxwoods and gambled it into six hundred grand. I bet the initial ten came from Gert's coin collection."

"Now *that's* an interesting take," Kenny admitted. "I can look into Foxwoods. I know a woman there who can tell me about the recent winners."

"Skeeter has a new Corvette convertible."

"I can help with that, too," Kenny said.

"Wow!" Cheyenne said. "This is exciting, but can we take a short break? I need to use the lady's room. I don't want to miss anything."

Cheyenne walked behind the bar and disappeared to the restrooms. Zack Sanders introduced his next selection, saying, "Washboard Blues by Hoagy Carmichael." The saxophonist began with a slow riff, as Zack worked the keys.

"She's beautiful," Kenny said. "Smart, too."

"I know, but what I don't know is what she's doing with me." The waitress refilled our coffee cups. "I need your help on another matter." I told him about Ester Diaz's drug-dealing boyfriend and his posse. I told Kenny that the boyfriend terrorizes Ester, holding her hostage in her own apartment, and that Ester was staying in a hotel, scared to death he'll find her there. I asked, "Do you still have friends in the DEA?"

"I have associates everywhere," Kenny said. "Give me his name and address."

Cheyenne came back to the table.

Kenny said to me, "Anything else about Skeeter Gruskowski?"

"He has a bad heart," I said.

"Why is he going to Chicago?"

"I think Chicago is only the beginning. Skeeter and Gage had Route 66 brochures. I think they're taking a road trip across America."

"Give me second," Cheyenne said, working her cell phone. "Route 66 is 2,500 miles long. Most of it has been replaced by major highways. That's quite the road trip."

"I know it is, and Skeeter paid his rent ahead two months," I said. "If he comes back at all, it will be too late for Victor Diaz. In two months Victor will be convicted and sentenced. I need to track Skeeter down now."

"Did you tell Kenny about Juan Rico?" Cheyenne asked.

"Who's Juan Rico?" Kenny asked.

"Diaz's accomplice in the break-in," I said. "We talked to him."

"Did it help?" Kenny asked.

"Yes, it helped. I believed him when he said they found Gert dead when they broke in," I said. I told Kenny about the bloody footprint. "Both Diaz and Rico have small feet."

"What about Skeeter?" Kenney asked.

"He's a big man."

"You have to look at him more seriously for the murder, Dermot. Skeeter might have a bad heart, but he might be the killer." Kenny stood from the table, leaving most of his drink in the glass. Obviously, he had no issue with alcohol. A lush would have gulped it down. "I'll get started on my end. It was a pleasure to meet you, Cheyenne." He kissed her hand.

"You as well, Kenny," she said with a smile.

Kenny Bowen left Greenburg's Nightspot, whispering something to the waitress on the way out. Cheyenne and I stayed for another hour and listened to music.

25

THE NEXT DAY Harraseeket Kid drove me to the airport, taking the Callahan Tunnel. In the tunnel my cellphone rang. I figured it for a dead zone, but apparently not. It was Kenny Bowen.

"That was fast," I said.

"Gruskowski opened a bank account and deposited $100,000. He bought four prepaid Master Cards and put fifty thousand on each. He also bought $60,000 in traveler's checks. This guy has money, Dermot."

"Nobody uses traveler's checks anymore."

"Gruskowski does," Kenny said. "I tracked down the Corvette. He paid $70,000 cash for it. When you add it up—the bank account, the prepaid cards, the traveler's checks, the car—he laid out $430,000 in one day."

"He's loaded."

"I'm starting to think your Foxwoods story holds merit. It is just possible that Skeeter cashed in the coins and got lucky on a longshot bet."

"I was thinking about the coins last night," *when I wasn't thinking of Cheyenne,* "and something came to me. If he sold the coins to a dealer, he might have had as much as a hundred thousand to bet."

"I'll check the coin dealers in the area."

"You work fast, Kenny, and I'm grateful as hell for that."

"The domestic stuff is easy. It's the international stuff that's tough. One more thing, Craig Gruskowski is staying at the Horton-Marlowe Hotel, which is located in Chicago's Gold Coast neighborhood. The place is first-class, I've stayed there myself."

"The Horton-Marlowe, got it," I said.

"Keep in mind that you might be chasing a murderer. People have killed for less reason than half a million bucks."

It was 11:00 PM when the plane landed at O'Hare Airport. I grabbed my carry-on, flagged a taxi, and drove to the Horton-Marlowe. The hotel was everything Kenny said it would be, a topnotch venue with all the frills you'd expect: oaken walls, gild-framed paintings, thickly carpeted lobbies and stairwells. I went to the front desk. With the carpeting muffling my footfalls, I felt like an authentic gumshoe.

As the clerk processed me in, I palmed him two hundred dollars and asked him about Craig Gruskowski. It was like swiping a credit card. He scribbled a number on my receipt and said, "His room number, but Mr. Gruskowski is out at the moment."

"Any idea where he might be?"

"The Blackhawks game," he answered. "The concierge procured two tickets for him and his buddy, premium seats, behind the Blackhawks bench."

"What did his buddy look like?"

"Younger, taller, probably Italian, in good shape. He walked like an athlete."

"That's quite a description," I said. "Were you a cop?"

He turned away and answered the phone. I rode the elevator to the tenth floor and went to my room. Exhausted from the flight and cab ride, I turned on the TV, reclined on the soft bed, and fell sound asleep. I never checked Skeeter's room.

26

SKEETER GRUSKOWSKI CAME out of the United Center on West Madison Street and said to Gage Lauria, "What a town! I'm home, Gage. Chicago has the biggest Polish population of any city in the world, bigger than Warsaw, bigger than Krakow. Did you know that?"

"Why would I know that?"

"I didn't know either 'til some dumb Polack told me at the beer stand." Skeeter howled into the night sky. "Nothing beats playoff hockey, nothing! Not the Super Bowl, not even the World Series."

They walked with the post-game crowd and went to a place called the Third Rail Tavern, a sports bar packed with Blackhawks fans wearing jerseys and caps. Gage ordered a draft beer. Skeeter ordered a double Blanton's bourbon and said to the barman, "Got any Polish beer?"

"Polish beer?" The barman frowned and shook his head as if he were dealing with an idiot. "We have Duvel Golden ale, that's Belgian. I think Belgium is close to Poland."

"Duval Golden, I'll take one." Skeeter leaned over to Gage and said, "I wonder why he's in such a foul mood."

"Maybe he looked in the mirror."

"That's it! He looked in the mirror and shattered the glass, like the old hag in Cinderella. Remember that one, Gage? Mirror, mirror on the wall, who's the fairest of them all?"

"That was Snow White."

"Snow White, Cinderella, Goldilocks what's the difference? The fact is he's an ugly fuck and his face broke the mirror. Where is the nauseating bastard? I need another drink."

"Shh, here he comes."

Skeeter and Gage drank round after round as the hours ticked away. With a slight slur in his scratchy voice, Gage said to Skeeter, "You didn't win that money at Foxwoods, no fuckin' way you won it there."

"What's it matter where I got it? We're having a good time, aren't we? We saw the Cubs yesterday, the Blackhawks tonight."

"It matters, Skeeter. I did a lot of time because I was a sap for the union. Arrested for embezzlement? I couldn't embezzle if I wanted to. I wouldn't know how."

"I know, I know, you took it on the chin."

"They accused me of mob connections. They called me a liar and a thief." Gage got off the stool and poked Skeeter in the chest. "Where did you get the fuckin' money? I wanna know."

"Quit poking me. I didn't do nothin' illegal. I got lucky, that's all."

"I don't believe you, not for a fuckin' second," Gage said. "We're gonna end up in prison. I know we are."

"I'm telling you the truth, Gage, it's cool. Nothing shady, I promise."

"If I had a buck for every time, ah, forget it."

"Everything's kosher, swear to God. You believe me, don't ya?"

"Doesn't matter," Gage sighed, "jail, the Aces & Eights, what's the difference?"

"Don't get discouraged on me. We're just beginning this journey."

"Sure we are." Gage drank more beer. "We're just beginning."

"You can be a real downer sometimes." Skeeter finished the Belgian ale and the glass of Blanton's, and he stood up. "Man, that stuff's strong. I'm practically hammered."

"Practically?" Gage held up his mug. "Me, too."

"I've had enough of this joint." Skeeter jerked his head. "Let's get outta here and hit Route 66, the Will Rogers Highway. Lake Michigan to the Pacific Ocean, the roadway that built a continent, the Third Coast to the West Coast!"

"You want to leave now, at this hour? We're half in the bag."

"So what," Skeeter said. "I called the hotel. The valet is bringing the car over."

"He's bringing it here, to the Third Rail?"

"I said I'd give him a whopping tip."

"What about our clothes?"

"He's packing them up, it's part of the deal."

"We paid for another night."

"Who gives a shit about another night? I'm itching to get going, Gage. We can sit around when we get back to Boston. I'm hungering for the road."

The valet came into the bar and handed Skeeter the keys. Skeeter bought him a drink and gave him a hundred dollar bill and bellowed, "Next stop, Joliet."

"Joliet, like Joliet Jake in *The Blues Brothers*?" Gage asked.

"You got it, Gage, *The Blues Brothers*, John Belushi and that other guy. I can't remember his name. Remember that song, Shama Lama Ding Dong? The toga party, when the girl's bra fell off. Dean Wormer. The food fight. What a movie!"

"That was *Animal House*, not *The Blues Brothers*."

"I couldn't hear you."

"Never mind." Gage smiled.

"I'll flag down penis face and we'll be on our way."

"Who?"

"The bartender, I have to pay the tab."

27

IN THE MORNING I stood under a scalding shower for thirty minutes, turning the bathroom into a steam room. I dressed and went to the seventh floor, Skeeter and Gage's floor, and found their room open and a maid stripping the beds. She told me they had checked out. I took the elevator to the lobby and asked the desk clerk, the retired cop I had tipped the night before, about Skeeter.

"He's gone," he said.

"I thought he had the room for another night."

"He must have changed his mind."

I went to the concierge and told him I wanted to rent a car, the fastest one available. He found a Ford Mustang for me, which the rental company delivered to the hotel. Before I drove off I approached the valet, handed him hundred, and said, "My friend checked out last night. He was driving a Corvette convertible. Know him?"

"Sure, Skeeter. I delivered it to him last night."

"Delivered it where?"

"The Third Rail." He must have seen the confusion on my face, because he said, "It's a sports bar on West Madison. I took the car there after my shift."

"Did he say where he was going?"

"Joliet." The valet blew his whistle for a taxi. "I gave Skeeter the keys, and he yelled out, Next stop, Joliet!"

"Thanks," I said, handing him twenty more.

I got into the Mustang. "Next stop, Joliet," I said to myself. I got directions on my cell and started driving, going through Cicero, Blue Island, and eventually reaching Joliet. I had no sooner got there when my phone rang. It was Kenny Bowen. I put him on speaker.

"Gruskowski paid a bill at the Joliet Route 66 Diner," he said. "He paid it today, but I'm not sure what time."

"I'm in Joliet on Route 52, going north."

"Perfect," Kenny said. "The diner is on West Clinton."

The diner was housed in the Hotel Plaza on street level. The windows were decorated with Route 66 decals—red, white, and blue shields with black numerals. I went in and sat at the counter. A burly waitress with faded tattoos came over to me, reeking of cigarettes.

"What'll it be?" she said with a gruff voice.

"Two men were in here earlier today." I showed her Skeeter's photo on my cellphone. "This is one of them."

"Lots of people come in. I don't pay much attention to them." She barely glanced at the photo. "Today's special is hash and eggs, any way you like 'em."

"I'm investigating a murder. The man in the picture might be able to help me."

"The other special is Belgian waffles with fruit and whipped cream."

She wasn't saying a word, Joliet's version of the Charlestown code of silence. I told her I'd have scrambled eggs and coffee. She wrote it down and went to the kitchen. After I finished the meal, she came back and said, "Anything for dessert?"

"A slice of humble pie," I said.

Her stone face broke into a smile. "The man in the photo was here with a younger man, a good-looking guy." She put her pad on the counter so she could speak using her hands. "The older man couldn't have murdered anybody, no way. Neither of them could have. They were fun guys, big tippers, too. They're traveling on Highway 66, the whole route, clear to L.A."

"Did they say where they were going next?"

"Do you have wax in your ears? I just told you, Route 66." She pointed to the street. "Why do you think they call this place the Route 66 Diner? Because we're on Route 66."

The helping of humble pie was growing larger and getting tougher to swallow. "Did they say anything else?"

"The older one, his name was Skeeter, he asked me if I'd like to join them. He said we could get married in Vegas." She rolled her eyes. "They might've said something about St. Louis."

I thanked her and went to the car and thought about my next move. I entered St. Louis into the GPS and continued west.

28

AFTER THEY SLEPT it off on the side of the road, they hit the pavement again. The red Corvette tooled along Route 66, ragtop down, cruise control engaged, motoring at a steady pace. Skeeter looked at Gage and said, "This is great, isn't it? Chicago yesterday, St. Looey today. Too bad the Cardinals are still at Wrigley."

"Getting clobbered by the Cubs," Gage said. "And the Blues got kayoed, so there's no hockey, either."

"We'll have plenty to do, all kinds of things. There's the Gateway Arch, the Delmar Loop, Ted Drewes Frozen Custard, the Ulysses S. Grant Historical Site."

"How do you know all this stuff?"

"I've been dreaming of Route 66 my whole life. I used to watch *Route 66* with my father, starring Martin Milner and George Maharis, two cool dudes, extremely cool dudes. They drove a Corvette, just like us. Believe it or not there was an episode in Charlestown. Milner and Maharis parked their Corvette in front of the Bunker Hill Monument, right there in Monument Square. Can you believe it?"

"I can't believe they found parking there," Gage said. "Is that why you bought the Corvette, to be like the guys on *Route 66*?"

"Why else would I buy it, to impress people?" Skeeter said.

"We're exactly like them, Gage. I'm Martin Milner, because I'm the leader, and you're George Maharis, because you're handsome and hip."

"Handsome and hip?"

"That's right, Gage, handsome and hip." Skeeter sped up. "We're hitting Ted Drewes for ice cream. We'll be there lickety-split. Lickety-split for banana splits."

Gage rolled his eyes. They drove up Chippewa Street to Ted Drewes Frozen Custard, ordered chocolate cones, and sat at a picnic table next to a small brass band. Gage opened the newspaper and read the front page. "The flooding in Texas won't let up. The Boston weather can be bad, but at least we don't have to worry about flooding."

"Unless my ex does a cannonball in the harbor." Skeeter slumped in the bench. "I shouldn't have said that. Gimme a minute. I need a second."

"Is it your heart?"

"Not my heart, Gage, my honey. I miss her. I screwed everything up."

They listened to the band play a couple of ragtime songs as they ate their chocolate ice cream cones. Skeeter sat still, not saying a word. When Gage finished his cone he said, "How come she left you?"

"She had her reasons," Skeeter said, and then enumerated them. "I forged her name on a second mortgage, a perfect forgery but she figured it out. I lost the house betting the Patriots in the Super Bowl, fuckin' Giants spoiling that perfect season. Then the car got repossessed, and the credit cards got canceled. Then the heavies came to our apartment, hired muscle from my bookie, scared the shit outta her."

"What if you stopped gambling?"

"Stop gambling?" Skeeter laughed. "Does a leper change his spots?"

"I think the saying is 'Does a leopard change its spots?'"

"Not if you went to parochial school in Charlestown." Skeeter slowly rose. "Come on, let's go. I'm feeling kind of blue today. The road'll do me good."

"Sure, Skeeter, let's hit the road."

They went to the car and continued up Chippewa Street.

I stayed on the highway for hours, driving through the small towns of Illinois, clicking them off like Domino tiles. In Springfield I stopped for coffee at a mom-and-pop place. The owner served me with a smile, until I asked him where the bathroom was located.

"We don't have sanitary facilities," the man said.

"Do you have any unsanitary ones, because I gotta go."

He didn't answer.

Outside, out back, beyond the parking lot and into the woods, I relieved myself on a sprawling oak. In Edwardsville I stopped for dinner, and after dinner I caught the end of an AA meeting in a veteran's hall. The speaker, an old coot with a lisp, said, "You know you have a drinking problem when you go to a bar and your drink is waiting for you, and it's not your regular bar."

That night I stayed in a camp-like motel. I opened the windows and slept well in the cool country air. In the morning I called Cheyenne and talked for an hour. It seemed like ten seconds. I didn't care that I was falling behind Skeeter and Gage while I was on the phone with her. I didn't care about anything else when I was talking to her.

At the Mississippi River I stopped at the Chain of Rocks Bridge, now a pedestrian crossing, and walked to the bridge's famed 22-degree kink in the middle. How did cars avoid crashes when it was open to traffic? I almost bumped into a jogger rounding it on foot, daydreaming about Cheyenne. Then I thought about Gert's crushed skull, her marred face. What kind of a mindless animal slaughters an old lady like Gert? A mixture of love and vengeance swirled in my head and made me anxious. It also spurred me forward.

From the Chain of Rocks Bridge, I continued southwest and crossed the Mississippi into Missouri on Route 70 and drove to St. Louis. I stopped at a tourist spot called Ted Drewes for ice cream. I ordered a cone and sat at a picnic table and an idea came to me. I went back to the counter and showed Skeeter's photo to the teenager who served me, handing him a twenty as an enticement.

"Have you seen this man?" I asked.

"Yes, sir, he ordered a chocolate ice-cream cone."

"When did he leave?"

"Two hours ago, maybe three," the boy said. "He was driving a candy-apple Corvette convertible. The car was mint."

"Thanks."

I drove on a southwest slant across Missouri, staying on Route 44, passing through Gray Summit, Devil's Elbow, and Rescue. In Rescue, Kenny Bowen called and told me that Skeeter used his credit card at Gus's Gas Station in Joplin.

"What will you do when you catch up to him?" Kenny asked.

"I'm not sure yet."

"He could be a killer, Dermot." A long pause ensued on the line. "I never thought I'd say this to you, but get a gun—strictly for self-defense."

"I've gotten by this far in life without one."

"Do it for me, please." There was another long pause. "I hate to do this, but if you want me to keep helping you, you must get a gun."

"You feel that strongly about it?"

"That's the deal. I couldn't live with myself if you got shot unarmed."

"Where will I get one?"

"You're in Missouri," Kenny said. "You can probably get one in a coffee shop along with a large regular and a jelly donut."

"Okay, okay, I'll buy one."

When I reached Gus's Gas Station in Joplin, I found an older man sitting in a rocking chair whittling a block of pine. He wore a straw hat with a pack of Chesterfields tucked in the hatband. A scattering of crushed butts and wood slivers circled his feet. He looked at me, whittled, and waited. I showed him a picture of Skeeter.

"I'm looking for this man," I said. "He gassed up here earlier."

"Let me take a guess," he said, whittling. "You work for an insurance company, and the man in the picture has money coming to him from a deceased uncle."

"What can you tell me about him?" I waited but he didn't respond. "There could be a couple of bucks in it for you."

"You city folk think everything's for sale." He blew the shavings off the block. "I sell artwork. My latest creations are in the office. See if there's anything you like. You might want to buy one."

I went into the office and looked at his collection. He had wood carvings of biplanes, tractors, covered wagons, and a beauty of the Gateway Arch, but the prices weren't listed. I took the Gateway Arch out to the whittler and the negotiations began. I offered him a hundred dollars.

"A hundred dollars," he said. "I spent hours carving it, and it's precise to scale. I think it's worth one fifty."

"One fifty, huh?" I played along, turning the figure this way and that. "Okay, one fifty, but not a cent more."

"Sold!"

After I paid him, he said, "The man in the photo gassed up here two hours ago, him and another guy. They said they were going to the National Cowboy Hall of Fame."

"Where is that?"

"It's in Oklahoma City on Highway 66."

I passed a sign that said Kansas State Line Five Miles, and when I crossed the border I stopped in the town of Galena. The Route goes through just a sliver of Kansas, thus Galena became Kansas's designated stop on the southwest passage. I took a quick stroll around the town, just to do it, and got back on the road. Before I could say Dorothy and Toto, I was out of Kansas and into Oklahoma.

29

SKEETER AND GAGE came out of the National Cowboy and Western Heritage Museum in Oklahoma City and got into the Corvette.

"That was pissa, pissa beyond pissa!" Skeeter said. "The murals of the Old West, with the horses and mesas and tumbleweed. The portrait of Clint Walker. That was awesome."

"I liked the buffalo heads mounted on the walls," Gage said with a smile. "You don't see that in Southie."

"No kidding." Skeeter pulled on to the highway going west. "Speaking of Southie, how did you end up at the Aces & Eights? The place is a dump."

"The owner made me an offer I couldn't refuse." Gage raised his face to the sun and closed his eyes. "He said you're hired."

"I see." Skeeter drove along with the top down, letting the warm air blow through the car. "I wish I could've been one of those frontiersmen back then, riding and roping, drinking coffee around a campfire, roughing it with the other cowboys."

"Like *City Slickers*," Gage said.

"Yeah, *City Slickers*. We're like Jack Palance, aren't we? He was a tough prick, Jack. Remember the one-arm pushups he did at the Oscars?"

"Yup. Where to next?"

"The next stop is the Texas Panhandle, the bustling town of

Amarillo for a high-stakes poker game. This guy I know told me about it, big-time poker he said."

"What guy?" Gage asked.

"Just some guy."

When they saw the Amarillo skyline Skeeter howled yippee ki-yay!

"Pull over soon," Gage said. "I gotta go."

"We need gas, too."

Skeeter drove in to a service station and parked at the pumps. They got out and circled the car, stretching their legs and rolling their necks, and then their carefree mood changed. A monstrous man, wearing a leather vest and mirror sunglasses, came up to them. Sweat and oil stained his red bandana. Tattoos covered his hairy arms and neck. He wasn't alone. A teenage girl with brown hair stood a few yards behind him.

Skeeter and Gage tried to walk by them, but the big man blocked the way and said, "Meet El Knucklehead. I'm talking about the bike not the girl." He pointed a big finger at a Harley-Davidson motorcycle. "You thought I was talking about the girl, didn't you? El Knucklehead is the 1936 Harley, the first hog ever to go the length of Route 66."

"Good to know," Skeeter said, trying to walk past him.

"Whoa, friend." The big man extended his hand. "I'm Maish, and I got a proposition for you and your buddy. The little gal I'm with is down on her luck. What I'm saying is she needs money." Maish leaned closer. "She'll take care of both you boys for a hundred bucks, the best money you'll ever spend. Believe me when I tell ya, she'll bang your bones off."

"She seems young," Gage said.

"She ain't young," Maish countered. "Well, not *that* young. It's a good deal. You'll walk away with a smile on your face, and she'll walk away with a little money in her purse. Talk it over and let me know what you think. I'll be with the little lady."

Maish walked back to the girl and waited.

"I don't like this guy," Gage said. "He's pimping that poor girl."

"He's bullying her, too." Skeeter looked over at Maish. "I hate bullies, especially hairy ones. Let's hammer him, Gage."

"What?"

"The two of us can take him. Let's whale his ass."

"With your heart?" Gage lowered his voice. "Bad idea, Skeeter. Besides, he probably has a gun. Let's just get out of here."

"I'm not running."

"You could have a heart attack punching him out." Gage reasoned. "I'm worried about your ticker."

"I didn't think of that." Skeeter unclenched his fists. "Then we'd need two ambulances, one for him and one for me. I guess I'll give the ugly bum a break this time and let him off easy. Let's go before I change my mind and bust him up."

"Smart move," Gage said, "very smart move."

Skeeter and Gage waved to Maish and said no thanks. Before Maish could make a counter offer, they drove away.

Skeeter sped along the highway, his left arm resting on the car door, his right hand clutching the steering wheel. He tooted and waved to a trucker as he roared by him, with the Corvette kicking into overdrive and the speedometer climbing to ninety.

He said to Gage, "I love the open road."

"Are you in a rush or something?"

"Not in a rush, but I'm supposed to meet a guy at a place called the Panhandle Quencher in Amarillo. I want to get there early and get the lay of the land."

"I'll look it up." Gage fiddled with his phone. "The Panhandle Quencher, we're right on top of it. Take a left up ahead on Nesmith Street."

"Nes-what?"

"Nesmith, as in Mike Nesmith."

"The name sounds familiar," Skeeter said. "Is he a Townie?"

"He's a Monkee."

"They give monkeys last names?" Skeeter said. "How do you know him? Does he live at the Stone Zoo?"

"He lives in England."

"England?" Skeeter took a left on Nesmith Street and stopped at a red light. "Mike is an English monkey?"

"The Monkees," Gage said. "Come on, Skeeter, they're a British rock-and-roll band. You must've heard *I'm a Believer*."

"Nope, never heard it. Did it just come out?"

"Yeah, it just came out," Gage said, shaking his head. "It's a big hit on the radio."

"I mostly listen to sports." The light turned green and Skeeter drove ahead. "Remember when that gorilla escaped from Franklin Park Zoo?"

"Sure, Little Joe, with the long arms. He pulled himself over the cage."

"I wonder if Little Joe had a last name."

"He did, it was Young. Little Joe was the great grandson of Mighty Joe Young."

"Ah, you're bullshitting me." Skeeter glanced at Gage. "Really?"

"I'm kidding."

"I knew you were kidding." Skeeter pounded the steering wheel with his right hand. "I told you we'd have a million laughs on this trip."

"I hope the next turn isn't Lennon Street," Gage muttered.

"I heard that," Skeeter said. "The Monkees. Mike Nesmith, Davy Jones, Micky Dolenz, and Peter Tork. I watch the reruns. I was practicing my bluffing for the poker game."

They parked in the Panhandle Quencher lot and went inside. Skeeter ordered a couple of beers at the bar and brought them to a table. They sat by a TV and watched a local rodeo.

"Who are you meeting?" Gage asked.

"A high roller named Lucky LeCam," Skeeter said. "He comes here every night at eight o'clock looking for card players. Lucky is an important man in Texas gambling circles, international circles, too. Some people call him Lucky the Legend."

"How will you recognize him?"

"He wears a yellow rose on his lapel," Skeeter said. "And there's another clue. He orders a shot and a beer, goes to a table, and plays solitaire."

"If he comes in, then what?"

"I'll ask him about the poker game," Skeeter said. "It's gonna be great, Gage, a poker game in the Texas Panhandle, just like Maverick. Remember Maverick, with James Garner?"

"Yeah, sure, I think." Gage's head shook slightly. "Are you *that* good a player? Do you even know how to play poker?"

"I'm outstanding, Gage, one of the best on the East Coast, maybe the entire country. No one can read my bluffs."

"I never heard you mention it before."

"That's 'cause I'm humble. I don't brag."

The barroom door swung open and an older man in a brown suit walked in. He took off his Stetson hat and held it in his left hand.

"I think that's him, Gage. I think that's Lucky the Legend. See the yellow flower?" Skeeter watched as the man crossed the floor to the bar. "Did you see that? He ordered a shot and a beer. It's gotta be Lucky LeCam."

"See if he plays solitaire," Gage said.

The man with the yellow rose put his hat back on his head so he could carry the drinks to a table. He finished the shot before his ass hit the stool, and then he took a deck of cards from his pocket and began to play solitaire.

"That's him," Gage said. "That's Lucky."

"Come on." They walked to the table and Skeeter said, "Lucky LeCam?"

"Yes, sir, that's me." He looked up. "You must be Skeeter from Boston."

"What did I tell you, Gage!" Skeeter joined Lucky at the table. "Did my friend call you? Did he tell you I was coming?"

"He sure did. He said you were quite a poker player." Lucky placed a black eight on a red nine. "Is that true, Skeeter? Are you good?"

"The best ever, better than Maverick, better than Doc Holliday," Skeeter said, unbridled. "Can you get me into the game? I have the cash."

"The cash is a good start." Lucky put away the cards. "Meet me here tomorrow night at eight and I'll tell you then. Are you sure you have the money?"

"I have the entry fee and more."

"Tomorrow night at eight." Lucky stood. "Bring the money." He looked at Gage. "Are you playing, too?"

"I'm a spectator," Gage answered.

"Each player is allowed one spectator, so that means you're in."

30

THE NEXT NIGHT at eight o'clock Skeeter and Gage went to the Panhandle Quencher and waited for Lucky LeCam. At eleven o'clock Lucky came in and explained his tardiness.

"It took some convincing. Those boys don't cotton to outsiders."

"But you got me in, right?" Skeeter said. "Did you get me in?"

"You're in." Lucky jingled his car keys. "Follow me. The game starts in an hour."

They followed Lucky out to the desert where you could see every star in the sky. Lucky parked next to an adobe building under a busy highway overpass, with eighteen-wheelers and work trucks thundering overhead. Skeeter and Gage got out of the Corvette and locked the doors.

Lucky came over to them and said, "Give me a minute to smooth the way," and he went into the adobe hut. Skeeter and Gage waited by the car.

"This is it, the big night." Skeeter popped the trunk. "Grab the satchel, Gage."

"What's in it?"

"A hundred and fifty thousand dollars, my stake for the game."

"A hundred-fifty grand? Are you nuts?"

"I feel lucky, Gage. I'm gonna show these clowns what card

playing is all about. I'm gonna fill straights and draw aces. Wait'll you see me in action."

They knocked on the door of the adobe hut and waited. A bearded Mexican holding an over-under shotgun opened it and nodded them inside. Skeeter said gracias, which came out grassy ass. Eight men, all smoking cigars and cigarettes, all drinking beer and liquor, turned and looked at Skeeter and Gage. A rawboned man who looked like a cowhand walked over to Skeeter and said, "My name is Wade Ralston and I'm from Lubbock. Lucky okayed you for the game, so I guess that's good enough for me. He said you weren't too bad for a Northerner." Wade gestured to an octagonal table. "You need fifty grand to get in."

Skeeter unzipped the satchel and counted out fifty packets of $100 bills and tossed them on the table. "Am I the only one with the entry fee?"

"Don't be a wiseacre, Boston," Wade Ralston replied. "It don't play well down here in Texas. We don't like mouthy types."

"I was kidding, Tex. Lighten up."

The players were verifying each other's bankrolls when a busty woman with brassy hair sat at the table. She peeled the cellophane off a deck of playing cards, broke the seal, and said, "Let's get started, boys."

Wade Ralston said to Skeeter, "This is Miss Jeffers, the dealer. Any objections?"

"No objections." Skeeter took a seat. "She's the prettiest dealer I've ever seen."

"Button it, Boston," Wade said. "We don't go for smart alecks down here. In Texas we respect politeness and heed decorum."

"Then take your hat off at the table," Skeeter said. "There's a lady present."

Wade's eyes looked up to the brim of his cowboy hat. Before he could bite back, Miss Jeffers said, "He's right, Wade. A Texan never wears a hat indoors, especially at the table."

"Yes, Miss Jeffers." Wade grumbled and removed his hat. "Sorry, ma'am."

The game commenced and the hours passed. Midnight, one, two, three in the morning. At five o'clock, three players remained at the table: Skeeter, a kid named Teddy, and Wade Ralston, with Wade holding most of the winnings. The others had busted out.

Miss Jeffers dealt the cards. Wade won the hand with three sevens. Teddy, with two pairs, joined the other losers, busting out. It was now a two-man showdown, Skeeter Gruskowski versus Wade Ralston. Skeeter lost the next three hands, the last with a pair of deuces. Wade, who was showing signs of the bourbon, unleashed an attack.

"Deuces?" He roared laughing, pounding his fist on the table. "Who the fuck bets ten grand on deuces?" Wade pounded again. "What do you think we're playing, Go Fish? Boston thinks we're playing fish."

Skeeter lost the next two hands and Wade rubbed it in, his voice growing hoarser and his pounds getting louder. Skeeter whispered to Gage, "I got Wade right where I want him. I'm ready to take him."

Miss Jeffers called for a break to let things cool down. Everyone stood and stretched, except Wade, who never moved from his lucky seat. Skeeter and Gage came back to the table.

"Seven card stud," Miss Jeffers said, opening a fresh deck of cards. "Any objections?"

Neither man objected. Miss Jeffers shuffled. Wade cut the deck. She dealt the first two cards down and the third card up, a king for Wade, an ace for Skeeter. Skeeter bet five thousand. Wade looked at his down cards and said, "I'll see your five and raise you ten. You gotta put in ten grand more, if you can count that high." Skeeter saw the bet. Miss Jeffers dealt the next card, another king for Wade, another ace for Skeeter. Skeeter bet five thousand. Wade bumped it ten, just like the first round.

"Everybody's in," Miss Jeffers said, and dealt the cards. A jack for Wade, a third ace for Skeeter. "Your bet, Skeeter."

"Twenty thousand," Skeeter said.

"I'll see your twenty and raise you ten." Wade plunked thirty thousand into the pot. "Your aces don't scare me, Boston. Nothing about you scares me."

Gage leaned in and whispered to Skeeter, "You have three aces showing and Wade is raising you. He's got you beat."

"Fuck him." Skeeter whispered, and threw in ten more. "I'm taking him on this hand."

Miss Jeffers dealt. Another jack for Wade. He now had two pairs showing, kings and jacks. A five for Skeeter. He now had three aces and a five showing. It remained Skeeter's bet.

"Five thousand," he said.

"Only five? Gettin' nervous, Boston?" Wade counted his bills. "Make it thirty, chump. Fuck thirty, make it fifty."

Both men were in. Miss Jeffers delivered the seventh and final card, a down card that Wade immediately looked at, and when he did he jumped from his seat and howled.

"You're gonna lose, Boston." Wade rubbed his hand together. "I bet a hundred grand. You might as well save your money 'cause you're a loser on this one."

"Hold your horses, Wade," Miss Jeffers said. "It's Skeeter's bet, not yours. You yourself said that poker carries with it a certain decorum."

"I apologize, Miss Jeffers," Wade said. "I got carried away."

"Pass," Skeeter said.

"Pass? You're smarter than you look. 'Course, you'd have to be." Wade counted out a hundred thousand dollars and dropped it in the pot. "You can't win!"

"Hand me the bag, Gage." Skeeter added a hundred grand to the pot and said. "Call."

"Ha!" Wade turned over his cards. "Four kings, asshole! And I know you ain't got four aces, because I got the fourth one right here." He held up the ace of clubs. "What do you have to say for yourself now, Boston?"

"Go fish." Skeeter turned over his down cards, the two, three, and four of spades, to go with the ace and five of spades showing. "Straight flush, you lose."

"Lose? What do you mean lose? I can't lose, I got four kings." Wade stared at the cards. "He can't do that. I have four kings."

Teddy, who had just been wiped out by Wade, said with a grin, "Don't be a sorehead, Wade. The man beat you fair and square. Don't give Texas a bad name."

"He must have cheated."

"He couldn't cheat," Miss Jeffers admonished him. "I dealt the cards myself. He might have got lucky, but he didn't cheat. And besides, you cut the deck, Wade. Right here in front of everybody, you cut the deck."

"Fuck, fuck, fuck!" Wade flung his cards in the air. "He cheated. The son of a goddamn bitch cheated."

"Watch your tongue, Wade," Miss Jeffers said. "Skeeter whooped you, and that's all there is to it."

"I didn't have to cheat to beat you, Wade." Skeeter shoved the cash into his satchel. "I had a great time tonight. Except for Wade, you're a good bunch of guys."

Wade came around the table at Skeeter. Gage stepped between them and said, "He's got a bad heart. Back off."

The Mexican with the shotgun got up. Lucky LeCam, who had watched the whole affair from his spectator chair, spoke. "Wade, at your request I bring moneyed players to these games. Don't ruin everything because you met your match."

"How the fuck do you lose with four kings?" Wade said. "Something ain't right here. Something happened."

"You lost," Lucky said him. "Live with it."

Gage and Skeeter left the adobe hut to head back to Amarillo. On the way out the door Skeeter said to the Mexican, "Mañana." It rhymed with banana. Once they hit the highway, Skeeter said, "Did you see the look on his face when I told him to Go Fish? He shit his pants, didn't he, Gage? I did the impossible tonight—a straight flush!"

"You showed big stones, hanging in 'til the last card."

"It wasn't big stones, it was pure luck. I had three aces, hoping for a full house. I figured Wade had a full house, kings up. I never figured him for four kings."

"To be honest, I thought he had you beat."

"I'd never let a bozo like Wade Ralston beat me." Skeeter wailed again. "I can't lose, Gage! I'm unbeatable, undefeated! I'm the Rocky Marciano of poker."

They parked at the motel close to the room and guardedly got out of the car. Gage held the satchel against his chest, looking left and right as he walked along. "I'm worried, Skeeter. There must be a half million bucks in the bag, probably more."

"That's chump change, Gage. By the time I finish kickin' ass in Vegas, we're gonna be millionaires, the both of us."

"We're going to Vegas?"

"You bet we are, but first it's Route 66," Skeeter said. "Next it's New Mexico, the land of enchantment. We'll start off in Albuquerque, the Duke City. They call it Duke City in honor of the Duke of Albuquerque, back there in Spain. He must've discovered it or something."

"Albuquerque has a hot-air balloon festival," Gage said. "People come from all over the world to go to it."

"We'll go up in a balloon when we get there. Hell, we'll buy a goddamn balloon. After Duke City, it's the Continental Divide, and after that it's Arizona." Skeeter unlocked the motel door. "Get the bag inside."

They had no sooner closed the door when they heard a knock. Gage locked the satchel in the room safe and said to Skeeter, "Don't answer it."

"Let me check it out." Skeeter peeked out the window. "It's Miss Jeffers." He opened the door. "Miss Jeffers? What are you doing here?"

"Visiting the winner." She dominated the room simply by stepping into it. "I was hoping you'd be alone."

Both Miss Jeffers and Skeeter looked at Gage, who took the hint.

"I'll catch you later," Gage said. "See you in the morning."

Miss Jeffers stepped forward, bumping Skeeter with her mammoth breasts. "You showed moxie tonight, Skeeter. I like a man with moxie."

"Moxie?" he said.

"You had three aces showing and Wade raised you," Miss Jeffers said. "That meant he could beat your aces, and you never blinked."

"That's true, I never blinked."

"You licked him but good."

Miss Jeffers unbuttoned her shirt and tossed it in the air. It parachuted to the floor. She unsnapped her bra and thrust her chest.

"Jesus, Mary, and Joseph, there *is* a God in Heaven," Skeeter said.

Skeeter's face beamed red, then darkened to crimson, then blackened to purple. He clutched his chest with his hands and collapsed on the bed.

"Nitro!" he gasped, pointing to the vial. "My heart—"

Miss Jeffers uncapped the vial and called 911.

31

I PULLED INTO a service station and parked at the gas pumps. They had mechanical dials to measure the gallons and sale price. A man wearing tattered coveralls with a Texaco logo came out of the shack, wiping his hands on a rag. I told him to fill 'er up. But unlike the era when Route 66 opened, the dollars spun like a slot machine, while the gallons rotated like a rusty cog. I bought Coke and a Milky Way from the vending machines and waited.

A big man wearing a black leather vest, accompanied by a teenage girl who was staring at the ground, approached me, intruding on my space. He brusquely introduced himself as Maish. I nodded, trying to ignore him, but he wouldn't have it.

"Ain't you got a name," Maish demanded. "Are you too good for us?"

"My name is Dermot."

"That's a funny name," Maish said. "Well, Dermot, meet El Knucklehead. I'm talking 'bout the bike, not the gal. It's a 1936 Harley, nicknamed El Knucklehead. You thought I was calling the little lady El Knucklehead, didn't you?"

"You'd have said La Knucklehead if you were talking about her."

"La Knucklehead?" Maish frowned. "Are you some kind'a smart guy?"

"Not really." I walked away from him, but I didn't get far.

"Hey, boy," Maish barked. "I asked you a fuckin' question. Are you a smart guy?"

He stood in front of me, blocking my way. His beefy arms and shoulders were tattooed with blue ink. I pointed at a bare patch on his left forearm and said, "You missed a spot."

"What's that supposed to mean?"

"Did the tattoo artist run out of ink? He missed a spot on your arm."

The teenage girl snickered. Maish regrouped. "I'm getting tired of your lip, sonny boy, real tired of it."

"Maish, smarten up. Be a good ole boy and leave me alone."

"What if I ain't in the mood to be a good ole boy?" He puffed his chest with air. "What if I'm in the mood to rumble?"

"Get away from me, moron."

"I ain't movin'." Maish stepped closer. "I ain't movin' an inch. What the fuck are you gonna do about it?"

"Do I have to spell it out for you?" I stared at him until he blinked, and I said, "I'll shove El Knucklehead so far up your fat ass the spokes'll be sticking out of your teeth."

Maish grumbled but didn't act. Most bullies don't. I paid the gas attendant and got into the car, but before I got the door closed, the young girl ran up to me. "Please take me with you. Maish makes me do things. The men pay him."

"Get in," I said.

"Maish will follow us."

"No he won't."

I got out of the car, my arms shaking with adrenaline, and walked up to Maish. He was sitting on El Knucklehead, revving the throttle and staring through mirror sunglasses. I turned the key and shut off the engine.

"What the fuck are you doing?" he growled.

"Don't follow us."

"I'll go anywhere I want, asshole. This is America."

"I'll tell the police you're pimping out a minor."

"The cops don't scare me. Half of them get their rocks off with her." He started the engine again. "I'll be right behind you, and when I get an opening, I'm gonna snatch her up."

"No you won't."

I shoved Maish hard. He toppled off the motorcycle and rolled to his feet with surprising agility, flashing a hunting knife. The mirror sunglasses shielded his eyes, making it difficult to read his next move, so I made a move instead. I grabbed a squeegee from a water bucket and threw it at his head. Maish turtled, giving me a chance. I sprinted to the car, threw it in gear, and drove at him. He dove out of the way, landing on the ground. I cut the wheel and spun around, spewing sand and gravel into the air. Maish hid behind the gas pumps.

I veered toward El Knucklehead and ran over it. Its motor went from idling to coughing to silent. I put it in reverse and crunched it again. Maish screamed threats and obscenities from the pumps. I shifted into drive for one more pass, bouncing over El Knucklehead lengthwise. When I finished the flattening, it looked like a chrome pretzel. I pulled onto the highway and watched Maish in the rearview mirror, jumping up and down like Yosemite Sam.

"Maish finally got what he deserved," the girl said and started to cry.

"You're safe now." I flew down the open road, putting as much distance between Maish and us as possible, with the tailpipe occasionally grazing the highway. I'd be paying for damages when I turned it in. "Where to?" I asked.

"Amarillo, any bus station."

When we got to a bus station, I gave her three hundred dollars and wished her good luck.

32

I GOT A room in a stucco motel and watched the sun fizzle to a flat orange ball on the horizon. Just above the dying sun a vague outline of the moon appeared, nothing more than a milky silhouette, and it began to take shape and rise. I rested on the bed and closed my eyes, and the tension of the clash with Maish frittered away. Soon I became drowsy, and soon I fell asleep.

Kenny Bowen's phone call awoke me in the morning. I said hello as I blinked open my eyes, barely awake.

"I have something from Amarillo," Kenny said. "I think it's something you can use. An ambulance rushed Gruskowski to the hospital on Tuesday morning. He thought he was having a heart attack, but it turned out to be false alarm. They let him out yesterday."

"Skeeter is in Amarillo?"

"He was as of yesterday," Kenny said. "I don't know if he's still there."

"I'm in Amarillo. I slept here last night."

"You're closing in on him." Kenny paused. "Did you buy a gun?"

"Not yet," I said.

"I have more," Kenny said. "A woman named Ellie May Jeffers accompanied Skeeter to the hospital. Jeffers is known to be involved in high-stakes poker games. She's a card dealer."

"Skeeter was probably playing poker when he had his scare."

"Probably at the hotel the ambulance went to," Kenny said. "I have Ellie May Jeffers's address. I think you should talk to her."

I went to Ellie May Jeffers's home on Hickory Street, a gray ranch house with white trim, all freshly painted. The lawn was lush and the shrubbery was landscaped. A flagstone path led from the sidewalk to the front steps. High-stakes poker must pay well in Texas. I rang the bell and waited, listening to the ticking of a sprinkler and staring at the rainbow in its spray. The inside door opened—the screen door remained shut—and standing in front of me was a blonde block of womanhood.

"Yes?" she said.

"Are you Ellie May Jeffers?"

"Who's asking?"

"My name is Dermot Sparhawk," I said. "You helped a friend of mine, and I wanted to say thank you."

"What friend?"

"Skeeter Gruskowski, you went to the emergency room with him."

"Who are you?" She stepped back. "Are you with the police?"

"I'm not with the police. I'd like to ask you a few questions about Skeeter."

"Your accent, you're from Boston."

She pegged me, not that I cared.

"I know about the poker game, and I know you were the dealer," I said. "I'm not looking for any trouble. I just want some information."

"What information?"

"Did something happen at the game that rattled Skeeter, a fight or an argument, maybe a misunderstanding? Why did he think he was having a heart attack?"

"Nothing bad happened. As matter of fact Skeeter cleaned up, and that's all I'm saying about the matter."

"How did the other players react to an outsider cleaning up?" I asked. "Were they angry? Is that what shook him?"

"I already told you, that's all I'm going to say about it. Skeeter won big, and Skeeter is doing fine. The hospital released him."

"Did he say where he was going next?"

She said no and closed the door. At least she didn't slam it. I stood for a moment and listened to ticks of the sprinkler and followed the flagstone path back to my car.

I called Buck Louis, and he answered the phone, saying Louis and Sparhawk Law Offices. I liked the way it sounded.

"Anything new on the Diaz case?" I asked.

"Nothing," Buck said. "The police are convinced that Diaz's accomplice killed Gertrude Murray."

"And the accomplice is still missing."

"I told the DA's office about Juan Rico, but I don't know if they issued an arrest warrant. And even if we get Rico to testify, his credibility is as bad as Diaz's."

"Who would believe that two junkies broke into an old lady's apartment to rob her, only to find her dead? We have to find Skeeter Gruskowski and bring him in."

"Are you catching up to him?"

"I'm closing the gap."

"Oh, before I hang up. Call Harraseeket Kid. He wants to tell you something."

33

WHITE STARS BURST like Klieg lights across the black New Mexico sky, and a full moon painted a silver line on the tops of the Sandia Mountains. Instead of car horns and hostility, there was quiet and calm. The contrast to Boston struck me, and I wondered why I was so drawn to the city. I called Harraseeket Kid, my trusty Micmac cousin, and his enthusiasm exploded over the phone.

"Wait 'til you hear this," he said. "The DEA busted Ester's boyfriend and his gang. He is going away for a long time. Ester said she can finally get on with her life."

"That's good news," I said. "Thanks for standing guard over her, Kid."

"No sweat. That Hotel Abruzzi is all right. Those gunners from Revere are all right, too. And so is your friend, Al. Hold on, Dermot, Ester wants to talk to you." Kid put Ester on the line, and she said, "Thank you, Dermot. Thank you very much."

Why was she thanking me? I never told her about my talk with Kenny Bowen regarding the DEA. "I didn't do much," I said.

"Sure you did. You set me up with Al at Hotel Abruzzi. I felt safe there."

"Al can have that effect."

"Anyway, thanks," she said.

"My pleasure." I sensed there was more. "Was there something else?"

"I heard something that might help your investigation," she said. "Victor has a new girlfriend. Her name is Bianca Sanchez."

"Bianca Sanchez." The name sounded familiar. "Does she live in Charlestown?"

"She lives in Roslindale, but she works in Charlestown."

"Where?"

"At Avakian's Market."

"Avakian's?" My mind raced in reverse. "Bianca, the cashier, I remember her. I talked to her about Gertrude Murray. She never mentioned Victor."

"Maybe she was protecting him," Ester said. "Is this good news for Victor?"

"I don't know yet." I thought about it. "Do me a favor, Ester. Don't tell anyone about Bianca until I get back."

"It's between us," she said. "Kid wants to tell you something else."

"Put him on."

"Dermot," he said with a gasp. "I hope this is okay, what I'm about to tell you. It has to do with Ester. We're kind of hitting it off. I know you told me to keep an eye on her, which I'm doing, but things started happening. I didn't plan on it."

"Ester is wonderful," I said. "You couldn't do better, and neither could she. Good luck with it, Kid."

"Thanks, Dermot."

In Albuquerque I went into a café on Lomas Boulevard. A shiny oak bar went the length of the wall, and behind the bar there were shelves of booze. My eyes went to the tequila bottles, every brand you could imagine. They were beautiful bottles with beautiful labels and beautiful worms pickled on the bottom, the lucky bastards.

After a burger and a Coke, I drove to Old Town Albuquerque, which was a tribute to the Old West. Block after block of adobe buildings surrounded Old Town Plaza. A sombrero band played Mexican music in a gazebo, while shoppers and tourists crowded into the marketplace, fighting for shade under trees and verandas. I did some shopping myself, buying Western duds for Cheyenne, including Caiman turquoise inlay cowboy boots and a Stetson 100x El Presidente Silverbelly cowboy hat. The shop shipped them to Boston free of charge. That's what happens when you spend seventeen hundred bucks in cash. I continued to wander around the plaza, taking in the sights, and I got a call from Kenny Bowen.

"How's it going?" he asked.

"I'm in Old Town Albuquerque, sweating my balls off."

"Good, then you won't mind sweating in a gym."

"What are you talking about?" I asked.

"I'm talking about our next lead," he said. "Go to Bass's Olympiad Gym on San Filipe Street. It's a two-minute walk from where you're standing. Ask for Clancy. He's the owner of the gym. Clancy might be able to help you."

"How do you know it's only a two-minute walk?"

"Because you're on the corner of Romero and Charlevoix," Kenny said. "I updated my phone. It automatically tracks the location of the person I call."

"So much for privacy," I said.

I went to the Bass's Olympiad Gym on San Filipe, and a female bodybuilder at the front desk greeted me. If I had her arms, I'd be breaking heads in the NFL. I asked for Clancy. She pointed to the free weights and said, "Clancy is over there. He's expecting you."

"I'm curious. How did you know it was me he was expecting?"

"You're accent."

"Is it that bad?"

"Yup, it's that bad."

I walked to the free weights and introduced myself to Clancy, who looked to be about sixty years old, and he was buffed to the bone. His head was balding but his hair was dark on the sides. Sinewy tendons striated his neck, thighs, and calves. Each time he moved, another muscle flexed through his skin. I never saw such vascularity. You could practically see the blood flowing through his garden-hose veins.

"My name is Dermot Sparhawk," I said. "I'm friends with Kenny Bowen."

"You're the moose from Boston," he said. "Kenny told me you'd be coming. Let's push some steel while we talk."

Clancy watched me on the bench press, making sure I didn't crush my windpipe. I spotted him on the squat rack, though he needed no help. We talked as we trained—intelligent talk, not jock talk—it reminded me of lifting with Kenny Bowen under Harvard Stadium. I learned that Clancy was actually eighty, which I couldn't believe. He eventually asked me what I needed, but only after I proved myself on the chinning bar.

"I'm not sure how much Kenny told you," I said. "I'm chasing a man who's into illegal gambling, backroom poker, things like that."

"Curls," was his response. Clancy ripped through a set of EZ-bar curls, pumping out ten perfect reps. Muscles pulsated in his biceps, like Popeye's after a can of spinach. Eighty? He dropped the bar on the mat and said, "Most gamblers go to Vegas these days. It's on the up and up, and the chances are quite high you'll come out of there alive. Around here, in the back alleys of Albuquerque, it's too dangerous, literally a crap shoot. The games attract desperate men, draymen and dicers gambling away the last of their money."

"My guy might like that atmosphere. I don't think he'd go for the glitz of Las Vegas."

"A man of the people, I didn't know there were any left." He thought for a moment and shook his head. "I still say it's too dangerous."

"How do you know all this?" I asked.

"I've lived in Albuquerque my whole life. High school, college, law school, work, this is my hometown. Go to Las Vegas. If your man is a gambler, that's where he'll be."

I thought about the pamphlets I saw in Skeeter's apartment and in Gage's room. Route 66 doesn't go through Nevada.

"The guy I'm after is a Route 66 fanatic. I doubt he'd vary off the path for Vegas."

Clancy disagreed. "Las Vegas is effectively a stop on Route 66, so is Santa Fe. Both are considered part of it, even though you leave the Mother Road to get to them. Believe me when I tell you, for gambling, Las Vegas is your best bet."

"It makes sense, going to Vegas to gamble." I thanked him for his help, but before I left, I asked, "How do you know Kenny Bowen?"

"I used to be an official at the NCAA track and field championships. That's where I first met Kenny. He threw the shot put for Dartmouth and won the meet. I also officiated at the Olympic trials when Kenny qualified for Athens."

"Were you an Olympian yourself?"

"Indeed, I was. I represented the United States in weightlifting, Rome 1960, with Tommy Kono and Norbert Schemansky. We had a hell of a team."

"Hence, Bass's Olympiad Gym," I said.

He extended his big paw for a goodbye handshake and said, "Keep pumping!"

34

SKEETER AND GAGE stood in line at a Las Vegas gambling house called The Can't Miss on North Rancho Drive, waiting to place bets with the sports book. Skeeter looked at the board.

"The Red Sox are minus 150 tonight. Price is pitching. What do you think?"

"They're paying the guy thirty-one million a year," Gage answered. "I'd bet it."

"The Blackhawks are underdogs, plus 115. I'm taking them, too."

"The Blackhawks are shaky, Skeeter. The goalie might be hurt. Like you said in Chicago, this is playoff hockey. I'd think twice before betting the Blackhawks."

"And the Celtics," Skeeter continued. "I'm taking the Celtics over the Hornets."

"I like the Celtics," Gage said. "They need a win to even the series."

A window opened up and Skeeter stepped forward.

"Hand me the bag, Gage." Skeeter unzipped it and said to the attendant. "I want the Red Sox, Blackhawks, and Celtics. One hundred thousand each."

"Are you out of your mind?" Gage said.

"I'm telling you Gage, I can't lose."

Skeeter counted out the money, which took quite a while. The attendant motioned to the pit boss, who came over and watched the transaction. When the deal was done, the pit boss handed Skeeter the tickets and started to walk away.

"Hold on," Skeeter said. "One more bet. Fifty K on River of Dreams to win, third race Aqueduct. He's gonna breeze!"

"River of Dreams," the attendant said. "Third race, Aqueduct."

"River of Dreams? Aqueduct?" Gage said to Skeeter, "You don't know anything about horse racing."

"I'm just as sure about this bet as I am about the others."

"That puts my mind at ease."

They left the sports book and went to the tables, losing thousands playing Caribbean Poker. They then tried their luck at the progressive tables and things got progressively worse. At three in the morning Skeeter said, "We're getting low on cash. Let's check the ball games."

They went to the electronic scoreboard to read the results, and it was a clean sweep—for the casino. The Red Sox lost to the Orioles, Price getting walloped. The Blackhawks lost in a blowout, the goalie getting pulled. The Celtics lost to the Hawks, the series slipping away.

"Fuck, we got swept," Skeeter said. "How the hell did that happen? I was on a roll."

"Hey, it could have been worse," Gage said.

"How could it be worse?"

"The Sox could have played a doubleheader."

The next day they went back to the casino. River of Dreams finished second at Aqueduct, getting nosed out by an upstart named Bushmill's Legend.

"Why didn't I bet River of Dreams to place instead of win?" Skeeter groaned.

"If you did, he'd have finished third," Gage said.

"It's bad enough without your wisecracks." Skeeter rubbed his stubbly chin. "Hey, I have an idea. Let's go to a brothel and blow off some steam. It's legal out here." He took a glossy pamphlet from his pocket. "Look at this, a place called the Raunch House."

"I think it says Ranch House."

"Whatever, let's check it out."

"Your heart, remember what happened with Miss Jeffers?"

"She caught me off guard," Skeeter reasoned. "I'll be ready this time."

35

I WAS STILL in New Mexico, twenty miles outside of Albuquerque and driving west, surrounded by pink sand and rim rock. I saw a sign that said Continental Divide, Elevation 7,882. Another sign said that Arizona was Spanish for arid zone. "You learn something every day," I said aloud. It was weird hearing my own voice. Going seventy-five with no cars in sight, I hit the eastern edge of Arizona, cruising through Sanders and Joseph City. When I passed Winslow I thought of Skeeter singing *Take it Easy* the first time I met him in the bricks. Skeeter was nowhere near the bricks now. In Flagstaff I got a room in a touristy hotel and called Kenny Bowen, who told me there was nothing new on Skeeter. He must have heard something in my voice, because he asked if everything was okay.

"The information I'm getting, I'm getting too late," I said. "I know where Skeeter gasses up, after he's gassed up. I know where he's staying, after he's checked out. By the time I get to these places, he's gone."

"You sound frustrated."

"I'm not frustrated, but the routine is getting old, and it's not working," I said. "What's more, I have a fear, and I have an idea."

"What's the fear?"

"Route 66 ends in Santa Monica. My fear is that if I don't catch them in Santa Monica, I'll lose them."

"What's your idea?"

"Instead of chasing Skeeter and Gage, I'll get ahead of them. I'll drive straight through to Santa Monica, no stops along the way, and let them come to me. Gruskowski and Lauria will probably keep gambling, giving me time to get the lead."

"Good idea," Kenny said. When a Rhodes Scholar says 'good idea,' the idea sounds that much better. "Go to California and wait for them. I'll focus on the Los Angeles area."

I pulled over to the side off the road and called Cheyenne, and we got into yet another endless conversation. We talked from sundown to dusk to darkness, and the talk was lively and loose, discussing everything that came to us. Nothing was off limits, nothing was out of bounds. When I hung up the phone, one word came into my mind: soulmate.

The next day I crossed the state line, going from Kingman, Arizona to Needles, California. In Amboy I stopped for gas and coffee. In Barstow I pulled over to eat. I passed the Mother Road Museum, which I would have liked to have visited, but I didn't have time to waste. I'd been driving all day, and when I came into San Bernardino, I decided to stop for the night.

I needed a meeting, and I found one called the Token Group. I activated the GPS and ten minutes later I parked and went in. A young woman was chairing, and it was clear from her attire that we weren't in Kansas anymore. She wore rings on her fingers, rings on her thumbs, loop earrings, loop bracelets, nose rings, lip rings, eyebrow rings. She had more rings than a frat-house coffee table. She also had more years in recovery than I had, humbling my smugness.

She talked about getting into a relationship too early in sobriety. Both she and her partner had been off the sauce for only a month when the whirlwind romance began, and not surprisingly, they both picked up a drink when the relationship intensified. It started with a single glass of wine. A glass of wine couldn't hurt her, she said, couldn't hurt anybody. Six months later she was hospitalized with a crack addiction. She finished her talk by saying, "We shouldn't have gotten into a relationship that early. Two dead batteries can't start a car."

After the meeting I went to a lookout in the San Bernardino foothills. I had read about the foothills in a novel and I'd always wanted to see them. They were burnt and rocky and grand, and they rose suddenly from flat brown ground. I smelled smoke in the air and the temperature was stifling hot. The Santa Ana winds blazed down the trodden slopes and vaporized the oxygen in its path, turning the lookout into a convection oven, and I was the bun baking inside.

A low rumble came from the east. The rumbling grew louder, nearly violent, and the lookout shook. Was it an earthquake? Then I saw it, a stampede of motorcycles rounding the bend, hundreds of them roaring like hungry lions. The riders were bearded, the men at least, and they wore no helmets. Clad in leather or denim and shod in engineer boots, they revved their motors and popped wheelies and passed each other and fell back, like a team of Olympic cyclists.

I hoped like hell Maish wasn't in the pack.

They thundered past the lookout and squealed on the soft shoulder and went up the road with expert aplomb—the back of their vests reading Hells Angels Berdoo—and then they disappeared into the darkening horizon, leaving behind a deadly wake of silence. I got out of there in case they circled back.

In the morning I left San Bernardino for Santa Monica.

36

I DROVE THROUGH Pasadena and Glendale and Hollywood on a sun-splashed day, cruising at a steady clip, and then the steady clip ended when I hit the freeway approaching Santa Monica. The traffic was far worse than Boston's, but the California drivers weren't as antagonistic, perhaps due to the pleasant weather. They didn't have to deal with snowplows shearing off sideview mirrors. I crawled along the freeway, a lane stripe at a time, daydreaming, and then the phone rang. It was Kenny Bowen.

"Gruskowski is back online," he said. "He's using his prepaid credit cards again."

"Good," I said. "I'm almost in Santa Monica."

"You're well ahead of him. He checked out of a hotel in Las Vegas this morning, and he bought gas in Bullhead City this afternoon."

"Where's Bullhead City?"

"The Arizona line, abutting Nevada."

"He's still driving southwest."

"I'll keep tracking him. The credit card makes it easier, but there's a downside to it. The hotels don't process the card until he checks out."

"Which is too late," I said.

"I'm working another angle. I'll keep you posted."

I went to the Henshaw Hotel, a four-star resort with water views, a health club, and a massage parlor. I checked in at the front desk and went to my room on the top floor. Tired from driving, I decided to stay in for the night. I order a cheeseburger platter with two cans of Coke from room service and ate by the window. The vistas were breathtaking at sundown, when the sky turned purple over Santa Monica Bay, but you really couldn't see the shoreline. Maybe you had to wait until high tide.

The morning brightness woke me with a start. I checked my phone. No call from Kenny. Two days passed and still no calls. I filled the time by going to meetings and talking to Cheyenne and hanging out on Santa Monica Pier. My skeeball scores were improving at the same rate my patience was declining. Kenny finally called one night, moments after I clicked off the television.

"I got him," Kenny said. "Skeeter is booked at the Henshaw Hotel in Santa Monica."

"That's where I'm staying."

"Perfect." Kenny shuffled papers. "He checked in yesterday."

I went to the front desk and asked for Craig Gruskowski's room number. The clerk, a more principled man than the clerk in Chicago, refused to give it to me, citing privacy issues and other legal restrictions. The hundred I offered didn't help. Rather, it cemented his high moral ground, prompting him to raise his peach-fuzz chin with pride. Integrity is a terrible thing when it comes to bribery. I stepped outside and stood under a streetlamp, thinking what to do next, when a parking attendant came up to me.

"Are you waiting for your car?" He paused. "The desk didn't call me."

"I'm getting some air," I said. He started to walk away, and I said, "Hey, did you park a Corvette yesterday?"

"Which one? We have three." He smiled at me. "I know the one you're talking about, the red convertible."

"How did you know?"

"The gentlemen talked funny like you. You're talking about Skeeter and Gage."

"Right, Skeeter and Gage." Now this was a guy I could work with. "I came in from Boston to meet them here." I peeled off two hundred dollars and held it out. "It's yours."

"For what?" He didn't take. "I didn't do anything."

"For their room number."

"I thought you knew them."

"I do." I peeled off another hundred. "I want to surprise them."

"I don't know about this," he said. "I could get in trouble."

"No trouble." I handed him the bills. "Take it. If you decide to tell me, I'll be in my room." I told him my room number. "The three hundred is a down payment."

"What do you mean?"

"You get another three for Skeeter's room number."

I went back upstairs and had barely stepped into my room when the phone rang. The parking attendant told me that Skeeter was staying in room 311. I went down to the third floor and knocked on the door. Nobody answered. I stood silently in the hallway and listened, but heard nothing inside. I knocked again louder. No answer. I thought about pulling a fire alarm, but decided against it. I could always do that tomorrow. With my cell phone I called the hotel and asked for room 311. The desk patched me through. I heard the phone ringing in the room, but nobody answered it. I went down to the lobby and out to the valet station and paid the parking attendant the three hundred I owed him. He timidly took it and said thanks, apparently worried about bending the rules. I said to him, "How would you like to make a little more?"

"How much?"

"A thousand."

"Are you kidding me?" he said. "What do I have to do?"

"Call me when Skeeter comes for his car." I could see he was nervous. "No one will know about our arrangement. You have my word."

"Yeah, the word of a briber," he huffed. "This better not cost me my job."

"I just want to talk to them."

"They don't pay shit at this place, so I guess I don't feel too guilty about helping you," he rationalized. "If it wasn't for tips, I wouldn't eat."

"Consider the money a tip, which is all it is anyway."

"If you say so, but there's a problem," he said. "My shift ends at eight and I won't be back 'til four in the morning. What if Skeeter comes for the car when I'm not here? Then we're both out of luck."

"Who's relieving you? Is he someone we can do business with, someone who will go along with us?"

"I think so," he said. "I got him the job, so he should be okay."

"I'll give him the same deal, a thousand, and you still get a full share."

"I get a grand even if he's the one who calls you?"

"That's right," I said.

"I'll make it happen," he said. "It's not that big a deal. I mean, it's not like we're robbing a bank, right?"

"Right," I said. "Use my cellphone number."

I gave it to him.

37

A DAY LATER Skeeter's car was still sitting in the hotel garage. I called Kenny twice and he told me Skeeter was still checked in. I went to the room hourly and knocked. I called on the phone. Skeeter and Gage weren't in. I even followed the maid in once. I saw a suitcase and a duffel bag on the floor, but the beds were made and the chocolates were on the pillows. The maid looked at me and shrugged.

Where had Skeeter and Gage gone? Did they figure out that I was following them?

I walked to the end of Santa Monica Pier and stared at the Pacific Ocean and let the yellow rays warm my face. In Southern California the sun shined a little brighter, the breeze blew a little cooler, and the sea glass came from champagne bottles tossed off yachts. Even the gulls cawed in harmony. My cellphone pinged. The parking attendant had sent a text. He was retrieving Skeeter's Corvette. I jogged off the pier and up Ocean Avenue to the hotel. It only took me a minute to get there.

I didn't see the parking attendant, and I didn't see Skeeter. I looked in the lobby and down the street and inside idling taxis, but I didn't see him. Was he hiding? Two Latino men in polo shirts and chinos walked through the revolving door and stood next to me at the valet desk. One of them glanced at his watch and said something in Spanish to his friend. His friend said nothing in response. Tires squealed from the garage below and the red Corvette rolled up to the surface and stopped in front of us.

My friend the parking attendant got out and said, "Mr. Gruskowski."

One of the Hispanic men stepped forward and said, "That's us."

"You're not Mr. Gruskowski," the attendant said.

"Mr. Gruskowski sold the car to me," the man said with the slightest of accents. "I have the title here to prove it. He signed it over."

"Excuse me." I stepped in. "I'm Gruskowski's friend. I'm surprised he sold the car. He loved that Corvette."

"He sold it to me yesterday," he said, not elaborating.

"Where?" I asked. "Here in Santa Monica?"

He said nothing and got into the driver side. His friend got in the passenger side. I walked up to the driver with my cellphone in hand and said, "If you don't tell me what's going on, I'll call the cops."

"Call them. I purchased the car legally from Craig Gruskowski." His accent was now completely gone. "Gruskowski's name and signature are on the title. He signed it over to me."

I couldn't stop them from leaving, not without getting into trouble. The car sale sounded legitimate and they themselves seemed aboveboard. Strong-arming them wouldn't work.

"Will you tell me what happened if I pay you?"

The driver looked at the passenger, who nodded his head. I counted out five hundred and held it so they could see it. I asked them what happened. After the driver tucked the wad into his pocket, he told me about a poker game in Tijuana, where Skeeter lost most of his cash on a can't-lose hand. Skeeter wanted to keep playing, so he sold the Corvette, a $70,000 car with less than four thousand miles on it, for $10,000 cash. Skeeter went on to lose most of *that* money within two hours.

"Skeeter went to Mexico City with his friend after the game," the driver said, holding out his forearm. "He sold the Rolex to me, too."

"Anything else about the poker game?"

"That's it."

The man drove off in Skeeter's former car, wearing Skeeter's former watch, while I stood on the sidewalk, flummoxed. I had chased these guys for three thousand miles, if you include the plane ride to Chicago, and I came up empty. I paid the parking attendant the money I owed him and asked for my car.

I had nowhere to go, the trail had ended, and so I drove to the airport and returned the Mustang, paying a hefty surcharge for the one-way rental and heftier charge for the damages caused by crunching El Knucklehead. I bought a plane ticket for Boston. The only upside to the trip was that I'd see Cheyenne when I got back.

38

THE PLANE LANDED in Boston at 11:00 PM, after a herky-jerky flight. My stomach was roiling when I hailed a taxi and told him to bring me to Charlestown, giving him the address. Cabbies don't need to know the city streets anymore. They simply enter the address, and the GPS does the rest. He took the Sumner Tunnel to I-93 and had me home in fifteen minutes.

When I entered the apartment I sensed a presence, as if someone had been here while I was away. Maybe Harraseeket Kid had come up to check things, or maybe I needed to get adapted to my own place again. I was wrong on both counts. Cheyenne came out of the bedroom wearing one of my button-down Oxford shirts and nothing else.

"I'm so glad you're home," she said, and gave me a big hug. "I missed you."

"I missed you, too."

I moved closer and wrapped my hands around her waist and guided her to the bedroom, kicking the door shut behind us. She turned off the desk lamp and let the moonlight illuminate the room.

Early in the morning we went to the Grasshopper Café and sat at a table facing Bunker Hill Street. Lynne the waitress took our order and said, "You two make a lovely couple." She went to the kitchen.

"How's the jet lag?" Cheyenne asked.

"You knocked it out of me last night, and again this morning."

"Glad I could help," she said. "It's good to have you home."

"I missed you, too." I reluctantly changed topics. "I have to figure out my next move on the case."

"What if you talked to Victor's girlfriend, the one Ester told you about."

"You heard about that?" I asked.

"Yes, I told Ester to call you," she said. "By the way, Harraseeket Kid is quite a character, and I think he's falling for Ester."

"I know he is," I said.

We watched the cars going by. The drivers in Charlestown are pretty good. They stop at crosswalks to let pedestrians cross. And the pedestrians are good, too, sticking to the crosswalks. Everywhere else in the city it's a free for all.

"What is Victor's girlfriend's name?" she asked.

"Bianca Sanchez," I said, "the cashier at Avakian's Market."

"You already interviewed her, right?"

"I did, but she never told me about Victor." I drank coffee. "I've been wondering why she didn't tell me, and I keep arriving at the same conclusion."

"And what conclusion is that?"

"I think Bianca told Victor about Gert's coins," I said. "If she told him about the coins, she's an accessory to the crime, thus culpable in the murder."

"What do you mean?" She pushed aside her coffee.

"If Victor gets convicted, which is pretty likely, Bianca will be on the hook too, *if* she told him about the coin collection."

"Maybe she didn't tell him about the coins," Cheyenne said. "So I guess you need to find out why she lied to you."

"I intend to do just that," I said.

After finished we breakfast, she asked, "Do you want to take a walk?"

We walked down Bunker Hill Street toward Hayes Square, and when we came to the projects, a car raced by us filled with laughing teenage boys. They swerved onto Monument Street, bouncing over a curb, and turned onto Medford Street without slowing down, all in daylight. In the old days they'd have waited till nightfall.

"That was scary," Cheyenne said. "I'm glad no one was walking a child."

"The loopers," I said. "They're going to kill somebody one of these days."

When we got home I saw Kid's truck parked out front. I told Cheyenne I'd be up in a minute and went to the basement to talk to him. He was sitting on the bottom step, cleaning one of his rifles. He eyed the barrel, nodded in approval, and set the gun aside.

"Hey, Kid," I said from the landing, hoping not to startle him into firing.

"Hey, Dermot." He waved me down. "Do you have a second to talk?"

"Always."

"Ester and I started seeing each other. It's getting kind of serious. I'd like to ask her to move in with me, if that's okay with you."

"You don't need to ask me. This is your home, Kid. I'm thinking of asking Cheyenne to move in with me, too."

"Look at the two of us. Who'd a thunk?"

I looked around Kid's apartment, and I could see why Ester felt safe there. He had a rifle cabinet lined with long guns. He had ammo boxes. The window shutters looked like parapets, ready to defend against attack. I contrasted the Kid's basement to Casa Abruzzi, where the Barese brothers were keeping an eye on Ester, and I asked myself: Who would provide better protection, Haraseeket Kid with a rifle or Andy 'the barber' Barese with a straight razor?

"I'll tell Ester," Kid said. I started for the stairs and he asked, "Where are you off to?"

"I'm heading for Avakian's Market to talk to Bianca Sanchez," I said. "Ester did a nice job tracking her down."

"She worked at it, Dermot." Kid fished in his pocket and handed me two lottery tickets. "Use these to break the ice."

"What do you mean?"

"Ask Bianca to check the lottery tickets," he said. "It'll give you an excuse to talk to her. Besides, my computer shit the bed, so I can't look them up."

"Good idea."

I walked to Avakian's Market, forming a plan along the way. My eyes glazed as I thought, always a strain for me, and they came into focus when I got to the store. Taped to the window was a Help Wanted sign that looked like it had been there since the market opened. The sign was faded and the phone number had no area code. I went inside and took out Kid's tickets and studied the lottery chart. The days and numbers ran together into a vertigo blur. The only thing I could discern was a red star next to one of the winning numbers. A delivery man with a two-wheeler bumped me going by, jolting me from the daze.

Bianca Sanchez came out of the back room and went behind the register, and one fact was clear: Victor Diaz had extraordinary taste in women. I went to the counter and asked her to check the tickets. If she was nervous, she didn't show it. She scanned them on the machine and said, "Sorry, no winners."

I tore the tickets in half and put them in my pocket, stepped closer and said, "I know about you and Victor Diaz, Bianca."

"Who?"

"Your boyfriend, Victor Diaz." I leaned forward. "You lied to me."

"I didn't lie. I just didn't tell you—"

""What is going on here?" Mr. Avakian said, coming out of the back room. "What's with the whispering?"

"I was asking Bianca what you paid your employees."

"That's not your concern," Mr. Avakian said.

"I saw the Help Wanted sign out front."

"Help Wanted? Is that still there?" He looked me up and down. "I could use a big guy like you around here. Are you looking for work?"

"I'll let you know."

"Think it over." Mr. Avakian then said to Bianca, "Where is Nick?"

"He's on a delivery at Flagship Wharf," Bianca answered. "Two cases of Sam Adams, two liters of Glenfiddich 21, and a big bottle of Smirnoff 100."

"The yuppies drink the best." Mr. Avakian nodded with approval. "The other a day a man ordered a case of Johnny Walker Blue Label, twelve bottles, each in its own gift box."

"Only top-shelf for the landed gentry," I said. "I'd better be going."

"Let me know about the job," Mr. Avakian said. "I'll put you to work right away."

I made eye contact with Bianca on my way out of the market, letting her know I'd be back with more questions.

39

I STEPPED OUTSIDE and noticed two men sitting in an idling car at the corner, with cigarette smoke drifting out the windows. A smoldering butt arced out like a fireball from a Roman candle and exploded into orange sparks on the asphalt. I walked along Terminal Street toward the Tobin Bridge and the car pulled up next to me. A revolver pointed out of the rear window. The hammer clicked, a gunman's ahem.

"Get in front," a man said. "Move it, get the fuck in."

I got into the car and looked in the back seat and saw Bo Murray.

"Should I buckle up?" I said.

"Shut up," Bo said. The driver was either Albert or Arnold Murray, one of Bo's twin brothers. Bo tapped me on the shoulder with the gun barrel. "Don't make me blow your brains all over the seat, Sparhawk. Drive, Arnold."

Arnold Murray, a known druggy, drove through Sullivan Square to Beacham Street in Everett. He turned for Chelsea, going over abandoned railroad tracks and bottomless potholes, into the maze of the meat-packing district, driving past loading docks and warehouses and alleys filled with debris. The putrid smell of processed fish and rotting meat filled the air, the smell of death. I hoped I didn't end up in a sausage run. Arnold parked in a dirt lot.

"It's quiet here at night," Bo said, "no one around to bother you."

"No one to witness nothin' either," Arnold added, and then he waxed philosophical. "If an asshole gets shot in Chelsea and no one hears it, is he still dead?"

"You should be at Harvard," I said to him.

"Button it, Sparhawk." Bo was in charge again. "What's going on with my mother's murder? I heard you left town for a while."

"Who said that?"

"I got friends," Bo said.

"Friends in the police department," I said, as if I actually knew. "You're a career criminal, Bo. The only time you went away was when the Feds raided Charlestown. The Boston cops protected you, and the politicians turned a blind eye. You must have made it worth their while."

"Shut the fuck up, Sparhawk," Bo said. "My friends told me Diaz didn't kill my mother. They said his accomplice did it."

"The cops are wrong. The accomplice didn't kill your mother."

"How do you know?"

"Whoever killed Gert has big feet," I said. "Your cop friends must have told you about the bloody footprints. I tracked down the accomplice, and guess what? He has small feet, just like Victor Diaz."

"Where is he?"

"He's in the Dominican Republic," I lied, hoping to throw Bo off the scent, thus protecting Juan Rico. "He took off."

"You went to the Dominican Public?" Bo tapped my head with the gun. "Answer me, Sparhawk. Is that where you disappeared to?"

"That's where I went, the Dominican Public."

"What's his name, the accomplice?" Bo said. "I wanna talk to him."

"His first name is Juan," I said. "I don't know his last name."

"You don't know his last name?" Bo sounded incredulous. "Do I look like an idiot to you? Tell me his fuckin' name."

"I never got his full name. For all I know his first name is bull-shit, too."

Bo grumbled then continued the interrogation.

"Who told you he was down there?"

"I don't know," I said. "I got an anonymous call from a woman with a Spanish accent. She arranged everything. She told me when and where to meet him."

"And he's still down in the Dominican?"

"As far as I know."

"Half the projects are from the Dominican," Bo said, more to himself. "This Juan, why did he want to talk to you?"

"He wanted to tell me that Gert was already dead when they broke in," I said. "I asked him to testify for Diaz, but he said no."

"Why the fuck didn't he just call you?"

"Maybe his plan didn't have unlimited minutes."

"Was that a wisecrack?" Bo snapped. "What about Avakian's Market? What were you doing in there? And don't say nothin', because I watched the whole thing. The old man got pissed off about something."

"I was checking my lottery numbers." I took the torn tickets from my pants pocket and held them up. "Two losers."

"Huh?" Arnold stirred from his stupor. "What did you call us?"

"Shut up, Arnold," Bo snapped. "Look, Sparhawk, I don't have long to go. The fuckin' cancer's eating me alive, but I won't die 'til I kill my mother's killer. So here's how it's gonna work. When you find who murdered my mother, you're gonna to tell me first."

"If I find out, I'm telling the police."

Bo pressed the gun against the back of my head and said, "Your girlfriend is quite the looker, a real fuckin' beauty. I'd hate to see anything untoward happen to her. Is that one of your fancy college words, Sparhawk, untoward? Or do you want me to dumb it down for you, so you understand it?"

"If you touch her I'll—"

"You'll what, kill me?" Bo laughed. "You'd be doing me a favor." Bo slumped in the back seat. "We aren't much different, you and me. We do what we gotta do to get things done."

"Like forcing a man into a car at gunpoint?"

"That's right, like forcing a man into a car at gunpoint," he said. "Are you above that, Sparhawk? Are you too refined to stick a gun in a man's face and tell him what to do? Is that what you're saying?" Bo coughed and laughed and said with a gasp, "Don't get all high and mighty on me. Your old man was a tough guy and a Townie, and you're a tough guy and a Townie, so don't go pretending you're a Brahman, just 'cause you went to college. I know you. I know what you're capable of doing. Find my mother's killer, dip shit, and get out of the car."

40

CHEYENNE AWOKE EARLY in the morning and went to Tufts to discuss her thesis proposal with a faculty advisor. I went to Uncle Joe's Diner for an omelet and coffee. The owner, Joe Lally, joined me at the table and said, "How's the investigation going?"

"Slowly, very slowly," I answered. "I hit a wall, Joe."

"You still think Victor Diaz is innocent?"

"I know he isn't the killer, but I can't prove it." I added cream and sugar. "It only counts if you can prove it."

"I haven't seen you around," Joe said. "You got some sun, I see, and you look relaxed and happy. Did you take a vacation or something?"

"Not a vacation."

I told Joe about my futile chase across Route 66, pursuing a criminal suspect. Then I told him about Skeeter Gruskowski and Gage Lauria. I told him about Cheyenne Starr. Joe stopped me and said, "Dermot Sparhawk in love? That's terrific news."

"Thanks, Joe."

"By the way, those guys you were talking about, I saw them."

"What guys?"

"Skeeter came in for lunch yesterday."

"He came here?" I put down my fork. "Are you sure it was him?"

"Sure, I'm sure. He was sitting right over there with another man, probably Gage, based on your description of him. You said

Gage played basketball. The guy with Skeeter looked like an athlete, moved like one, too."

"Skeeter and Gage were here yesterday?" I said. *Joe's memory of them seemed pretty sharp, almost too sharp.* "They must have made quite an impression on you."

"They did," Joe said. "Donald spilled a pitcher of ice water on the table, and Skeeter was sympathetic about it, didn't make a fuss or anything. And Gage was so quick, he scooted out of the way, didn't get wet."

"I can see why you remember."

"People aren't always so patient with Donald, especially when he's ogling their mothers or following their wives to the car."

"He almost knocked down a waitress the last time I was here."

"Betsy, she's always good to him. Donald is a loose cannon, as the old saying goes, but he's practically family to me. He grew up next door on Walford Way."

"How did Skeeter seem to you?"

"What do mean?"

"Was he secretive?" I asked. "Was he keeping a low profile?"

"Not at all," Joe said, smiling. "On the contrary, he was loud and boisterous, but in a fun way, nothing cocky. They both seemed normal to me, two customers having lunch."

Interesting, surprising, too. I dropped a twenty on the table. "Thanks, Joe. I have to check on something."

"Wait." He put his hand on my shoulder, keeping me in the booth. "Don't go yet. There's something you have to see." Joe pointed to the police station in Hayes Square. "The loopers are about to strike. This will be good."

Ten minutes later a dented SUV flew down Bunker Hill Street and skidded to a stop in front of the police station. A gang of white kids wearing hoodies hung out the windows laughing. They blew the horn and revved the engine and patched out in the sandy gutter. A red-faced cop rushed to the street. The driver put it in reverse, bumped a police cruiser, and took off. The cop stood flatfooted on the sidewalk, barking into his collar mic.

"Those kids are ballsy," Joe said.

"Reckless, too."

From the diner I walked to Skeeter's apartment on O'Reilly Way and knocked on his door. Nobody answered. I was getting used to people not answering when I knocked. I went outside and looked up at his windows. They were dark and closed shut. I went round the building, not sure what I'd find, and bumped into Harry from Housing. Before I could say a word, Harry said, "Let me guess. You're looking for Skeeter Gruskowski."

"I heard he was back in town."

"I saw him yesterday with Gage Lauria. They were telling me about a brothel in Vegas, all the juicy details."

"I tried his door but he didn't answer."

"He's probably out." Harry propped the broom on his shoulder like a soldier carrying a rifle. "I'll tell Skeeter you were looking for him."

"I'd rather surprise him, Harry."

"Sure, a surprise." Harry paused. "You're doing good these days. You look good, too. For a while there I thought you were heading for the big barroom in the sky. No offense."

"None taken," I said.

"Are you still living on Bunker Hill Street?"

"Yup, same house," I answered.

41

CHEYENNE AND I went to the Navy Yard Bistro for dinner, sitting at a table that gave us a twilight view of the moon, the window framing it like a masterpiece. After dinner we strolled to Dry Dock 2 and out to the end of Pier 4, and by the time we reached the pier's edge, the skies had turned dark. Across the harbor the city lights twinkled to life on hotels and skyscrapers, and on the East Boston side of the water, tugboats came home to dock.

We walked along the waterfront and stopped at Kormann & Schuhwerk's Deli for coffee, and after that we went home to my apartment. On the first floor, Buck Lewis's door was open, and he yelled out for us to come in. He wheeled into the parlor and said hello to Cheyenne, and then we talked about the Diaz case.

"Skeeter is back in town," I said. "I tried his apartment but he wasn't in."

"His return surprises me." Buck locked the wheels. "Do the police know he's back? Should we tell them?"

"The cops don't care about him," I answered. "They already have their man, but they must have their doubts. They know Diaz didn't commit the murder because of the footprint."

"They're assuming the accomplice did it," Buck said.

"And Rico isn't coming forward," I said. "I'll talk to Skeeter. He's the key to this thing."

Cheyenne and I said goodnight to Buck and went upstairs to my place, soon to be our place—I hoped. I clicked on the air conditioner to cool things down, but Cheyenne had other ideas. She wanted to heat things up.

I was lying on the bed when Cheyenne came in wearing my old BC football shirt that looked like a dress on her. On her feet she wore black stiletto pumps that shot her up to six-three, and on her head she wore a cowboy hat that shot her up to my height. She moved toward me in a straight line, slowly disrobing, and crawled in next to me, and we proceeded to reenact the big bang theory, Charlestown style.

We lounged atop the sheets afterwards and praised each other's performance to the point of laughter. Rain started to fall, and the pitter-patter of raindrops added to a romantic moment. We sighed deeply and enjoyed long silences, and although we didn't say it, we knew that life couldn't get any better. Cheyenne rolled on her side and said that she wanted to show me something.

"You mean there's more to see?"

"Funny boy, it's in the car." She got out of bed. "Wait here, I'll be right back."

"No you stay here," I said. "I'll get it for you. What is it?"

"No I *need* to get it. It's a surprise for you, well really, for us." She pulled on her jeans and my BC football shirt and the stiletto pumps, gathered her hair and tucked it into the cowboy hat. "I'll be back in a jiffy. I hope you'll be pleased when I show you."

I rested my head on the pillow and enjoyed the glow of street lamps and the hum of a transformer. A distant police siren grew louder then faded into the night. An ambulance sped over the Tobin Bridge and down the Leverett Circle Connector, probably for Mass General. Firecrackers popped and bottle rockets hissed. A cherry bomb exploded and kids cheered. In a month, when the Fourth of July got here, the projects would be louder than Pearl Harbor. I loved the sounds of the city.

Tires screeched in front of the house. I heard a thud and tires screeched again. A woman screamed in Spanish. I threw on my clothes and raced downstairs and saw Cheyenne on the street, her legs sprawled on the tar, her head bleeding, her beautiful chestnut hair soaked red. The cowboy hat flopped down the street in the breeze. I went to Cheyenne and felt for a pulse, which was faint. I kissed her cheek and called 911.

I should have gone to the car myself. What was so important that she had to get it herself?

"Fuckin' loopers!" I groaned into the night.

42

I STAYED THE night in the hospital as Cheyenne fought for her life. Her father, George, was there, too. We didn't say much to each other. In the morning the doctor told us that Cheyenne had a fractured skull, a broken leg, and a broken back. She was also in a coma. The doctor said, "We'll just have to wait and see."

A nurse joined us in the room and said to me, "I need you to fill out some paperwork, please."

George said, "I'll do it. I'm her father and her healthcare proxy."

As the doctor left the room, he said, "I'll let you know if there any changes."

The rage must have shown on my face, because George said to me, "Do not compound the problem by doing something irrational, Dermot."

"George—"

"I know you love Cheyenne, and I know she loves you," he said. "I want you to go home and get some sleep. When you wake up, I want you to go to an AA meeting."

What's with the *I want you* bullshit? "George, the last thing on my mind right now is an AA meeting."

"After the meeting, call your sponsor and tell him what happened. You'll be no good to Cheyenne if you start drinking."

"I know that, George."

"And do not seek revenge. It was an accident. Do you understand what I am saying to you?"

I told George that I understood, but I was merely placating him. What I really wanted to say was fuck off. The nurse and George left the room together. I left the hospital, enraged. Sitting in my car, feeling the sting of George telling me to leave, pissed me off.

I thought about the first time I saw Cheyenne at an AA meeting in Powder House Square. George was with her, though I didn't know he was her father at the time. She sat in front, with her chestnut hair shining. I remembered when she grinned at George. I remembered because that was the moment I fell in love with her.

I peeled out of the hospital lot.

I didn't go home to sleep, as George suggested, and I didn't go to a meeting, either. I drove back to Charlestown with one thought in mind: hunt down the loopers. The morning traffic fueled my anger as I idled on North Washington Street, waiting to go over the Charlestown Bridge. For months now a construction crew has been working in the left lane, making no measurable progress, turning a minor project into the second coming of the Big Dig. In six days God created the earth. In six months these guys were still jackhammering the same corner.

I blew the horn. The driver in front of me threw up his hands as if to say, 'What can I do?' The bridge workers milled about, checking their watches for the next coffee break. A gurgling pickup truck edged in front of me and coughed diesel fumes into my face. The lettering on it read Massachusetts Environmental Police. The green police turning the sky black. Angry as hell, I resolved to save my rage for those who deserved it: the loopers.

I started my search at Uncle Joe's Diner. The owner, Joe Lally, knew about the loopers' strike at the police station before it happened, but Joe had the day off. Donald the busboy tripped and landed on a table, scattering plates and cups. The patrons recoiled as foodstuff covered their clothes. Betsy the waitress was ready with a mop and bucket.

I visited the stores on Bunker Hill Street, asking about the loopers, but nobody told me a thing. I did the same on Medford Street, on Terminal Street, in City Square, and in the Navy Yard. Nobody knew about the loopers, or so they claimed.

Hours later on Main Street, a few blocks past Zumes, I came to a ramshackle store that had somehow escaped gentrification, despite its prime location. A gang of white kids, all wearing baseball caps, loitered in front, shoving each other and exchanging taunts. I didn't bother to ask them about the loopers, because it would be a waste of time. The code of silence is a sacredly held norm among Townie teens.

I went into the store.

The cashier rocked out of his chair and trudged toward me, his body odor arriving before he did. He placed his grimy hands on the counter, showing long fingernails caked with dirt. If he stole from the store, it wasn't soap. Saving the worst for last he exhaled stink into my face, confirming he didn't steal mouthwash, either. The disgusting bastard made no attempt to look presentable. Wormy stubble crawled on his cheeks, almost looking alive, as if he'd been bobbing for maggots in a garbage pail.

"Yeah?" he barked, baring his brown-edged teeth. He probably flossed with used pipe cleaners. "Whadda you want?"

I want you to shower, shave, gargle, spray on deodorant, wash your filthy clothes, and comb your fucking hair.

"I want your help on something," I said slowly, so as not to swamp him with too much at once. "What do you know about the loopers? I'm told they hang around here."

"Loopers?" He glanced at the kids on the sidewalk. "I can't help you on that one, chief. Don't know about no loopers."

Bingo, he knew.

"Nobody in Charlestown seems to know about them."

"That's because they don't exist. They're a myth, a made-up fairytale like Santa Claus or the Easter Bunny. Do you want to buy something or don't ya?"

"Sure." I looked at the lottery board on the wall behind him. "Give me a Megabucks."

"It's worth two and a half million tonight."

"I'll take three of them, quick picks on separate tickets." I reached into my pocket and took out a wad of bills. "Give me a quick pick on the daily number, too."

He stared at the wad, not quite drooling, as he punched the buttons and the tickets spit out. He handed them to me, and I gave him a hundred.

"Got anything smaller?" he asked. "With those punks hanging outside, I don't keep much cash in the drawer."

"Nothing smaller, but I have something larger." I peeled off another hundred and dropped the bills in front of him. "Tell me about the loopers."

He looked at the kids outside and he looked at the money on the counter. His unshaven face contorted as he weighed loyalty against payola, and it didn't take him but a greedy second to make up his mind. He snatched up the cash and said, "There's a kid named Jimmy Molony on Dunstable Street. He's just a boy, thirteen or fourteen, and he lives with his mother. He might know something about the loopers."

"Jimmy Molony, Dunstable Street."

"Don't tell anybody I told you about him," he said. "I don't want those punks smashing my windows."

"It wouldn't be bad if they did," I said. "It'd let in some fresh air."

43

I WALKED TO Dunstable Street, a long U-shaped street with a hundred or more apartments on it, located in the Mishawum Park development. If I randomly went down the street knocking on doors, I'd arouse suspicion—not a good move in this tight-knit neighborhood. I stood on the sidewalk, thinking, wondering how to find Jimmy Molony's address, when luck came my way. A food-pantry client walked up to me.

"What are you doing on this side of town, Dermot?" She shielded her eyes from the sun as she looked up at me.

"I'm looking for the Molony family."

"Gina Molony," she said. "Her husband took off and left her to raise Sean and Jimmy by herself."

"I'd like to talk to her."

She looked at me for a moment, deciding whether or not to tell me where Gina lived, and must have judged me okay, because she said, "Gina lives over there on the ground floor."

I went to the apartment and rang the bell. A lean woman with tired eyes answered it. She had been attractive at one time, but life had beaten the sparkle out of her.

"My name is Dermot Sparhawk," I said.

"I know who you are." She wore a threadbare bathrobe with cigarette burns on the sleeves. "I see you in the newspaper, raising money for the food pantry."

"I'd like to talk to Jimmy."

"My Jimmy? Why?"

"I want to ask him a few questions."

"Questions about what?" She snugged the robe to her throat. "What questions?"

"It's about the loopers."

"Jimmy doesn't know anything about the loopers."

"They ran over my girlfriend and damn near killed her."

"Jimmy had nothing to do with that."

They never do. "Of course he didn't, but he might know who did."

"He ain't a rat, either." She stepped away and tightened the belt. "You have no right to come here."

"I just want to talk to him."

"Keep away from my Jimmy." She started to close the door and said, "Get out of here or I'll call the cops."

"Yes, ma'am."

That went well.

From Mishawum Park I took an Uber to the hospital to visit Cheyenne. Nothing in her condition had changed. She remained in bed, eyes closed, mouth opened. An orchestra of monitors beeped, a saline bag dripped, and an intravenous port protruded from her arm. I sat in a chair next to her and prayed the rosary, probably because my mother had prayed it. A lot of good it did her. She died of cirrhosis of the liver. Her saline drip was vodka. When I finished, I put away the beads and leaned back in the chair and watched Cheyenne's face. Her father came and said, "It is time for you to go home, Dermot. Get some rest. I'll call you if anything changes."

I didn't want to leave, but there was no arguing with George.

When I got out to my car I punched the front fender with everything I had, denting it. I punched it again. A woman getting into a car in the next row looked at me and quickly locked her door. My hand throbbed and my knuckles bled.

44

AT HOME I sat and rested my feet on a hassock and ice on my hand. It felt good to relax, especially after getting chewed out by an irate Charlestown mother. I should have known better than to question the goodness of her son. I sunk into the chair and opened a book I'd been reading titled *Shadowboxing: The Rise and Fall of George Dixon*. I had just finished the last chapter and was browsing the acknowledgements when my eyelids got heavy and slammed shut.

When I awoke it was dark. The apartment sat in blackness, the only light coming from a digital clock-radio across the room. I felt isolated, safely beyond the reach of the outside world. And with the lights off, the chances were high that no one would bother me tonight.

Wrong.

The doorbell rang. I thought about ignoring it but couldn't, and I went down to answer it. Outside, waiting on the porch, stood a longtime food-pantry client, an older Hispanic woman who lived in the bricks. She looked skittish—fidgeting and scanning the area. I opened the door and asked her if she was okay.

"I waited till dark so nobody could see me," she said. "I have to talk to you about something important."

Looking over her shoulder and back at the street, she moved away from the porch light, apparently afraid someone might see her. I invited her into the foyer and closed the door behind her. It was eighty degrees out, and she was shaking.

"What's wrong?" I asked.

"I saw the car hit your girlfriend."

"What?"

"It was parked on Monument Street," she said. "When your girlfriend came out, the car hit her on purpose. I thought it was you."

"On purpose?" I said.

"The car headed right for her."

I thought it was an accident and so did the police.

"Were young kids driving?" I asked. "Was it the loopers?"

"No, not them," she said. "One man drove. He aimed at her."

"One man, not a group of teens?"

"One man," she said.

"What did he look like?"

"A white man," she said. "I couldn't see him that good."

Something she said earlier threw me, a small thing that didn't fit. "You said you thought it was *me* getting run over. Why did you think it was me?"

"I'm not sure why."

"Try, it's important."

She looked at the floor, looked outside, looked at me. "When she got hit I watched it from right there." She pointed across the street. "That's where I was standing."

"A perfect view," I said.

"I thought it was you that got hit. It was rainy. All I saw was the BC shirt, and I thought it was you getting out of the car."

"I can see why," I said. "Forgive me for asking, but I forget your name."

"Carmen Cardosa, but don't tell anybody I talked to you."

Carmen left, and I started to shake. Fuck, this is my fault. Cheyenne got hit because of me. I was the target. This was no accident. George's words came back to me, that I'd be no good to Cheyenne drunk. I needed a meeting, and I knew where to go to get to one.

45

I WALKED TO the Teamsters building in Sullivan Square for an AA meeting, and when I got there I saw Skinny Atlas standing at the door, handing out raffle tickets for the Big Book. Skinny had grown up in a section of the South End called the New York Streets, an established community that got bulldozed in the name of urban renewal, destroying a vibrant Boston neighborhood. His knowledge of the New York Streets helped me solve a lucrative case, my first big moneymaker.

I was talking to Skinny about the Red Sox and their lack of power hitting when my sponsor, Mickey Pappas, came in. Mickey added his own thoughts on the subject, harkening back to the twilight years of Ted Williams, when he batted .388 at age thirty-nine—no steroids, no juiced-up baseballs. The Mick and I grabbed a cup of coffee and sat up front. There are always seats up front.

An old codger chairing the meeting identified himself as a low-bottom drunk who had spent most of his life living on the streets of Boston. And then everything changed.

"The grace of God came into my life," he said. "Today I have an apartment and a job, and my self-esteem is skyrocketing, all because I surrendered. My friends call me FHG, former homeless guy. I'm proud of that name."

Mickey and I hung around after the meeting, and that's when I told him about Cheyenne getting run over. Mickey had been out of town and hadn't heard about it. I told him about the loopers, and the scuzzy cashier in the scuzzy store, and my encounter with Gina Molony.

"Why didn't you call me as soon as this happened?" he said.

Before I had a chance to answer, Skinny Atlas interrupted us and told us to lock up when we left, leaving us alone in the hall.

"A woman in the projects saw the car hit Cheyenne," I said. "She said there was a man driving the car. The loopers work in teams. I saw them in Hayes Square, bumping a police cruiser. Five or six of them were hanging out the windows, taunting a cop."

"Brazen little bastards," Mickey said.

"The witness thought Cheyenne was me." I said. "Carmen Cardosa had mistaken Cheyenne for me. If Carmen mistook Cheyenne for me, maybe the driver did, too."

"If that's true, you're in danger," he said.

"I know I am." I thought about the kidnapping at the hands of Bo Murray and his brother Arnold. "On the other hand, Bo Murray made a threat against Cheyenne, so maybe Cheyenne *was* the intended target."

"Jesus, Dermot, I hope you're not fuckin' with Bo Murray. He is flat crazy, out of his goddamn mind. Bo killed a young girl and got away with it."

"I heard."

"You heard? You say that like you heard it might rain tomorrow. We're talking about a mindless killer who just got out of the can." Mickey studied my face. "It could have been Bo Murray or one of Bo's dimwitted brothers. Or it might have been somebody else altogether driving that car, somebody you're not thinking of."

I told Mickey that I wanted to be alone for a while, that I needed a few minutes to clear my head. "I'll call you later," I told him.

Mickey gave me a hug and left.

A few minutes later I locked the door and went to the parking lot. Storm clouds blocked the moon and stars, and a dense fog shrouded the street lamps, rendering the lot nearly unnavigable. In Sullivan Square, beyond the fenced lot, traffic thundered around the rotary, and up on I-93 horns blared, adding background ruckus to the din below.

I shuffled across the asphalt square, feeling my way to the car. A noise got my attention, enough so that I stopped and listened. A cat or a rat or some four-legged thing scurried away. I felt relieved, but it would be short-lived. An SUV bounced into the lot and skidded to a stop in front on me. A horde of teenagers, armed with guns and hockey sticks, jumped out and surrounded me.

The loopers.

One of the boys stepped forward, a scrawny kid wearing a Boston Bruins cap, and aimed a pistol at my chest.

"You scared the fuck outta my mother," he said.

"You must be Jimmy Molony," I said. "I didn't mean to scare her."

"You gawked at her, too, ya' fuckin' pervert."

"I didn't gawk at anyone."

A kid wearing a Dropkick Murphys T-shirt yelled, "She has a pissa body, Jimmy. I stare at her, too." They all laughed, except for Jimmy, who said, "Shut your yap, Sully."

"I wanted to talk to you," I said, "but your mother answered the door."

Jimmy raised the gun, which looked too big for his adolescent hand, and pointed it at my recoiling head. "I heard your woman got run down, but it wasn't us. We didn't do it."

"I believe you," I said.

"Shoot him anyway," a boy yelled, prompting more laughter.

"Kneecap the prick," came from the back.

For the Irish, kneecap is a verb, not a noun.

Jimmy came closer. "If you go near my mother again, I'll blow your brains out." He tucked the pistol into his belt. "And keep the fuck outta Mishawum. Understand?"

"Yeah, sure, I understand."

They piled back into the SUV and sped toward Rutherford Avenue. I stood in darkness and waited until they were gone. I was never scared during the skirmish, because I knew it was a warning. When the threat is real, you never see it coming.

46

I VISITED CHEYENNE in the hospital and watched her from the foot of the bed. Lying motionless under a blanket with her head propped on a pillow, she seemed at peace, not suffering, but not conscious, either. Her father wasn't there and I was glad for that. I reclined in a chair and nodded off to the beeping monitors.

A flash of sunlight roused me from a restless sleep. I stretched my arms overhead, leaned left and leaned right. My neck cracked and my back popped, but it felt good, like a chiropractic adjustment. Cheyenne was in the same state, with her head on a pillow and comatose to her surroundings. I stayed for an hour. After a good cry, I kissed her cheek and left the hospital.

It was time to face Bo Murray, a dangerous man with erratic judgment, a man who has killed but was never convicted. Bo had leveled a threat against Cheyenne, and he delivered on it, or so it seemed. But then I had wrongly assumed that the loopers ran down Cheyenne. Being wrong about the loopers was one thing. Being wrong about Bo Murray was something else altogether. The loopers wouldn't chop you up and use you for lobster bait.

I parked in the projects and knocked on their door. Albert Murray—the name Albert was stitched on his bowling shirt—opened it and stared at me the way he stared at everything, with confusion on his face.

"What the fuck are you doing here, Sparhawk?"

"I'd like to talk to Bo."

Bo was sitting on a couch with an oxygen tank at his side, showing neither surprise nor anger at my visit. He told Albert to let me in, and as I stepped into the room, Arnold Murray, Albert's twin brother, came out of the kitchen aiming an Uzi submachine gun at me.

"Don't do nothin' stupid," Arnold said, with his finger shaking on the trigger. If he had a flashback, he'd shred me.

"I won't, Arnold," I said, nice and slow.

Arnold and Albert were identical twins, the dueling banjos of Boston, and they were dangerous as hell. The drugs didn't help matters, dulling the minimal neurotransmitters they were born with. Bo leaned forward on the couch.

"You better be here to tell you found my mother's killer," he said.

"Did you run down my girlfriend?"

Arnold raised the Uzi. Bo pointed a finger at me.

"You got balls, Sparhawk. I didn't run her down, so you fucked-up coming here. But I'm a tolerant guy, so I'm gonna give you a Mulligan on this one. I could have Arnold strafe you dead right now, but I want you alive. I want you to find my mother's killer, so I can kill him myself."

Arnold lowered the Uzi, Bo sat back, and I said, "If you hear anything about the driver, I'd like to know about it."

"You're asking me for help?"

"Yes, I am."

"Don't ever come here again."

I went to the door, hoping I wouldn't hear the burping of an Uzi, and when I got outside I damn near fainted.

47

I WENT BACK to my apartment and reviewed the last thirty-six hours. The loopers didn't run over Cheyenne, because they work in teams. Bo Murray didn't do it, because he would have gloated. Most importantly, whoever ran her down, thought he was running me down—or so the theory goes. But what if Cheyenne was the target after all?

The confusion was too much.

I clicked on the Red Sox game. They were playing San Francisco tonight at Fenway in an inter-league contest, which meant the Giants could use a designated hitter. I was hoping to enjoy an evening of meaningless escape when the doorbell rang. I went down to the foyer and saw Harry from Housing on the porch. I let him in.

"Sorry to bother you at home," Harry said, "but Skeeter just went into his apartment."

"When?"

"Two minutes ago. I heard his air conditioner go on, so he's probably in for a while."

"Thanks, Harry. Was anyone with him?"

"He was alone," Harry said. "Don't tell him I told you."

"I won't."

I went to Skeeter's apartment and knocked. The door opened and standing in front of me wearing a Las Vegas T-shirt was

Skeeter Gruskowski. His mouth opened and closed, not saying a word. I stepped inside.

"I've been looking for you," I said.

"Is something wrong?"

"I'll ask the questions. Where have you been?"

"Vacation," he said.

"You stayed at the Henshaw Hotel in Santa Monica."

"What's going on here?" He swallowed hard. "Were you in Santa Monica or something?"

"Yes, I was. I stayed at the Henshaw, too."

"Why didn't you call me? We could've had a few drinks." He waited a second and said, "The place is tops, isn't it? Santa Monica is out of this world."

"My girlfriend got run down on Bunker Hill Street."

"That was your girlfriend?" he said. "I heard about it."

"She's in a coma."

"You're talking like I did it. I didn't have nothin' to do with that. And you're in my face." Skeeter stepped back. "I didn't even know you had a girlfriend."

"The driver probably didn't know either, because the driver thought he was hitting me. I was the intended target."

"I don't know what you're talking about, not a clue."

I had birddogged this man across the country, never quite catching up, and I felt my anger rising. "Where did you get the money?"

"It's none of your goddamn business where I got it."

"I think you stole Gert's coins," I said. "I think you went into her apartment, whacked her on the head, and robbed her."

"Fuck you, Sparhawk, I never—"

"Even at face value, the coins must have been worth twenty thousand dollars, but a coin dealer would give you five times that amount."

Skeeter clutched his heart but said nothing. I continued.

"And then you went to Foxwoods, just like you told Gage Lauria, and gambled the twenty into a pile of money."

"You talked to Gage?" Skeeter muttered.

"You robbed and murdered Gert Murray for the silver coins."

"Wait a second," he inched forward. "I didn't kill Gert. She was my friend. And I didn't rob her, not really."

"Not really, Skeeter?" I stepped closer to him, hoping to sniff a lie. "You either robbed her or you didn't."

"It's not what you think."

"You'd better explain."

Skeeter walked around the room and gestured with his hands, as if preparing a defense, and then he stopped in front of me, ready to make his case.

"Gert and I were neighbors, more than neighbors, we were practically family," he said. "We watched out for each other, you know, kept tabs on each other. She was getting forgetful, dementia I think. For two or three years now she'd forget what she was doing, so she asked me to take care of certain things for her."

"What things?"

"She lost her keys a couple of times, so she gave me a spare set. Things like that."

"What else?"

"The coin collection you mentioned, she asked me to look after it for her, in case she got robbed. I was looking out for her."

"Sure you were."

"I wanna show you something." He led me to a closet and opened the door. "Look for yourself. There's her collection."

I looked inside the closet. There must have been fifty glass containers filled with coins. Mason jars, pickle jars, milk bottles, a Pickwick Ale bottle, every type of bottle, jug, or jar you could imagine, all brimming with silver. There were stacks of cardboard coin holders filled with coins. Gert Murray's collection appeared to be intact.

"If you didn't steal the coins, where did you get the money?" I asked.

"I was getting to that part," Skeeter said. "There was this lottery ticket."

"You'd better elaborate."

"Like I said, Gert was getting forgetful, so she gave me things to hold. The night she got killed, she gave me a lottery ticket. Damned if it wasn't a winner."

"She gave you a winning lottery ticket?"

"I didn't know it was a winner 'til a couple of days after she died, swear to God. The first time you came here asking me all those questions, I had no idea the ticket hit. I didn't know 'til days later. What was I supposed to do at that point, give it to the state?"

"So you cashed it in."

"Yes and no, I sort of cashed it in."

"Sort of?"

"There's this guy I know, he cashes lottery tickets for people who want to be private about it, guys like me who don't want the world to know they won money. What he does, he goes to the lottery in Braintree and cashes the tickets down there. It's on the up and up, but he charges a fee."

"Why didn't you cash it yourself and save the fee?"

"I wanted to keep it confidential," he said. "On account of Gertrude Murray, I wanted to show a little respect."

"Cut the shit, Skeeter. Why the secrecy?"

"To tell you the truth I was worried about Bo Murray. What if Bo found out it was Gert's ticket? I know he's away, but he has a long reach, even from jail."

"Tell me more about the lottery go-between."

"His name is Cawley, lives in Jamaica Plain."

"Cawley's the guy that went to Braintree to cash the ticket for you."

"Yeah, he's the guy."

"What's his first name and where can I find him?"

"Michael Cawley, he's a lawyer and a finance guy, but he's semi-retired. You can find him at Franklin Park Golf Course. He's the pro there."

For some reason I believed him.

"I talked to Bo Murray earlier today," I said.

"You went to Fort Devens?"

"Not Devens, I talked to him in Charlestown. He's out and he's itching to get his hands on the man who killed Gert."

"Jesus, you can't tell him about the lottery ticket. Bo's crazy. He'll kill me if he finds out. Promise me you won't tell him, Sparhawk."

"I'm not too good with promises these days." I thought about the winnings. "Did you blow the whole thing?"

"Yeah, but it doesn't matter," he said. "I wanted to lose it."

"Give me a break, Skeeter."

"With my bum heart, what's the money gonna get me, a marble headstone, an extra bagpiper? Plus, I'd lose my subsidized apartment. It ain't Beacon Hill here but I like it here. On top of all that I have a disgruntled ex-wife. If I went on the books, I'd have to give her half."

"So you went to Cawley instead."

"I'd rather pay Cawley's vig than my wife's alimony."

I walked to the window, thought about Skeeter's story, and tried to punch holes in it but couldn't. Senseless as it was, the story rang true. I stared out to the twilight. On a flat rooftop across the courtyard, three boys ran in circles, skirting the edge of the building, oblivious to the three-story fall. They shoved each other and taunted each other and disappeared into a stairwell—future loopers, no doubt.

"I just wanted a good time," Skeeter said. "I didn't care about winning or losing. I wanted the adventure, the thrill of seeing the Southwest, just like Martin Milner and George Maharis. With my bad ticker, I'm rounding third and heading for home."

"You're exaggerating."

"I never exaggerate," he said. "I wanted one last fling before they plant me. And you wanna know something? My bucket list is fulfilled. How many guys can say that in life? Even if Bo kills me, I'll go out with a smile on my face, an empty-bucket smile."

"Is there any money left?"

"Not a nickel," he said.

"And obviously the Corvette is gone."

"It's buses and subways from now on." The lighthearted banter ended, and his tone grew desperate. "Please don't tell Bo. He'll kill me." He perspired and held his chest. "Please, Sparhawk, don't tell him."

"Calm down, Skeeter. I won't tell him if what you say is true, but if you had anything to do with Gert's killing, you'll be seeing Bo real soon."

I started to leave and stopped.

"Do you have a copy of the lottery ticket?"

"Yeah."

He gave it to me.

In the hallway, amid the stink and dead air, I stood thinking. The lottery ticket was the key to this thing. I knew with complete certainty that the ticket would point me to the killer, and yet I had no idea where to begin my search for him. But with little bit of legwork and a little bit of bulldog, I would find the bastard. I was closing in.

I drove to Franklin Park Golf Course to talk to Cawley, the man who cashed the ticket for Skeeter. I went through the gate and told an attendant in the booth that I wanted golf lessons.

"Talk to Michael Cawley. He's the golf pro here."

"Where can I find him?"

"In the clubhouse. Tall guy wearing a purple shirt."

I found him sitting at a table sipping a bottle of Amstel light. His reddish hair was short and curly, and his long arms were tanned and sinewy. I sat in the chair across from him and said, "Michael Cawley?"

"That's me, need a lesson?"

"Maybe later," I said. "Right now I'd like to ask you a few questions. I'm investigating a murder, and Skeeter Gruskowski is in the middle of it."

"Skeeter?" He rested the bottle on a cardboard coaster. "Who are you?"

I told him who I was and said, "Gruskowski said you cashed a lottery ticket for him. Is that true?"

He didn't answer my question. Instead, he said, "Dermot Sparhawk, you played football at Boston College. I went to Holy Cross."

I was about to ask him if he knew Superintendent Hanson, another Holy Cross man, but I didn't want to ruin my day. "About Skeeter—"

He put up his hand in a stop gesture.

"I don't discuss my business dealings with outsiders. Confidentiality is important in my line of work."

I nodded my head as if I understood.

"Can you tell me this much? Do you cash lottery tickets for people who want to protect their privacy?"

"Cashing lottery tickets is one of my offerings."

"Can you tell me how you know Skeeter?"

"Sure. My brother worked with Skeeter at the Conley Terminal in South Boston. Longshoremen, they became good friends."

I gently grasped the salt shaker and slid it like a chess piece.

"If I wanted you to cash a ticket for me, how would I go about it?"

"The process is very simple." And then Cawley explained the simple process, losing me after the first sentence. "It's a legitimate transaction," he said. "All the taxes are paid, so the government is happy. The clients' privacy is protected, so they don't have to worry about leaches pestering them. Everything gets filed in court. Everything's on the up and up."

"And what do you get out of it?"

"Ten percent of the gross," he said.

"Not bad."

"Yeah, not bad at all," he said and took another sip. "If I like a client, I might give him a discount. For example, if the client was my brother's friend, I might take ten percent of the net instead. So—just to pick a random number—if the gross was $1.4 million and the net was say $900,000, I'd take ninety grand, not a hundred and forty grand."

"Charitable."

"I think so."

48

AFTER ANOTHER TRYING visit with Cheyenne—she was still comatose and totally inert—I left the hospital and took an Uber to Charlestown, getting out at Avakian's Market. Gert's lottery ticket was troubling me, and I wanted to ask to Bianca Sanchez about it. I went inside but she wasn't there. In her place stood a new cashier, a goofy kid with scraggly black sideburns and buck teeth. He looked like a computer geek, not a liquor store attendant.

"Can I help you?" he said.

"Where's Bianca?"

"She's off tonight," he answered with an air of smugness. "Actually, she's off forever, as in permanently—period."

"Why would Mr. Avakian fire his star employee?"

"She wasn't his star employee, I was. I just worked in the back."

"So that's why I haven't seen you before. I don't know, she seemed like a star to me."

"She's no star. She dated that guy that killed the old lady in the projects."

"She dated Victor Diaz?"

"Yeah," he said. "Mr. Avakian promoted me to night manager." He shifted into his new role, plugging the store's wares. "Mega Millions is worth $80 million tonight. Do you want to play?"

"I'd have a better chance of getting hit by—"

"Not in this store. Look at all the winners we sold this month. The red star means the ticket was sold in this store." He pointed to a lottery chart on the wall, the same chart I looked at when Kid asked me to check his tickets. "Last week we sold a Lucky for Life that hit—a thousand bucks a day for life. Not bad, eh? See the red star next to it?"

"I see it." I looked at my copy of Skeeter's winning ticket and searched the chart for it. I found the number listed, but it wasn't marked with a red star. I said to the geek, "How do you know to mark the number with a star? Do the winners tell you?"

"Sometimes they do, but they usually don't," he said. "We get a printout from the state lottery each week, an official report."

"You find out about the winning numbers weekly, but not the names of the winners, is that what you said?"

"Yes," he replied with irritation in his voice. Maybe the pressure of the new position was getting to him, or maybe he was hiding something.

"I don't mean to pester you," I said.

"You're not pestering me. Why did you say that?"

"No reason."

No red star, it had to mean something. Gertrude Murray was killed the night she bought the lottery ticket, the same night she gave the ticket to Skeeter. Skeeter said he didn't know it was a winner until days later, and he didn't hire the go-between Cawley until days after that.

Mr. Avakian came out of the back room, holding a clipboard.

I said to him, "You fired Bianca."

Avakian looked up and said, "It's none of your business."

The new kid said, "I told him she was a scuzz, her boyfriend killing that old lady."

"Shut up and go in the back," Avakian said.

"Victor Diaz didn't kill Gert, Mr. Avakian," I said.

"The police arrested him for it. Victor Diaz knew about Gertrude's coins, because Bianca told him."

"Maybe Diaz wasn't after coins," I said.

"He had the coins in his pocket when they arrested him."

"Maybe he was after a winning lottery ticket."

"Winning lottery ticket?" Mr. Avakian adjusted his thick glasses and said, "What are you talking about?"

"Gert Murray bought a winning ticket here the night she was murdered." I showed him a copy of it. "What's going on here, Mr. Avakian."

"Nothing's going on," he said. "I don't answer to you. Get out of my store."

Bianca lived in Roslindale in the Washington-Beech projects, once a dreary maze of dirty red bricks that had been transformed into clapboard townhouses. I drove down Washington Street, going by the composer streets—Liszt, Brahms, Haydn, Mendelssohn—and parked at the Pleasant Cafe. I knocked on her door. Bianca opened it and closed it just as fast. I jammed my foot into the door wedge and said, "I need to talk to you."

"Take your foot out of my door or I'll call the cops."

"I'm sure the cops would love to know about Gert's winning lottery ticket and the part you played in her murder."

"What are you talking about?" She opened the door a bit.

"The lottery ticket, I know all about it. I'm on my way to the police station to tell them about it."

"I had nothing to do with Gertrude Murray's death," she said.

"Gertrude Murray bought a lottery ticket the night she was murdered," I said. "It turned out to be a winner worth one-point-four million dollars."

"I don't know anything about it."

She blocked the doorway, while I remained in the hallway. I moved ahead with caution. "You sold her the winning ticket," I said, guessing.

"What if I did?" Her voice grew stronger. "I sell lottery tickets all day long, or I used to until you got me fired."

"You sold Gert a ticket, and when you found out it was a winner, you told Victor Diaz about it." I paused, but she didn't react, so I continued. "You told him about the lottery ticket, and that's why he robbed Gertrude Murray."

"You're wrong, asshole. I didn't know I sold a winner that day, but even if I did, I'd have no idea who bought it. How could I know who bought it?"

"Come on, Bianca, you remember selling it."

"I don't." Bianca came closer to me. A faint smell of perfume wafted from her body and filled my nostrils. In a husky voice she said, "I had no idea Mrs. Murray bought a winning lottery ticket. I wouldn't know unless she told me."

"She didn't live long enough to tell you," I said. "You also told Victor about the coins?"

"No, I didn't."

Bianca sounded believable. Was it a coincidence that Diaz robbed Gert for the coins on the same day she bought a winning ticket? It didn't seem probable, but it was possible. I hated explaining things by coincidence. It's the lazy way out. There had to be an angle I was missing, another explanation.

"Suppose Mr. Avakian got wind of the winning ticket," I said. "Could he have identified the person who bought it?"

"Maybe," she said. "The tickets are timestamped."

"Could he find the buyer using the timestamp?" I asked.

"It's possible, but not likely."

"How is it possible?"

"Surveillance cameras," she said, "the store has surveillance cameras. If Mr. Avakian knew the time of purchase, he could play the surveillance video and find the buyer that way."

"That sounds pretty easy," I said. "Why did you say it was possible but not likely?"

"Mr. Avakian is a total klutz with computers," she said. "He doesn't even own a cell phone. He uses the store phone that has one of those old answering machines with a cassette."

"Do you know how to watch the tapes?"

"I don't have access to them, asshole."

"How does the store get notified of a lottery winner?" I asked.

"The lottery sends a report," Bianca said. "If we sell a big winner, we tape a printout of the ticket under the glass counter, so the customers can see it. Then we put a red star next to the number on the lottery chart that lists the winners."

That's what the geek told me. "But the lottery doesn't notify the store the night you sell the ticket."

"No, they send a report. I think they send it once a week."

"That shreds my theory," I said. "If Avakian didn't know he sold a winner the night of the murder, he'd have no reason to look at the video to find the buyer, in this case Gert Murray."

"Mr. Avakian has a friend at the lottery," she said. "When we sell a big winner his friend calls the store and tells him about it."

"One-point-four million must qualify as a big winner," I said, mostly to myself. "Did the lottery man call Avakian the night Gert won?"

"I don't know."

"Was Avakian working that night?"

"He works every night." She let go of the knob and dropped her arms to the side. "I think the lottery man is an old friend of Mr. Avakian's, maybe a childhood friend, because he calls on holidays, too. His name is Norm."

"Norm," I said, removing my foot from the door jamb. "Do you know his last name?"

"No, I don't. And don't come here again." she said and slammed the door shut.

49

I NEEDED TO get Mr. Avakian's fingerprints to see if they matched the partial print the police found found in Gertrude's apartment. I went to Avakian's Market and waited outside until my mark came around. And then I saw him, a man wearing a stained raincoat and high-top sneakers with no laces. He might have just got out of jail. They take away your shoelaces when they book you. When he reached me, I said to him, "I'd like you to do a job for me."

"A job?" His eyes were lifeless. "I can use the money."

"It'll take five minutes."

"Five minutes?" His interest grew. "How much?"

"Twenty bucks."

"What do I have to do?"

"Buy a bottle of wine from the old guy guy at the counter."

"What kind of wine do you want?"

"It doesn't matter," I said. "Just make sure it's in a bag."

I handed him twenty for his services and twenty more for the wine, and he went into the market. I watched the transaction from across the street, making sure that Mr. Avakian served him, which he did, ensuring his fingerprints would be on the bag. A minute later the man came out and walked over to me.

"Can I keep the change?" he asked.

"Keep it," I said.

He walked away twenty bucks to the better. I walked away wondering if I should have bought a jug for a fellow drunk.

50

I PHONED KEIRA MCKENZIE, a fiery redhead who works as a lab technician in the forensics unit of the Boston Police Department. We had worked together on a case a couple of years ago and hit it off, both professionally and personally. She was smart, beautiful, and sophisticated, everything you'd want in a woman, with one glaring exception—she was married. I left her a message and ten minutes later she called back.

"How have you been?" she asked.

I told her that I was doing fine, and she told me that she was expecting her first child, and the small talk tapered off.

"I need a favor," I said.

"And I thought you were calling to say hello."

"I'd like you to run some fingerprints for me."

"Keep talking," she said.

"I want to know if they match a partial print found at the Murray murder scene," I said. "Are you familiar with the case?"

"I should be," she said. "I was on the team that processed it. I saw you when we rolled out the body."

"How did I miss you?"

"You were in shock, Dermot," she said.

I explained my tunnel vision, telling Keira about my close relationship with Gertrude Murray, and then I said, "What do you think about running the prints?"

"You're asking me to violate protocol. The police frown on that sort of thing."

"I don't want to get you into trouble."

"On the other hand, I did the lab work on the case, which means I have direct access to the evidence."

"It sounds like you're considering it," I said.

"Possibly. Meet me at Doyle's tonight at seven o'clock, and bring the evidence with you. I'll decide then."

"Thanks, Keira."

"How did you get the prints?" she said.

"Nothing illegal, I promise you. The prints are on a bag with a bottle in it. I don't drink anymore, so you can have the bottle."

"You're a big spender, you know that." She laughed.

"Thanks, Kiera. I'll see you at Doyle's."

I arrived at Doyle's Cafe at seven, and the first thing I saw was a huge monochrome photo of heavyweight champion John L. Sullivan, the Boston Strong Boy, with his bare fists clenched and ready to go. I walked to the end of the bar and carved out a spot by the TV. I told the barman I'd like a Coke, no ice. At quarter past seven Kiera McKenzie came in and pulled out the stool next to me. I asked her how she was feeling. She said that she was fine, and that the morning sickness had passed. She positioned herself on the stool.

"Question number one," she said. "Why are you asking me to check the fingerprints? Why didn't you ask the Homicide team working the case, or the DA's office?"

"I can't because I didn't get a warrant for the prints," I said. "I just want to know if they match."

"And you think the prints are related to the Murray murder, is that correct?"

"That's correct," I said. "But I also have a personal reason. A car deliberately ran down my girlfriend. She's at Mass General in a coma."

"Oh, my God that's terrible. I am so sorry. Is she going to be okay?"

"We won't know until the swelling in her brain goes down." I looked away, fighting tears, composed myself and continued. "Cheyenne wasn't the intended target. I was. The driver mistook her for me."

"That's awful. Why were you the target?"

I finished my Coke. "I think the man who ran down Cheyenne is the same man who killed Gertrude Murray."

"I'll have to think about this, Dermot. No promises."

"Thanks, Kiera."

"I assume you brought the evidence with you," she said.

"The prints are on the paper bag inside this bag." I handed her a plastic shopping bag that contained everything. "I would bet the house that the prints on that bag will match the prints at the murder scene."

"Don't get your hopes up. I'm still not sure I'll run them." The barman came over and Kiera waved him away. "You're asking me to take an awfully big risk, you know. I have a family to think about now."

"I know you do. If you can't do it, I understand."

Kiera grabbed the bag and left Doyle's, and I watched the start of the Red Sox game. A scrub called up from Triple-A Pawtucket jogged to the mound in the top of the first inning. No doubt the manual scoreboard operator had the yellow number plates ready.

51

I VISITED CHEYENNE in the hospital and for the first time since the accident she was awake. My heart filled with joy, and I smiled and leaned over the bedrails and kissed her but she gave no response. Maybe she was still out of it. I asked her how she was feeling, and in a monotone voice that held no emotion, she said she felt terrible.

"I can't walk. I can't use my right arm. According to the doctors, I'm lucky to be alive." Her eyes looked to the ceiling, and she talked as if I wasn't there. "I'll be spending the next year in a rehabilitation hospital in Arizona, so they can teach me to walk again."

Avakian's face came to me as she described her pain, and my lust for revenge nearly erupted. I would kill him. "I'll go with you to Arizona and support you every step of the way, Cheyenne. I'll take care of you."

"No." She strained for a Kleenex box on the table but couldn't reach it. *She couldn't reach the box.* I pulled out a few tissues and passed them to her. She dabbed her eyes and said, "I'm going to Arizona alone. I need time away from you."

"Away from me?" What was she saying? "Why? What are you saying? I love you."

"I love you, too, Dermot, I really do. But I need to be alone for this." She cried.

"Can't we get through this together?"

"No, no, we can't." She sniffled and shook her head as tears rolled down her cheeks. "I love you, but I can't do it. I cannot live with the uncertainty."

"What uncertainty? What do you mean?"

"Please let me finish." She rubbed her swollen forehead. "You have no idea what you're like, do you? You're a good man, but there is something about you that attracts danger. More than that, you don't just attract danger, you confront it. You never walk away from it. This isn't easy for me to say." She breathed deeply. "I will always love you, but I can't be with you right now. When I saw that car bearing down on me, I knew it had something to do with you. I'm not saying it was your fault, because it's not, but the car hit me because of you—I know it did. And I can't live that way. I have to say goodbye, Dermot."

Goodbye? No way!

"Cheyenne, I know it was my fault. Let me fix this, I can fix it. It will never happen again. I'll stop being a private investigator."

"No, Dermot, that would kill you. You would resent me if you stopped. You're a lone wolf, and you need the excitement, and I understand that, but I can't live that way."

A nurse came into the room and told me that I had to leave, that Cheyenne needed her rest. I walked out to the corridor.

What the hell just happened?

Inside the parking garage, while sitting in my car, I gasped for air. In college I played in a game against Notre Dame and got the wind knocked out of me. This was worse. I didn't sob at Notre Dame. How could she end it like that? The snap of a finger, poof, finished. Didn't our love mean a damn thing to her? I wanted to die. The top truss of the Tobin Bridge would do it. A swan dive onto a concrete pier. No splash. A perfect ten. That would teach her.

After I caught my breath and stopped crying, the finality of the loss began to sink in, the outcome of it, too. It was back to the solitary life for me, a life of gray days and empty nights, a life of monotony, a dull life, a life where you settled for less, because you knew you deserved less.

As I drove to Charlestown, I thought about the night Cheyenne got hit. We made love and basked in the afterglow and talked about our future. She said she wanted to show me something that was out in the car, and threw on my BC football shirt and her cowboy hat. I offered to get it for her, but she said no. She went to the car herself, and she got run down. I never should have let her leave the bed.

All because she wanted to show me something in the car.

The next thing I knew I was in front of my house, home but lost, and I boiled inside as reality set in. I was a fool. I had duped myself into thinking I deserved a woman like Cheyenne. What a nitwit. At that moment I made a vow to myself. I vowed I would never get close to a woman again. I would never put a woman in danger like that again.

Laden with hatred and overcome by grief, I climbed the stairs to my apartment and went inside to the bedroom. When I reached to click on the fan I saw my college football helmet on the shelf, sitting next to the All-America plaques and the Butkus Award. With all the accolades and honors and trophies, why did I feel like such a loser? I crammed the gold helmet on my head, snapped the chinstrap, chomped the crusty mouth guard, and glared through the gray bars of the facemask.

Grunting like a wild boar in the forest, I dropped into a three-point stance, bulled my neck, and exploded into the wall, ramming my head through the horsehair plaster. I replanted my feet, spit out grout, snorted dust, and rammed it again. Slats cracked and noise rumbled in the framework. I backed up five feet and ran at it again and again, leading with my head, seeing stars when I hit beams. I kept ramming until I burst through the wall and tumbled to the parlor floor, and I rammed until the entire wall was flattened to a scrap heap.

I lay atop the rubble crying, my teeth gnawing the mouth guard, my heart destroyed. I banged my head on the floor, adding to the constellation of stars spinning in my brain. If I had a speck of integrity, I'd have done it without the helmet.

52

"YOU'RE LUCKY IT wasn't a weight-bearing wall," Harraseeket Kid said, looking at the destruction. "Buck thought a plane hit the house."

"I forgot about Buck."

"What's wrong with you?" Kid said. "A splinter could've gouged out an eye."

"I didn't think of that."

"You broke the studs and furring." He studied my eyes, moving closer. "Maybe you should go to a doctor, see if you have a concussion."

"I'm fine, Kid."

"I still think you should see a doctor. You might need brain surgery—to put one in."

"Cheyenne left me," I said.

"What?"

"She ended it."

"Fuck." Kid unexpectedly embraced me. "No wonder you snapped."

"She said I was dangerous."

"You *are* dangerous, but in a good way," Kid said. "You defend the little guy from the lowlifes out there. Scumbags don't listen to nice talk."

"Cheyenne nearly died because of me." I crunched through the ruins and went to the window and looked to the bridge. "I can't blame her for moving on."

"This is bad." Kid looked at the wreckage. "I'm worried what you might do."

"I'm cool, Kid, nothing to worry about."

"Yeah, real cool." Kid pointed at the kitchen table. "You have a gun?"

"It's not loaded."

"That's a military-issue forty-five," he said, apparently impressed. "That's a hell of a side iron. Where did you get it?"

"It belonged to my father," I said. "He took it from a dead second lieutenant in Vietnam."

"It's a classic." Kid ejected the magazine. "I'll clean it, make it good as new."

"Don't waste your time. If I use it at all, I'll use it as a prop."

"A prop?" He examined the scuffed magazine and blew on it. "You're not going to point an empty gun at someone, are you?"

"Maybe."

"Don't do that, Dermot," Kid said. "A gun should always be loaded, especially if you aim it at a man. I'll refurbish it and load it."

"Do whatever you want."

Kid told me that he'd clean up the room and start the renovations. I tried to talk him out of it, but he insisted, saying that he liked that kind of work. I was too tired to argue. I gave him some money to get started.

"I won't replace the wall," he said. "I'll frame it out in pine and make it an open-air room, like the yuppies on the hill."

The next morning the doorbell rang. Standing on the front porch with her red hair blowing in the breeze was Kiera McKenzie. I let her in and led her up to my apartment, not my smartest move.

She looked at the mess and said, "What happened?"

"I'm remodeling."

"Really?" She stared at the flattened wall. "Remodeling, huh?"

"It's a long story."

"I'm sure it is." She eyed the football helmet, with a chunk of plaster sticking out of the cage. "Interesting choice of tool."

"What have you got, Kiera?"

"Plenty," she said. "I found two sets of useable prints on the bag. One of them belonged to the wino, Jonas Q. Sherman, who is in the system for vagrancy and various misdemeanors. The other one belonged to you."

"Me?" I was surprised by this. "How do you know it belonged to me?"

"Your soda glass," she said. "I smuggled it out of Doyle's for elimination prints. You'll be happy to know you're not in the system. More importantly, you're not the murderer."

"That's a relief."

"The third set of prints, which most likely belonged to Mr. Avakian, was too smudged to use against the partial at the murder scene."

"No problem, I'll get another set off him."

"Don't bother," she said. "I stuck my neck out once, I won't do it again."

"I didn't mean to put you in the middle."

"Sure, you did," Kiera said. "That's why you called me, and that's okay, but you'll have to find another way to nab Avakian." She paused. "I thought of a way you can get him."

"How?"

"Find the car."

"What car?"

"The car that hit Cheyenne," she said. "His prints will be on it, or his DNA, or something to tie him to the crime. There always is."

"How am I supposed to find the car? I don't even know what it looks like."

"You're the private detective, Dermot, you figure it out." She picked up her briefcase and smoothed her pleated skirt. "By the way, how is Cheyenne doing?"

"She's awake."

"That's good news. I'd love to meet her someday."

"Sure, someday," I said.

I walked Kiera out to her car and waved goodbye as she drove away. I thought about what she said. If I could find the car that ran down Cheyenne, I could nail Mr. Avakian for the murder. I thought about it some more, and I knew how to find it. It would be ugly and illegal and could land me in jail, but I knew how to find it.

53

THE NEXT DAY I went to Little Mystic Channel and found Rod Liveliner fishing against the railing. His Igloo cooler contained two whopping stripers, which explained the broad smile on his leathery face.

"You'll be eating good tonight," I said. "They must weigh twenty pounds each, lunkers, as you say."

"Once in a while they wander into the shallows." He reeled in the line. "I know you're not a fisherman, Dermot."

I leaned next to him on the railing.

"That favor you mentioned, is it still on the table?"

"I pay my debts," he said, "and the debt I owe your father is a lunker and a half."

"I thought you'd say something like that."

"What's the favor?" he asked.

I told him what I needed.

At midnight I went to Avakian's Market and waited in a dark alley behind the building, where his car was parked. The lights in the store went off and Avakian came out, accompanied by the geek who'd replaced Bianca. The geek was boasting about the great job he was doing, and Avakian was nodding with approval, making the kid feel good. I put on a ski mask and took out the forty-five, pulled back the slide and let it snap. Avakian turned. I aimed the gun at his head. The geek stood frozen. I told him to screw, and he ran like hell out of the alley, with his arms and legs awkwardly pumping. I told Avakian to get in the car.

"What are you doing?" he said. "Is it money? Do you want money?"

"Give me the keys," I said. "Shut up and get on the floor in back."

He got in face down. He begged me not to shoot, cried and slobbered, and said he had a family. I drove down Terminal Street and out to the Mystic Piers, which was vacant in the late hours of the night. I steered behind a derelict warehouse and parked at a rotting wharf, where Rod Liveliner was waiting in a boat. I tooted once. Rod put on his hood.

"Get out of the car," I said to Avakian.

"What are you doing?"

I put a stocking hat on his head and pulled it down over his eyes, blindfolding him, and we boarded the boat.

"If you touch that hat, I'll shoot you," I said.

"I won't, I won't."

Rod and I removed our ski masks. The cool air felt good on my face. Rod gave me an apprehensive look, as if to say *I hope you know what you're doing*. I had assured Rod that nothing bad would happen, that I would take Avakian at gunpoint with an empty gun, guaranteeing he wouldn't get hurt. Rod wasn't convinced, but he acquiesced. I also told Rod that my goal was to scare Avakian to the point of pissing his pants, so that he would tell us where the car was located, the car that hit Cheyenne. After that, we'd bring him back to the dock unharmed.

"What do you want from me?" Avakian's voice muffled through the hat. "Whatever you want, it's yours."

I guided Avakian to the rear of the boat and sat him on the deck. Rod shifted into gear and moved out from the dock. He piloted through the harbor, passing the Coast Guard station and Castle Island and Boston Light, taking us out to open waters. As we churned farther from shore, an aura of serenity took hold of the boat, a quiet I didn't expect. The rippling surf and soothing breeze fostered a mood of tranquility on board, as if nature were abetting the crime. The combination of kidnapping and calmness struck me as odd, a fatalistic mismatch that couldn't last, as if portending disaster, but I knew everything would be fine if we stuck to the plan.

The cityscape of Boston soon disappeared from view, and an hour later all signs of land were gone. Rod churned on. He told me that the boat was fitted with twin 250-horsepower outboard engines, and that we had plenty of fuel in the tanks, enough to go for hours. The time passed slowly and the motors roared. Rod yelled over the noise, "We just passed the nautical three-mile line."

"Nautical mile three?" Avakian said. "What does that mean?"

"Be quiet," I said, pressing the gun on his forehead. Avakian shit himself, and something inside of him flipped. He started talking gibberish, talking in a disjointed mantra of syllables, like a man speaking in tongues. None of it made sense. His words blended with the other sounds, with the waves and wind and engines, and I began to question the wisdom of my plan. What was I thinking? I joined Rod at the wheel and said, "This is stupid. Turn around."

"We've come this far. Let's see it through."

"Avakian shit himself."

"So what," Rod said. "Nothing bad's gonna happen. He'll tell us where the car is, and we'll bring him back safely. And then you make an anonymous call to the police, telling them about the car. It's simple."

After a long period of time Rod yelled out, "Stellwagen Basin." He sounded like a train conductor announcing a station. "We're here."

"Kill the engines," I said.

Rod and I put on ski masks. I removed Avakian's stocking hat. He opened his eyes and focused on the gun in my hand. I dragged over an anchor and tied the rope around his waist.

"What are you doing?" Avakian said. "Please don't do this."

"It's a new interrogation technique," I said. "I ask a question, you answer it. If I don't like the answer, I dump you into the ocean. Do you understand the ground rules?"

"I'll do whatever you want."

"That's what I wanted to hear, Mr. Avakian." I sat next to him. "Now tell me, where is the car?"

"What car?" He grabbed my leg. "I don't know about any car."

"Where is the goddamn car?"

"I don't know what you're talking about."

I looked at Rod, who shrugged his shoulders. I said to Avakian, "Gertrude Murray bought a lottery ticket from you the night she was killed."

"She bought them all the time."

"The ticket she bought hit for one-point-four million dollars. A man named Norm Yorsky called your store and told you about it. Yorsky works for the lottery."

"I know he works for the lottery." Avakian seemed bewildered. "Norm and I are old friends. We grew up in Watertown."

"Yorsky told you about the winning ticket."

"He always tells me about winning tickets. It's an excuse to talk."

"You used the timestamp on the ticket, you searched the surveillance video, you found the person who bought it: Gertrude Murray. You went to her apartment to steal the ticket, and something went wrong, and you killed her."

"I didn't kill her," he said. "I don't even know how to work the surveillance video, and I didn't hear Norm's message 'til the next day."

"Do you expect me to believe that?"

"It's the truth."

I sat on the edge of the boat as waves crashed over the gunwales, splashing everything and everyone on board. The icy spray soaked my ski mask, and I said fuck it and took it off. Rod yelled at me to keep it on, but I didn't listen. I stared at Avakian.

"You?" he said.

"Yeah, me. And I don't care you know it's me, because I am going to get what I need, and we are going to march into the police station together and tell them everything."

"Tell them what?"

"We are going to tell them about the murder of Gertrude Murray and the maiming of Cheyenne Starr."

"Cheyenne who? You're crazy."

"Like hell I'm crazy," I said. "I went to your store and looked at the lottery chart. Gert Murray's number wasn't marked with a red star. The other winners you sold were marked with red stars, but not hers. When you saw me studying the chart, you knew I figured out you killed Gert, so you ran me down. Except you didn't run me down, you ran down my girlfriend instead."

"I didn't run anyone down," he said. "It's impossible. I don't even—"

"It was dark and rainy," I said. "You confused her for me and you mutilated her." Then I floated a bluff. "And there's the fingerprint."

"What fingerprint?"

"The one you left at Gert's apartment," I said.

"I've never been to her apartment. I don't even know where she lives."

"You followed her."

"Followed her? That's impossible," he said. "Even if I heard Norm's message that night, which I didn't, Gert was already gone. The store was closed when he called."

"A friend of mine bought a bottle of wine from you. I watched while you sold it to him. I gave the bag to a fingerprint expert."

He didn't respond, so I resumed.

"The prints on the bottle matched the prints at Gert's apartment," I said, lying to get the truth out of him. "You killed Gert and you tried to kill me."

"I didn't."

"Tell me where the car is, Mr. Avakian, the car you used to hit my girlfriend. Tell me or you're going overboard."

"The fingerprint matched the one at Gert's?"

"That's right," I said.

Avakian started to say something, but stopped and got to his feet. An odd expression swept across his face, not a grimace but a look of submission that said all was lost, that there was no use in going on. I've never seen a look like it before.

"No more lies." He picked up the anchor and shuffled to the edge of the boat. "I can't do the time, not at my age." He fell backwards into the ocean like a scuba diver.

"What the fuck?" I shrieked, as the rope unwound. "Gimme a hand, Rod!"

We grabbed the rope and pulled, going from dry to wet fibers, jerking the line as fast as we could. Avakian must have sunk thirty feet or more into the water. We kept pulling and got into a rhythm and pulled in unison. Avakian appeared on the surface, his head under water, his body slack in a deadman's float. I reached over the gunwales and yanked him into the boat. He wasn't breathing. I pushed on his chest and blew into his mouth. He lay inert. I blew and pushed and blew and pushed. A spittle of spray came from his mouth, followed by a gush of salt water. He coughed and gasped for air.

He was alive.

I untied the anchor from him and flopped on my back. Avakian was on his back, too, breathing more easily now. I crawled to the side of the boat and vomited, spewing an acidy discharge into the waves. What had I done? I puked again, half of it spurting out my nose. I only meant to scare him. After ten minutes I was doing okay, and Avakian was back to normal—or as a normal as a man can be after a kidnapping and suicide attempt.

"I killed her," Avakian said. "I didn't mean to, but I killed her. I don't know what got into me. I only wanted the ticket." He looked up to the dark sky and shook his head. "I will not go to jail for this." He stood and grabbed my arms. "Give me three days, that's all I'm asking for, three days. I'll make arrangements to leave the country, and you'll never see me again."

"Why should I give you three days?" I said.

"If you don't, I'll tell the police you kidnapped me, and all three of us will go away." He looked again at the starless sky. "I know you won't kill me, because you just saved my life."

"We could change our minds," Rod said, taking off his mask.

"You won't," Avakian said. "You seem like descent men."

"Maybe I don't care about going away," I said. "Maybe I'll march you into police headquarters and soon as we dock."

"You'll gain nothing by doing that," Avakian turned to me. "Nothing you tell them can be used in court."

Avakian was right. Nothing he said could be used in court, not his confession, not his admitted motive, nothing. Besides, I kidnapped and coerced the confession out of him, crimes that could land me in prison myself.

I said to him, "Victor Diaz will go away for your crime."

"Diaz doesn't deserve to go to jail because of me. And I won't let that happen. Once I get settled, once I'm safely tucked away, I'll write a confession and mail it to the Boston police."

"Do you expect me to buy that?" I said.

"I'll write the confession here, in Charlestown. I'll leave it with my lawyer and tell him to deliver it to the police when I'm gone. He won't know it's a confession, because if he knew, he'd be culpable in my escape. When the police get the confession, Diaz will get released."

"Right-o, he'll be released," I said. I doubted Avakian would confess, and I doubted it would result in the charges being dropped against Diaz, but what could I do? I had no leverage. I had fucked it all up, and I didn't want to go to prison.

"We have to get back," Rod said, opening up the throttle.

Before long, Boston Light came into view, and then the airport and Castle Island, and we soon came to the Navy Yard and then to Mystic Piers. I hopped off the boat and secured the line, and Avakian stepped onto the pier.

"Now what?" he said.

"You'll need these." I tossed him his car keys. "You got three days."

Avakian got in his car and drove off.

I said to Rod, "That went well."

"Terrific," he deadpanned. "I have to return the boat."

I untied the line and tossed it on the deck, and Rod churned away from the pier.

I went into St. Jude Thaddeus church and sat in the front row and faced the tabernacle. I didn't pray. I didn't ask for forgiveness. I sat silently. I took out my rosary beads, and feeling like a fraud, I put them away. I heard the big doors open, and one by one, parishioners drifted in for morning Mass. The sacristy bell rang. Fr. Dominic walked to the altar and genuflected. I left the church, taking a side aisle. I went by the marble holy-water font, but I didn't dip my fingers, fearing they'd sizzle off.

I stood on the top step of the church and looked across the street and saw the dim lights of the Horseshoe Tavern burning in the window. The Horseshoe opens early to accommodate the morning drinker and the third-shift crowd getting off work. I crossed Bunker Hill Street and opened the door. The smell of stale beer punched me in the face. I went to the bar. Without saying a word, the barman, a Townie named No Nose, placed a shot of Old Thompson and a mug of Narragansett in front of me. I hadn't been to the Horseshoe in six years, yet he remembered my order. I grasped the shot glass, which is dubbed a shaker glass, because it is large enough that a shaking hand doesn't spill the first vital sip. It felt good in my hand, natural, like a football in the hand of a quarterback.

I moved the shaker back and forth on the mahogany countertop, never lifting it off the wood. Circles of varying sizes scarred the bar, circles etched by alcohol. The small circles were made by shot glasses, the medium by beer bottles, the large by beer mugs—permanent tattoos engraved by booze. I gazed into the cracked mirror behind the bar. My face reflected between bottles of gin and rum and vodka, the long necks of the liters resembling prison bars. I let go of the shaker glass. If I was going to do prison time, I was going to do it right—in a cell, not a bar. I would surrender to the authorities and confess my crime.

I dropped a twenty on the bar and walked outside to the curb, and that's when my cell phone rang. It was my sponsor, Mickey Pappas, who said, "An image of your face came to me, so I took it as a sign to give you a call."

"Thanks, Mick."

"You don't sound so good. Did something happen?"

"I just ordered whiskey and beer at the Horseshoe."

"Christ," he said. "Did you drink?"

"No, I'm on the sidewalk out front."

"Stay there, I'm on my way."

I watched the parishioners exiting the church after Mass. Frail yet smiling, they moved with caution down the steep granite stairs, clutching the railings, feeling for the next step with a dangle foot. I wondered what sins they were carrying inside. I doubted kidnapping was one of them. Mickey's Toyota Avalon pulled up in front of me. I got in the front seat.

"The Horseshoe Tavern, are you serious?" he said, pulling away. "What's going on?"

I told him what I did to Avakian.

"You're out of your fuckin' mind." After circling Charlestown twice, he drove under the Tobin Bridge and into the Navy Yard at Gate 4. "I've heard some crazy things before, but this is the craziest—and I'm a Townie."

"I know."

"Let me see if I got it right," he said. "You kidnapped Mr. Avakian to find the car that ran over Cheyenne. You thought he knew where it was, and you tried to scare it of out of him."

"That was my thinking."

"Thinking?"

"Maybe I'm giving myself too much credit."

"Unbelievable." Mickey shook his head so vigorously, I thought it would spin off his neck and into orbit. "Alcoholism," he said. "You switched obsessions from alcohol to Cheyenne. Obsession. You're obsessed with finding the guy who ran her down. That's why you kidnapped Avakian, because you're obsessed with finding out."

"And I *did* find out, Mick, that's why he jumped overboard."

"He didn't get any help jumping, did he?"

"He jumped on his own. Nobody pushed him," I said. "Why would I save him if I pushed him in?"

"True enough, just asking."

"But I can't live with the guilt. It's eating me up inside, like I'm going insane."

"Okay, okay, slow down."

"I'm turning myself in, because if I don't, Diaz will go away for twenty-five, maybe longer. I know the truth. I know Avakian killed Gert. I'm the only one that can help Diaz."

"Whoa, whoa. Wait a second now, we need to talk this out." He parked next to the Navy Yard Bistro. "Give me a minute to think."

"There's nothing to think about," I said. "Diaz's freedom depends on me."

"Hold it, will ya? Christ almighty, gimme a chance to think," he said, drumming the steering wheel with his blunt fingers. "This is complicated, very complicated. I want you to listen to me real closely."

"Go on, I'm listening."

"Don't be selfish," he said. "You gotta think about Rod Liveliner. If you turn yourself in, you'll take Rod down with you, and maybe the guy that lent him the boat."

"I won't rat out Rod."

"Your confession will rat him out. The cops aren't stupid. They have cameras all over the harbor, probably the Mystic Piers, too. If you spill, they'll find out what happened, all of it, and it's say-onara Rod." Mickey lowered the widows and killed the engine. "Avakian murdered Gert Murray and he maimed Cheyenne, and you caught him. Avakian knew he'd be going away, so he weighed his options and tried to deep-six himself. And I don't blame him for taking the Dixie dive, because I'd have done the same thing."

"What about me? What about Diaz?"

He rubbed his face with two open palms.

"First of all, you didn't kill Avakian."

"I tied an anchor to him."

"I didn't say you were smart, but he's alive, you didn't kill him." Mickey faced me. "I know you're feeling bad, and I know you want it to go away, but it's not that simple because of Rod. Here's what I want you do. I want you to tell Fr. Dominic what happened, all of it. Will you do that for me?"

"Go to confession?"

"Exactly," he said. "If you're going to spill, spill to Fr. Dominic."

"And Diaz goes to prison?"

"Give it time. Maybe Avakian will confess like he said he would."

"What if he doesn't?" I asked.

"Give it a week, Dermot," Mickey said. "See what's up in a week. Decide then."

I knocked on the rectory door and Fr. Dominic opened it. He looked at me and said, "What's wrong, Dermot? I noticed you left Mass early today."

"I need help."

"I thought you might. Come in."

54

BUCKLEY LOUIS SAT in a wheelchair behind his big oak desk in our Navy Yard office. We were looking toward the harbor at the storm clouds looming on the horizon. The Red Sox had already canceled tonight's game.

"The DA's office sent a report." Buck picked it up and read from it. "The police found an abandoned car and ran forensics on it. They got the fingerprints, DNA, too." Buck placed the report on the desk. "It's the car that hit Cheyenne Starr."

"What?"

"DNA, blood, it's definitely the car that hit her."

"Where did they find it?"

"Mystic Piers," he said. "There's more. The prints on the car matched the partial print in Gertrude Murray's apartment. Do you understand what I'm saying?"

"You're saying the man who killed Gert is the same man that ran over Cheyenne."

"That's right, the same man."

I already knew this, thanks to the boat ride with Avakian, but I had decided not to tell Buck about the Avakian kidnapping. Why burden him with my boneheaded play?

"This proves that Victor Diaz is innocent," I said.

"Not yet, not until the cops catch the accomplice. If the accomplice's prints don't match the prints on the car, Diaz is off the hook."

"Tell me more about the car."

"It was sitting at Mystic Piers for days. One of the shippers figured something was wrong when a tire went flat. He checked it, saw the dent, saw the blood, and called the police."

"The car had been there for a while."

Lightning flashed and thunder growled. The skies opened up. Whopping raindrops pelted the office windows and bounced off the walkway surrounding Dry Dock 2. People scattered for cover, holding newspapers over their heads. Seagulls flew up and perched under warehouse eaves, waiting for the downpour to end. A commuter boat docked at Pier 3. After the ramp had been secured, passengers raced off the boat to awaiting cars with glowing headlights. Everything changes when it rains.

"Gertrude Murray and Cheyenne Starr," Buck said, "what do you think connects them? I'm only bringing this up because sooner or later the police will be asking."

"They both kept great company," I said.

"Get serious."

"Okay, I'll get serious. I'm the connection. But Cheyenne was a victim of circumstance. The driver mistook her for me. I was the intended target."

"And why would the driver want to hit you?" Buck asked.

"He probably thought I was getting close to identifying Gert's killer."

"Yeah, I came to the same conclusion, and so will the cops."

55

I WAS WALKING up Bunker Hill Street when I saw a gray sedan idling in front of my house. The tinted windows and curly antenna got my attention. The LEDs behind the grille increased my suspicions, and my suspicions were confirmed when Partridge stepped out of the car. I went up to him.

"Detective Partridge," I said. "Touring the neighborhood?"

"Hanson wants to talk to you, hop in."

"Where's your affable partner, McClellan?"

"Get in the car, Sparhawk."

I got in the front seat and buckled up, hoping for blue lights and sirens. Instead, Partridge puttered along, taking in the sights. After dillydallying through the city, choosing the least direct route, he rolled into police headquarters and escorted me inside. As we were walking into the building, Partridge said, "I have to warn you, Hanson is ripping mad at you."

"Is that supposed to be news? He's always pissed at me."

"McClellan dropped a massive snapping turtle into Hanson's pool. Hanson got on his raft with a gin and tonic in hand and floated to the deep end, and the snapper attacked, biting through rubber. Hanson sank in front of his party guests."

"I stand forewarned."

"I didn't get to the warning part yet. McClellan made an

anonymous call to Hanson and told him that you threw the snapper in the pool."

"Great."

"Like I told you, too much combat in Kandahar for McClellan. The poor guy is soft as shit and getting softer by the week."

And he's armed with a gun.

In the front lobby Detective McClellan greeted me with a wiseass smirk on his face, and after he finished taunting me, he and Partridge took me to an interrogation room. I sat at a long table and looked at my cellphone. I had missed a call from Kiera McKenzie, the forensics expert who examined the bag for prints. Partridge's car ride and Kiera's phone call couldn't be a coincidence.

I was in trouble.

McClellan said, "You got big problems, Sparhawk, and I mean big fuckin' problems." He walked to the door and peeked out the small window. "And not just of the turtle variety."

"It doesn't look good for you," Partridge added.

"Here comes Hanson." McClellan hurried back to his seat. "Your ass is grass."

The door burst open and Hanson stormed in, wearing his customary attire: navy blue suit, purple tie, starched white shirt, all of which complemented his silver hair and darkening face. He sat across from me and opened a folder, but the folder was a prop. It could have been upside down for all the attention he paid to it. He tightened his Windsor knot with a tug, locking in the anger. He was now ready to take my head off. Partridge and McClellan sat quietly and waited for the beating to begin. Hanson didn't disappoint them.

"Where were you two nights ago?" he said.

"Home," I said. "Why?"

"I'll ask the questions, Sparhawk. Can anyone verify that?"

"No," I said, hoping my voice didn't quaver.

Hanson stared at me. I tried not to blink. He got up and walked around the room and came back to the table and stood over me.

"Kiera McKenzie ran fingerprints for you. Am I correct in saying that?"

I told him he was correct.

"Why did you go to Ms. McKenzie?" he asked. "Why didn't you come to me?"

"The way I obtained the prints was iffy."

"Iffy, as in inadmissible in court," Hanson said. "Dumb move as usual, Sparhawk, you worked against your own self-interest."

"I know."

"Here's something you don't know. The prints you gave to Ms. McKenzie matched the partial print at the Murray murder scene, which means they also matched the prints on a car we recovered at Mystic Piers. What do you have to say about that?"

I didn't answer. *Why did Kiera tell me the prints were too smudged to use?*

"Ms. McKenzie told us about the first test she ran, which she limited to the bag. Those prints were useless. She later dusted the bottle inside the bag and guess what she found—usable prints. The prints on the bottle matched the prints on the car and the partial in Gertrude Murray's apartment. Ms. McKenzie told us that the bottle came from Avakian's Market, so guess what we did next."

"You went to Avakian's."

"Boy, you're smart." He closed the folder. "We talked to the employees. One of them, a squirrelly twerp who thinks he's a fuckin' genius, told us something interesting. Do you know what he told us?"

"I'm sure you're going to tell me."

"He told us that a big man wearing a ski mask kidnapped Mr. Avakian at gunpoint two nights ago. The twerp called the Avakian family and told them about it, but they never called the police, because they were waiting for the kidnapper's demands."

"That's awful."

"According to the twerp, the masked man forced Avakian into his own car," Hanson said. "Tell me, Sparhawk, do you have any idea who the masked man might be?"

"Don't know."

"Avakian hasn't been seen since." Hanson walked round the room in tightening circles, a hawk closing in on prey. "Why did you suspect Avakian of the murder, Sparhawk? You must have had a reason to get his prints."

"It was a hunch."

"A hunch?" He scoffed. "Come on, you can do better than that."

"I was asking around town about the silver coins Gert collected. When I went to Avakian's Market I got a bad vibe."

"A bad vibe?" He grunted. "What's that supposed to mean?"

"Something struck me as fishy."

"Are you getting smart?"

I told him I wasn't.

"Here's what I think happened," Hanson said, never sounding more confident. "You figured out that Avakian killed Gertrude Murray. In turn, Avakian figured out that you pegged him for the murder, so he tried to run you down. But the poor prick is half blind and hit Cheyenne Starr instead. You figured out that Avakian hit Cheyenne, you wanted revenge, you kidnapped him, and you killed him. How does that sound for a crime theory, Sherlock?"

"Solid work, Dr. Watson, but there's one major flaw. It wasn't me."

"I'm going to nail you, Sparhawk, and I'm going to enjoy doing it. Oh, there's one more thing. Don't leave town." He went to the door. "By the way, I know about the snapping turtle. If you go near my pool again, I'll drown you."

Hanson left the room. If he had tail feathers, they'd be preening.

Detective McClellan roared laughing and said, "Ehhh! Hanson's gonna drown you the next time I throw a snapper in the pool. Ehhh!"

"You're fucked in the head, McClellan."

"You're not too sharp yourself, Sparhawk. Ehhh!"

The only thing sharp about McClellan was the shrapnel in his head. I opened my mouth to say something, but Partridge cut me off. "Get out of here, Sparhawk."

56

I WAS DRINKING coffee at the kitchen table when the doorbell rang. I ignored it and kept working on the *Boston Globe* crossword puzzle. I filled in twenty-one across, eight letters, the clue was 'opening,' the answer was premier. The bell rang again. This time I went down to answer it. Rod Liveliner was standing on the porch, looking over his shoulder toward Bunker Hill Street. I invited him in, but he said no and asked me to come out to join him. The whole thing struck me as strange, but I complied, joining him on the porch.

"What's wrong?" I asked. "Is it about the boat?"

"Joe Gun wants to see you at his club tonight."

"Joe Gun?" Joe runs an after-hours club in a Charlestown industrial park, in an area that turns into a ghost town when the sun goes down. It's the perfect location for illicit activities. "Why didn't he call me himself?"

"Joe doesn't like phones, too risky."

"I gave *you* my number. Why didn't you call me? Why trek over to my house?"

"I'm getting nervous, Dermot. All this stuff with Bo Murray and Skeeter and Victor Diaz, let alone the Avakian thing. I don't want a phone record, no offense. The last thing I need is to end up in court with some asshole lawyer carving me up."

"Did Joe say what it was about?"

"No, they just said they wanted to talk to you."

"They?"

"Joe and his friend Smitty. You know Smitty, the guy Joe played basketball with, they said it was very important." Rod crossed his flaking forearms in front of his chest. "They drove to Little Mystic Channel to talk to me. It must be important."

At two in the morning I drove to Joe Gun's place, which was housed in a dilapidated building next to an elevated section of I-93. The noise from the highway was deafening, even in the wee hours of the morning, but the club itself was shielded from the outside world, with acoustic tiling and thickly insulated walls.

I went inside and stepped into a different domain, a make-believe domain where it was always happy hour and last call never comes. There must have been two hundred or more people drinking cocktails as if it were the Roaring 20s, hollering and singing and toasting to life. Watching it, I thought of *The Great Gatsby*—without the gowns and tuxedos. They gathered round tables and stood in circles. Some leaned against the forty-foot bar, as three bartenders hustled to keep up with the demand. Five or six waitresses delivered drinks to the cash-paying customers, who threw around tens and twenties, expecting no change.

I saw Joe Gun sitting at a table, overseeing his realm, accompanied by Smitty, his lifelong friend. I weaved through the tippling throng and sat in the chair between them. Joe was drinking a lime beverage in a tall glass. Smitty had a can of Red Bull.

"Rod gave me your message," I said.

Joe Gun's white-blond hair was thick and wavy, and he combed it straight back so that it looked like a lion's mane. His pal Smitty had big blue eyes that continually scanned the club, checking for potential problems. Twenty surveillance cameras couldn't take in what Smitty's two eyes took in, and they sure as hell couldn't interpret the data the way Smitty could.

"Coffee?" Smitty said.

I said yes and he signaled for a waitress.

"We were just talking basketball," Joe Gun said, "specifically the Boston Celtics, the greatest sports franchise ever assembled. Who do you think was their best player of all time?"

I played along.

"Paul Pierce and Kevin Garnet took home a banner," I answered, knowing I was about to get a lesson in Celtic lore.

"You're still young," Joe said. "Bird was better, and Russell and Cousy were the best. And you can't forget Cowens and Havlicek. Havlicek won eight titles, and so did Heinsohn."

"Heinsohn won ten if you count his coaching," Smitty added. "Sam Jones won ten, too."

"What do we talk about next, the Bruins?" I said. "Bobby Orr and Phil Esposito?"

The coffee came. Smitty slid the mug over to me and said, "Are you still looking into Gertrude Murray's murder?"

"I am," I said.

"Still trying to prove Diaz didn't do it?" Smitty went on. "Or his accomplice?"

"Diaz didn't kill her, and neither did his accomplice."

Smitty looked at Joe Gun, who leaned forward and said, "Sometimes people drink a little too much in here, and sometimes the drink loosens their tongues. Are you following what I'm saying? And sometimes they say things they might later regret, or they say things they might not remember at all. You of all people know what I'm talking about."

"Sadly."

"Crystal Light lemon," Joe said, holding up his glass. "Anyway, getting back to what I was explaining, sometimes they lie, trying to impress the saps around them. You never know what to believe is what I'm saying."

"What did you hear, Joe?"

Joe Gun and Smitty looked at each other. Their tacit exchange conveyed more than words ever could. Townie telepathy. Smitty nodded, Joe leaned farther forward. "This conversation we're about to have never happened, understood?"

"The Charlestown code of silence," I said. "We'll be like *Get Smart*, the cone of silence. You can be the chief, I'll be Max."

"Wise guy," Joe said. "There's this guy who drinks here, a lawyer, and he got a little sloshed one night and started crying in his beer. Self-pity is pathetic, especially when the whiner is drunk. Anyway, this lawyer I'm talking about, he started moaning to me and Smitty, slobbering all over us like a two-year-old child."

"And?"

"And he said he was responsible for Gertrude Murray's death." Joe Gun glanced over his shoulder. "He said Gert's murder was his fault."

"Did he say why?" I asked.

"He didn't elaborate, and I didn't ask, because Smitty and I figured Diaz killed her. Then we heard maybe he didn't. Then we heard you were ruffling everyone's feathers downtown, so that's why we asked you here tonight, to tell you what we heard. The lawyer I'm talking about, the one with the loose lips, his name is Remus Shonta."

"Shonta, I've seen his office," I said. "He's in Sullivan Square, across from the Teamsters building."

"Shonta specializes in wills," Joe said. "He writes and files wills in probate court. He's a back-office lawyer, which is a good thing, because he'd wither in front of a judge. The poor bastard drinks like a whale, hardly coming up for air."

"Is he here tonight?"

"He just left."

I drank some coffee and sat back in the chair. The joint was now completely jammed and the atmosphere was getting rowdier. The bartenders shifted into overdrive, and the waitresses raced and delivered trays of drinks.

"Do you ever get raided?" I asked.

"Never," Joe said. "The cops were the first people I talked to before I opened. There are more guns in here tonight than in the armory in Dorchester." Joe Gun lit an expensive cigar and blew out the match with a stream of smoke. "The good thing about running an illegal saloon is everything that happens inside it is legal, like smoking."

Investigating Remus Shonta seemed like a waste of time—knowing that Avakian had killed Gert Murray—but I went to his law office the next morning anyway. When I got there the receptionist asked for my name. I told her, and she told me to take a seat, and she went into Shonta's office. Five minutes later she came out and said, "Mr. Shonta is tied up all morning. Can you come back later this afternoon, say four o'clock?"

"Tell Shonta I'm friends with Bo Murray," I said. "If he doesn't talk to me now, I will go to Bo with what I know."

She stiffened. "Please wait here," she said, and went back to his office.

A moment later a puffy-faced man with a pink complexion came out. A gray rumpled suit covered his plump body, and scruffy stubble of gray dotted his blooming jowls. He stared, apparently not sure what to make of me, and invited me into his office. He sat behind his desk. I sat across from it.

"So, you're friends with Bo Murray," Shonta said.

"More like enemies, you know how it is in Charlestown."

"The receptionist said you were his friend."

"I lied."

"What's going on here?" Shonta's eyes watered in an effort to focus. "I could call the cops, you know."

"You won't," I said. "I work for the law firm that represents Victor Diaz, the man accused of murdering Gertrude Murray."

"I heard about the murder, it's an open-and-shut case."

"You heard wrong. Diaz didn't kill her." I paused for effect. "A reliable source told me that you were responsible for Gert's death. You admitted it to him. Would you like to tell me about that?"

"Me? I don't know what you are talking about. I never said any such thing, and you can't prove I did."

"I figured you'd say something like that." I got up and walked to the door. "Have a good day, Mr. Shonta."

"That's it? That's the end of it?"

"Not by a long shot," I said to him. "When Victor Diaz goes to trial, and as you know it will be a very public trial, we will subpoena you to testify."

"Testify to what?"

"To why you said you were responsible for Gertrude Murray's death. You can tell it to a jury. We'll also subpoena the man who overheard you saying it at Joe Gun's club, and I can tell you this much, he won't be happy about getting dragged into court. And, of course, Bo Murray will be there when you spill what you're hiding."

"Jesus, it's not what you think. I didn't—"

"I don't care what you did or didn't do, Mr. Shonta. You don't look like a killer to me, but I know you're holding something back. All I want is information. If I get it in court, fine. If I get it right here, right now, that's fine, too. Tell me what you know, and I'll be on my way."

Shonta tapped his left index finger on the desktop, stopped, opened the bottom drawer and took out a bottle of Old Thompson. Needless to say, the seal was already broken. He poured an inch into his coffee cup and drank it in a swallow.

Pride goes out the window when the thirst is upon you.

"I was Gertrude Murray's lawyer," he said. "I wrote her will, which included the administration of a small life insurance policy."

"How small?" I asked.

"Twenty thousand dollars," he said. "One of the Murray twins, he said he was Arnold but I can't tell them apart, came to my office and asked me why his mother was here the day before. I told him I couldn't discuss it with him, period. Arnold, if that's who it was, pulled out a gun and aimed it at my head. He was shaking and sweating, and I got scared, so I told him about his mother's will. What else could I do?" Shonta poured another stiff one but didn't drink it—yet. "I told him that the proceeds were to be divided equally among the three sons, but that there was a stipulation clause in the will."

"Explain."

"If any of the Murray boys were in prison at the time of Gertrude's death, they would be excluded from the will."

"What else?"

"That's it."

That's it? "If that's it, why do you feel responsible for Gert's death?" I asked.

"She was murdered the day before Bo got out of prison."

It began to sink in.

"Thus eliminating Bo from the will," I said while I thought. "You feel responsible because Gert was murdered before Bo got out."

"That's right."

"And you think Arnold killed her because you told him about the stipulation."

"Yes, I do," he said, with his hand shaking. The whiskey must not have kicked in yet, but it will. It always did for me.

I couldn't picture Arnold killing his mother for a bigger piece of a tiny pie. But it's not so tiny if you're an addict, and Arnold was an addict. Remus Shonta drank the whiskey that had been aging in his mug.

"You never told me your name," he said.

"Didn't the receptionist tell you?" I was surprised she hadn't. "My name is Sparhawk, Dermot Sparhawk."

"Sparhawk?" He gripped the edge of the desk with both hand and steadied himself.

"Are you okay, Shonta?"

"Fine, fine, I got dizzy," he said in a pant. "It's nothing."

"What's going on?"

"My blood pressure, it's low, and sometimes I get lightheaded. Sometimes I even faint." He refilled his cup, this time with two inches. "Will there be anything else?"

"That's all for now," I said. Why did he get spooked when he heard my name? Maybe it was the alcohol. I wrote my phone number on a piece of scrap paper and handed it to him. "If the booze gets too much, call me."

"I suppose you're a member of assole-holics anonymous."

"And proud of it," I said. I let his comment pass.

I was the same way when I was in my cups.

From Shonta's office I drove to the projects, still feeling like I was wasting my time, and parked in front of Bo Murray's building. I climbed the stairs to the second floor and banged on his door. Bo greeted me in his usual manner.

"What the fuck do you want?"

"I'm looking for Arnold," I said.

"Arnold ain't in." He stepped into the hallway and flexed his bony arms. "What do you want with him?"

"I need to talk to him about an important matter," I said.

"You'd better tell me what's going on, Sparhawk."

"Tell Arnold to call me."

"I'm not tellin' Arnold nothin', asshole."

I drove from the projects to the lowly hellholes that attracted the outcasts of society. Flophouse lobbies, fleabag motels, abandoned buildings slated for demolition, anywhere the castaways might go. I parked on Southampton Street, aka Methadone Mile, a derogatory term I detested, and went into Samantha's Tap, a refuge for addicts and alkies of every stripe. Samantha's Tap made the Aces & Eights look like it deserved a rave review in the *Improper Bostonian*.

I went inside.

Junkies and dopers commiserated at tables, drinking sugary soda and bartering for butts. A glue sniffer cowered in a corner—I could smell the pungent fumes when I walked by him. Weather-beaten winos, who no longer occupied the lowest rung of the social ladder, thanks to the addicts, drank white port and muscatel from pint bottles they'd rustled in. I saw a Townie named Billy sitting dazed in a booth. Dozing next to him was a reedy woman zonked out on something that left her near catatonic. I sat across from them and loudly cleared my throat, which prompted no reaction.

"Hey, Billy," I said, hoping to roust him. "Billy, I'm looking for Arnold Murray."

He wouldn't or couldn't answer me, his drug-addled brain unable to respond. I countered his inertia with an unethical ploy. I laid a twenty and a ten on the table in front of him. He came to life like a concussed fighter after a whiff of smelling salts.

"Huh?" Billy said. "Arnold?"

"Arnold Murray," I said. "I'm looking for him."

"He ain't here today," Billy slowly drawled. "Don't know where he is. Maybe he's at Forneau's in Egleston."

"I checked Egleston Square."

"Try Chelsea, the place by the creek, I think it's called Rosen's Cafe," he said, and with that the conversation ended. Billy's head fell to the table, counted out. I put the twenty and ten in his shirt pocket and slid out of the booth. As I was getting to my feet, his female companion said with a wheeze, "Lemme catch my breath. I shouldn't smoke, but I got asthma."

"Excuse me?"

"My asthma is bad today, very bad." She shook loose a cigarette from a generic pack. "I think I can help you with Arnold Murray."

"I'm listening."

"Try Joe Gun's. Arnold's drug dealer drinks at Joe's." She yawned and sniffled and started to fade. Her pupils constricted to two black dots, dots as tiny as typewriter periods. "Arnold meets him there sometimes, at Joe's. But whatever you do, don't tell Joe Gun about the dealer. He'd skin him."

"Thanks," I said, handing her ten dollars, feeling guilty for giving her a downpayment toward her next jag.

I thought about Arnold's motive for murder, trying to analyze the whole picture, or as much of it as I could see. Did Arnold partner up with Avakian? It didn't seem likely. I thought about the $20,000 life insurance policy. Divided by three, Arnold gets sixty-seven hundred, divided by two he gets ten grand, an increase of thirty-three hundred, which was more than enough incentive for a jonesing burner like Arnold to do something desperate—but murdering his own mother?

I decided that Arnold's wasn't the killer. Addicts don't take the long view. They look at the immediate, the moment in front of them, as they scheme for the next fix. They aren't Wall Street investors, waiting for quarterly earnings. They're slot-machine players, waiting for the clang of coins.

And besides, the Murrays loved their mother. They might be screw-ups, and they might be stupid, and they might be murderers, at least in Bo's case, but they wouldn't kill Gert. No man kills his own mother. Although a friend of mine stepped over his dead mother to go out for a night of drinking. But he didn't kill her. She was already dead when he walked past her. When the ambulance came the next day, she was as cold as the linoleum floor she lay on.

That night at three in the morning I went back to Joe Gun's, and the atmosphere was the same as the last time I was there, raucous with festive drinkers. I looked around for Arnold Murray and didn't see him. The person I did see, however, was Joe Gun, who was sitting at the same table with Smitty, and I again sat between them.

"How did it go with Remus Shonta?" Joe asked. "Did he own up to it?"

"Not exactly," I said. I told them about Gertrude Murray's will and the will's stipulation. Joe and Smitty's reacted the way I had initially reacted: benignly.

"So what, there was a stipulation," Smitty said.

I repeated it. "Remus Shonta told Arnold Murray about the stipulation, that if any of the Murray boys were in prison—"

"Yeah, yeah, you already said that. What am I missing?" Joe Gun said.

"Gertrude Murray was murdered the day *before* Bo got out of prison," I said.

"And you think Arnold killed Gert to cut Bo out of the will. Arnold gets half instead of a third." Joe looked a Smitty, and Smitty said, "Arnold didn't kill her."

"How do you know?"

"Arnold was here the night Gert got murdered," Smitty said. "The police called and told us about it. They called us because they knew Arnold comes here sometimes. The word got around the club, and everyone started buying Arnold drinks."

"Arnold was here?"

"Sorry, Dermot," Joe Gun said. "I'm afraid we sent you on wild goose chase. Smitty and I are Arnold's alibi. He couldn't have done it."

"Shonta must have assumed what you assumed," Smitty concluded, "that Arnold rushed to kill Gert before Bo got sprung. That's why Shonta felt responsible for her death."

"I guess you're right," I said.

I had come full circle on the Shonta lead, and like a dog chasing its mangy tail, I was back where I started, having accomplished nothing. I knew the runaround with Shonta would prove to be a fiasco because of the fingerprints on the car, fingerprints that belonged to the killer, Mr. Avakian. The Murray murder had been solved, and the murderer was probably out of the country by now, never to be heard from again.

But I had to follow-up on Joe Gun's tip. And if I looked at it objectively, it wasn't a complete waste of time. Shonta provided a piece of information I didn't know before, the stipulation in Gert's will. Maybe the information would come into play later, completing the picture of what really happened the night of Gert's murder, or maybe I had wasted my time and was trying to rationalize it. I drove to the Cape and got a motel room in Dennis Port, just to do it, just to get out of the city for a night.

57

WHEN I GOT home the next evening I found a note on the kitchen counter from Harraseeket Kid, telling me to go to the basement. When I got there I saw Kid with Ester Diaz, and sitting next to Ester was Bianca Sanchez, the clerk I got fired. They looked at me.

"What's going on?" I said.

"Juan Rico will testify," Ester said, referring to Victor's accomplice. "He will tell the judge that Gertrude Murray was already dead when they broke in."

"What changed his mind?" I asked.

"Bianca called a friend," Ester nodded at Bianca. "Her friend convinced Juan to do the right thing."

"That's good news for Victor," I said.

"Rico will do time for this," Kid added.

"Which makes his testimony that much more impressive," I said.

We talked about Juan Rico's loyalty to Victor, and after we praised him for five or ten minutes, Kid said, "Ester is definitely moving in with me. We're getting her things tomorrow."

"I can't wait." Ester smiled. "I appreciate all you've done, Dermot."

"Glad to help."

Bianca told us that she needed to get going, and I said I had things to do, and the two of us left the basement together. She went up the stairs in front of me, and when we hit the first landing, she lost her footing and fell backwards into me. My hands slid up to her armpits, brushing her breasts along the way. She sighed and turned and we kissed. A pang of remorse surged through me. The loss of Cheyenne, I couldn't shake it. I've never been so blue in my life, never so lost, and I guess I didn't give a damn anymore, because Bianca and I were still kissing. I felt no guilt—guilt requires a conscience, and mine was gone. We went up to the moon crater I called home, took off our clothes without saying a word, crawled under the dusty covers, and stayed under them all night.

In the morning she made coffee and carried two cups to the so-called bedroom, the coffee giving us an excuse not to talk.

"I'd better get going," she said. "I have a busy day."

I asked her if she needed a ride. She joked, saying I had already given her one she would never forget. We laughed, but it was a hollow laugh.

"I parked near the monument," she said.

"Way up there?"

"No one will know I stayed the night." If she parked at the monument, blocks from the house, she must have planned the tryst. I had assumed it was an impulsive act, an irresistible urge on her part, but it seems I was merely a stop-gap to fill the void left by Victor. Worse things have happened to me. Bianca said, "It's not you, it's Ester."

"I don't understand."

"Victor's sister, Ester," she said. "I don't want her knowing my business. That's why I parked near the monument. I thought maybe we'd, you know, and we did."

"Now I understand." It became clear that this was a one-off, which was probably for the best. "I'm sorry about your job."

"I loved working there." She got out of bed and dressed. "They treated me like family. Mr. Avakian trusted me to drive him home at night."

I drank the last of my coffee, and when I placed the cup on the end table, a weird feeling came over me. "You drove him home at night?"

"Every night," she said.

"Why?"

"He has night blindness. Mr. Avakian can't see so good after dark, so I was his nighttime driver. He called me his personal teamster."

"He doesn't drive at night?"

"He has a restricted license. I think they call it a daytime license, but even in the daytime he's a terrible driver. And at night, forget it. He couldn't steer out of the alley behind the store without bumping a wall or a pole. One time he hit a fire hydrant."

"At night," I said.

"Yes, at night."

I was on my feet putting on my own clothes. Avakian couldn't have run over Cheyenne, not if he couldn't see her.

"I wonder why he didn't update the chart," I muttered to myself.

"What chart?"

"The lottery chart," I said. "Why didn't Mr. Avakian put a red star next to Gert Murray's winning number?"

"Mr. Avakian doesn't update the chart, Nick does."

"Who's Nick?"

"His son." She got out her keys. "Nick hates the market, but he's the only heir. Mr. Avakian is leaving everything to him. But instead of being glad about it, Nick complains about it. He complains like a baby, a big baby."

"I remember him now—he *is* big." And he probably has big feet and blood-stained shoes. "I forgot how big he was."

"Nick is a loser," Bianca said. "The old man is the brains of the place. Nick is nothing but a deadbeat looking to cash in."

I had kidnapped the wrong man. Mr. Avakian was taking a dive for his son.

58

I DROVE TO the auto-body shop to talk to Glooscap about the Avakian matter. When I got there he was sitting inside his office smoking his trademark bulldog pipe. His Native American profile remained stoic while he puffed. The pungent smell of burning tobacco filled the air with a strong vanilla scent. I sniffed hard to get some into my nostrils.

"I can tell something is weighing on your mind," he said. "Am I right in saying that?"

"You're right."

"Please tell me about it."

I told him about Stellwagen Bank and Rod Liveliner and Mr. Avakian's attempted suicide and Superintendent Hanson and Captain Pruitt and Bianca Sanchez and Nick Avakian. I told him about the impending threat of Bo Murray and his moronic twin brothers, Arnold and Albert. I told him about Joe Gun and Smitty and Remus Shonta and the stipulation in Gert's will.

Glooscap, who never utters a vulgarity or an off-color remark, never turns a slang phrase or a wisecrack, and never cuts corners with contractions, deliberately puffed his pipe and said, "Rod used extremely poor judgment in bringing you to Stellwagen Bank. He should never have done that. Rod is partly to blame for the mess you are in."

"It's my fault," I said. "Rod told me he owed my father a favor from Vietnam, and I talked him into taking me out there. I took advantage of him."

"You most certainly did." Glooscap rested the pipe in an ashtray, as lingering smoke drifted from his nose. "Kidnapping, Dermot? I cannot believe it."

"I know."

"I can only surmise that your love for Cheyenne blinded you to the insanity of your actions. What were you thinking? What are you going to do now?"

"I toyed with the idea of telling Bo Murray about Nick Avakian," I said. "After all, Nick murdered Gert. But that would be akin to putting a hit on Nick. I thought about strangling Nick with my bare fucking hands—sorry for the language—but I'm beyond that now, even though he nearly killed Cheyenne."

"You do not sound beyond it to me."

A clattering noise came from the garage area, a can tipped over, a tool skittered across the floor. The office door opened and Cheyenne's father, George, came in. He walked to the middle of the small room. I got up and stood in front of him, searching his eyes for a sign, an indication, trying to read him. I took a chance and embraced him and said, "George, I am sorry."

"I know you are."

"I never meant for Cheyenne to get hurt." I turned and extended my hand. "This is my uncle, Glooscap."

George looked at Glooscap and said, "Which tribe?"

"Micmac, from Antigonish, Nova Scotia," Glooscap answered. "You?"

"Cherokee, from New Echota, Georgia, the last Capital of the Cherokees," George said, and then looked at me. "I know this is hard for you, Dermot. Cheyenne loves you very much. She has been crying for days. She wants you to know that she loves you, but she cannot be with you right now."

"But maybe some day?"

"Maybe, but you have to let her go for now." He held my shoulders in a fatherly way and said, "What I'm about to tell you is most difficult." He handed me an envelope. "These are Cheyenne's ultrasound results. The night she was run over she was going to the car to get these pictures."

"She's pregnant?"

"Cheyenne *was* pregnant. She lost the baby," George said. "I am sorry to be the one to give you the horrible news. Cheyenne asked me to tell you, because she couldn't bring herself to tell you in person."

"She lost the baby?"

"Yes, she lost the baby."

"I have to see her."

"Cheyenne left for Arizona this morning," George said.

"I'm on the next plane."

"No," he said with force. "She loves you, but she is asking you to leave her alone. Please don't contact her."

"We lost our baby?"

"You are not to blame, Dermot. It was the accident, not you. I have to go now."

George walked out of the room.

"Fuckin' Nick Avakian," I screamed. "I'm gonna kill him."

"Wait." Glooscap got to his feet. "Do not act foolishly, Dermot. Please, do not—"

Glooscap staggered forward, reaching for me, and collapsed on the floor.

An ambulance took Glooscap and me to Mass General, where a medical team rushed him into ICU. I called Harraseeket Kid from the waiting room and told him what happened. Kid showed up twenty minutes later. An hour after that, a young Asian doctor came to the waiting area and updated us on Glooscap's condition. She said that Glooscap was stable, but they were running more tests. We asked to see him, she told us not yet. She came back an hour later and led us to his room. Along the way she filled us in.

"His vitals are perfect," she said. "His heart is strong and his oxygen levels are superb. He has the pulse rate of a marathoner. We are trying to ascertain what caused the collapse, but at the moment we still don't know."

Glooscap was sitting up in bed, watching the Red Sox game when we came in. Except for the tubes and monitors, he looked the way he always looked, hale and hearty and ready for life. He told us that he was feeling fine, that there was nothing to worry about, and that he couldn't understand what happened in the garage. Glooscap hit the mute button and instructed Kid to take care of a few things at the shop, tedious tasks that had to be done.

"I just got here," Kid complained. "I came to see how you were doing."

"I am doing much better, just a harmless scare," Glooscap told him. "I might be laid up for a few days, so please take care of those things for me."

Tension filled the air, as Kid stared at his father, insulted by his dismissal. Then Kid shrugged. "Yeah, sure," he said. "No sweat. I'll take care of everything."

"Dermot," Glooscap said to me. "I would like you to stick around after Kid leaves. We need to talk about something."

Kid took the hint and left the room. I waited for Glooscap to begin, but his eyelids sagged and he fell asleep. I stayed for an hour, waiting for him to wake up, but his breathing deepened and slowed. I heard snoring. The monitors beeped evenly, almost hypnotically, and his blood pressure and pulse remained per-fect—perfect for a trained athlete half his age. Confident that he was in good shape, I left the room and headed for Charlestown.

I crossed the locks behind the Garden to Paul Revere Park, and that's when it happened. The Murray twins, Albert and Arnold, got out of a car and pointed guns at me. They had parked under the Zakim Bridge, hidden from public view, a surprisingly smart move on their part. One of them, I can't tell them apart, told me to get in the back seat. I did as he instructed. You don't argue with buffoons holding guns.

"Drive, Arnold," Albert said. He tapped my head with the gun barrel and told me not to move. Bo had tapped my head in the same way. "We're going for a ride, Sparhawk, and you're gonna keep your mouth shut. Get on the floor facedown."

He covered my head with a blanket. We drove for what seemed a long time, a twisting route that went up and down hills. My stomach filled with nausea. We finally pulled into a garage. I knew it was a garage because of the smell. It reminded me of Glooscap's shop. The engine shut off, the garage door came down.

"Get out," Albert said. "Sit over there."

He pointed to a wooden chair next to a workbench. Arnold, the driver, went to the 'shitter to take a leak.'

"What now," I asked Albert.

"Now we wait."

We waited for hours. Night had fallen. The Murray twins kept the garage dark, the only light coming from a low-wattage desk lamp on the workbench. They kept their guns trained on me, dying for an excuse to shoot. I did my best not to give them one. Albert's cellphone rang, breaking the silence. He answered, mumbled something incoherent and hung up. He looked at Arnold and said, "Let's go."

Arnold opened the garage door. They got into the car and drove away, leaving me behind. What was going on? I stepped out to a quiet street and saw the Boston skyline in the distance. Based on the position of the Hancock Tower and the Prudential Building, I was north of the city, probably in Cambridge or Somerville. The quiet street led to Hampshire Street, which was in Cambridge, and I plotted a course to Central Square, where I hailed a cab.

"Where to?" the cabbie asked me.

"Charlestown," I said. "Avakian's Market, 725 Terminal Street."

The cabbie clicked the meter and drove to Charlestown, taking the Prison Point Bridge. He cruised along Chelsea Street, next to the Navy Yard, and I wondered if I'd ever see the harbor again after I killed Nick Avakian. The cab went under the Tobin Bridge and turned on Terminal Street, where the dark skies were illuminated with blue light—police blue. Five cruisers and a fleet of unmarked cars surrounded Avakian's Market. A cop stepped into the street, stopping the cab, and told the driver to turn around. The street was closed he said. I paid the driver and got out. The cop told me the street was closed to pedestrians, too.

"I'm friends with Hanson and Pruitt," I said.

"Good for you," he replied. "Get back in the cab and go home."

I heard gunfire and bullhorns and more gunfire. The salvo of shots was followed by yelling and confusion. Cops were running everywhere. Radios squawked and sirens chirped. I got back in the cab and the driver took me home.

59

SHE CALLED THE next morning and and told me to meet her at Uncle Joe's Diner at eight o'clock. When I got there I saw Kiera McKenzie sitting in a booth reading a newspaper, her red hair pulled back off her face. I sat across from her and noticed a cup of coffee waiting for me. I added cream and sugar and drank some. She folded the paper and put it on the bench she sat on.

"I finished processing Avakian's evidence at five this morning," she said. "The crime scene was a mess."

"I heard about it."

"Do you know what happened?"

"I don't know anything for a fact," I said. "But I think Bo Murray killed Nick Avakian, because he found out that Nick murdered Gert."

She looked out to the street. "Bo was right about Nick killing his mother. Nick's prints matched the partial in Gertrude's apartment. I'm sorry to tell you that they also matched the prints on the car that ran over Cheyenne."

Kiera confirmed what I suspected, that Nick was the killer.

My eyes filled with tears, and I turned away. I didn't trust myself to speak.

"But I'm guessing you already knew that," she said, as Betsy the waitress refilled our cups. We sat silently for a minute, long enough for the 93 bus to stop and pick up riders and drive on to the Navy Yard. Finally, Kiera said, "I wonder how Bo Murray found out about Nick Avakian."

I had a pretty good idea, but I would never divulge it.

"I don't know," I said.

"No one seems to know, and no one has seen Mr. Avakian since the kidnapping. Maybe Bo was behind the kidnapping, too."

"Makes sense."

"I also need to apologize to you, Dermot."

"Apologize for what?"

"I told Hanson about the fingerprints on the wine bottle before I told you." She drained her coffee cup in one final gulp. "I had to, it's my job."

"I'd have done the same thing."

"I tried to warn you, but I couldn't get through." She looked at her cup. "I left a message. I hope you got it in time."

"Everything's fine, Kiera."

"Hanson and Pruitt will come at you hard on this," she said. "The media, the newspapers, they all want answers. Last night was a complete nightmare. It made national news."

"I saw the police cars and heard the bullhorns and gunshots." I smelled the cordite in the air, too. "Hanson and Pruitt must be a little perturbed."

"You are the master of understatement," she said. "Nick Avakian is dead. Bo Murray is dead, suicide by cop. A store clerk got shot. He'll probably die. And Mr. Avakian has vanished. It is safe to say that Hanson and Pruitt are not happy. They're looking to hang this on someone, Dermot." Kiera stood from the table. "I hope you can handle them."

"Me, too."

60

THEY CAME AT me hard, just as Kiera predicted. Superintendent Hanson and Captain Pruitt pinned me in an interrogation room and hammered me with questions about Avakian's Market, accusing me of abetting Bo Murray in Nick Avakian's death. My only hope to stay out of jail was to lie through my teeth. No lawyer, con man, or politician could have done it better. At one point I thought Hanson had boxed me in.

"How did Bo Murray know about Nick Avakian, Sparhawk?"

"Why would I know?"

"How did Bo know that Nick killed his mother?" Hanson leaned across the table. "Bo was no genius, we both know that, so how did he figure Nick for killing Gert?"

"Why are you looking at me," I asked.

"*Someone* told him, and you're the only one who suspected Nick Avakian. That's why you gave Kiera McKenzie the wine bottle with Nick's prints on it, because you suspected him."

Actually, I suspected Mr. Avakian

"That's true, I suspected him."

"And then you told Bo about the matching prints," Hanson continued. "And that dumb bastard acted on it and blew Nick's head off."

"I didn't know about the matching prints until *you* told me, Superintendent. I asked Kiera to check the bag, not the bottle, and the prints on the bag were smudged. I didn't find out about the matching prints until *after* the police found out. Bo had friends in the department."

"What's that supposed to mean?"

"Half the police force grew up in Southie, Dorchester, and Charlestown, where Bo ran his rackets." I leaned closer to Hanson. "Hell, you yourself knew about the prints before I did."

"I'll tell you what we're going to do," Hanson said, gritting his perfect teeth. "We are going to sit here, and you are going to tell us everything you know."

"I don't know much."

"You are going to tell us why you suspected Nick Avakian in the first place. You are going to tell us how you got word to Bo Murray about Nick Avakian. And you are going to tell us what the hell happened to Mr. Avakian. Do you understand me? You are going to tell us every goddamned, infinitesimal, minuscule thing there is to tell, so start talking."

I thought it over. This was no time to be coy.

"I hope you have time," I said, "because it will take a while."

"Talk!"

"Before I start I want to make one thing clear," I said. "I did not tell Bo Murray about Nick Avakian."

In the end I told them virtually everything, except for one self-incriminating detail: the boat ride to Stellwagen Bank with Rod Liveliner and Mr. Avakian. Why sign my own prison sentence, and why get Rod in trouble? I told them about the winning lottery ticket, and when I did, their attitude changed. The lottery ticket was new information. It gave them Nick's motive for robbing Gertrude Murray.

Hanson said, "How did *you* know about the winning lottery ticket?"

"The missing red star," I said. And then I lied like a bastard, hoping to keep Skeeter Gruskowski out of it, but I doubted I could. "When I saw the missing star next to the winning number, I got curious and went to lottery headquarters in Braintree. After some wangling I got the name of the man who cashed it."

"Who the hell was it?" Hanson asked.

"A Jamaica Plain businessman named Michael Cawley," I said. "He cashes lottery tickets for people who want to protect their privacy. He takes a piece of the winnings, of course, but it's a legitimate business from what I understand. Cawley cashed the Avakian ticket. If you want to talk to him he's the golf pro at Franklin Park Golf Course."

Hanson leaned back and tapped a gold pen on the table and then he came forward with a smile on his face.

"You are full of shit," he said. "How did you know the ticket was sold at Avakian's? The chart must have dozens and dozens of numbers without red stars."

I couldn't protect Skeeter. I had to tell the cops what I knew, and when I finished telling them, Hanson waded in. "You're telling me that you followed Gruskowski across the country on Route 66, and you didn't catch up with him until he came back here to Charlestown."

I told him he was correct.

"And you're telling me that because Gertrude Murray was getting forgetful, she gave Gruskowski a winning lottery ticket to hold."

"Yes, but Gruskowski didn't know it was a winner until days later, days after the murder," I said. "And Gertrude never knew at all. She was murdered before she found out."

"According to Gruskowski he didn't know until days later," Hanson said. "He could have been snowing you, Sparhawk."

"Maybe, but I don't think so."

"Then Gruskowski gave you a copy of the ticket, and you went to Avakian's Market, and you checked it against the chart, and you noticed there was no red star next to it."

"That's right."

"Jesus." He tossed the pen on the table. "Keep going."

I told them about Norm Yorsky, Mr. Avakian's friend at the lottery, who called the market and left a message about the winning ticket. I speculated that Nick Avakian heard the message, reviewed the surveillance tape, identified Gertrude Murray as the buyer, and saw an opportunity to escape a lifetime of working at the market, a job he hated. Gertrude's winning ticket was Nick's ticket to freedom. Nick went to rob her and killed her in the process.

I went back to the red star again. I told them that I was looking at the chart a week earlier, checking my lottery tickets—actually Kid's tickets—and that Nick Avakian must have seen me scanning the chart. I further speculated that Nick started to worry that I'd make the connection to Gertrude Murray's ticket. Nick decided to get rid of me by running me down with a stolen car, but he hit Cheyenne instead.

Hanson and Pruitt looked at each other but didn't speak. Then Hanson talked about Victor Diaz and admitted that he had nothing to do with Gert's murder. As they were talking about Diaz, I thought about Bianca Sanchez, and I decided to keep her name out of it if I could. She had enough troubles, thanks to me.

By the time the interrogation ended, Hanson and Pruitt seemed somewhat satisfied with my take on the matter, but that was another assumption on my part. I was getting used to making assumptions.

Hanson pointed at me and said, "We still don't know what happened to Mr. Avakian. And we still don't know who told Bo about Nick Avakian."

Pruitt said, "Maybe Bo whacked Mr. Avakian before he took out Nick. It wouldn't be the first time he kidnapped someone. Remember the bank manager's wife?"

"Of course I remember." Hanson stared at me. "I still think you got word to Bo about Nick Avakian."

"Why would I?"

"Revenge," he said. "Nick ran over Cheyenne." He got up from the table. "I can't prove it, not yet, but I'm staying on it until I do. I will go through every phone call and every email you ever sent, and I will nail you. Now get out of here!"

He didn't have to tell me twice.

61

I DROVE TO Glooscap's garage and went in. As usual, the smell of pipe tobacco filled the work area, and when I entered his office, he was blowing a cloudy stream from his mouth. He looked at me and took another puff. I sat in a chair.

"How are you feeling?" I asked.

"I made a quick recovery. They let me go this morning."

"I know they did." I leaned forward and rested my elbows on his desk. "You faked the heart attack to save me from myself."

"I do not know what you are talking about." He studied the smoldering bowl, sniffed it, and bit on to the stem. "I felt light-headed, fainted, and that is all there is to it."

"The doctor said you have the heart of a stallion. Your pulse could power a compressor."

"That is good to know."

"You got word to Bo Murray," I said. "You told Bo that if he kidnapped me, you'd tell him who murdered Gert."

"That is absurd."

"You wanted Bo to kill Nick before I did."

"Is that what you think?"

"You saw my anger, you knew I'd act on it, and you pretended to get sick. You did it to to stall me," I said. "You tied me up long enough for Bo to do his thing. Bo ordered the twins to kidnap me and detain me until he whacked Nick Avakian."

Glooscap said nothing in response, and in his stillness I wondered if I'd hurt his feelings. Here was Glooscap, my uncle and my father's half-bother, doing something he would never do under ordinary circumstances: fingering a man for murder. He did it to protect me.

I said, "I appreciate that you always look out for me."

"I still do not know what you are talking about, but if you will indulge me, I would like to move on to another matter." He struck a wooden match and relit the bowl. "I am inviting a friend to join us. I want you to listen to what we have to say. Agreed?"

"Sure, agreed."

"Good." Glooscap dialed his cell phone. "Ah, you are in. Can you drop by the garage to discuss the matter we talked about earlier? Very good, I will see you then." He hung up.

"What's this about?" I asked.

"You shall see," Glooscap answered. "Be patient."

An hour later the door opened and Rod Liveliner came in, his face gray, his movements stiff. I wondered if he had slept since the Avakian incident.

"Please have a seat, Rod," Glooscap said. "Dermot, I am concerned about you. Your judgment is impaired, and your anger is escalating. I am afraid that you might do something foolhardy and end up in prison for a long, long time."

I hung my head.

"Your decisions have been crackpot. You kidnapped a man, and you were planning to kill Nick Avakian. I saw the vengeance in your eyes."

"He stole everything from me, my future wife, my future child, everything."

"I love you. You are blood, my brother's boy. I will to do anything to safeguard you."

"What am I supposed to do now, crawl into a cave and hide?"

"In a manner of speaking, yes," he said. "That is why I asked Rod to join us. I believe you two can help each other."

Glooscap turned to Rod as a prompt to speak.

"I'm sure it's just paranoia," Rod said, "but the man I borrowed the boat from is asking questions, and I'm getting nervous. The way the cops can test for DNA these days, it wouldn't take much to put Avakian on that boat."

"Hundreds of gallons of seawater splashed over the decks," I said. "The evidence had to be washed away."

"I'm just saying I'm nervous." Rod rubbed the back of his sunburned neck. "I don't want to end up in an interrogation room, Dermot. I'm a lousy liar."

"I can teach you a few tricks," I said.

"Dermot!" Glooscap shouted. "No more levity, this is a serious situation."

His outburst silenced the room. After a moment he said, "Here is my proposal, a proposal I feel very strongly about. I have already spoken to Rod about this idea, and he is on board with it, so it is up to you, Dermot."

"I'm listening."

"Leave Charlestown," Glooscap said. "If the police cannot find you, the police cannot question you. Go away. Let your head clear. Give yourself a chance to regain perspective, to get on solid footing again. Rod will procure a vessel large enough for a distant sea voyage, and you two will go on a long trip together." Glooscap leaned closer to me. "What do you say, Dermot? Will you do that for me? You will be helping Rod, too."

The idea of leaving town held a certain appeal to me, and the appeal increased when I thought of Superintendent Hanson and Captain Pruitt coming at me again.

"How much do you need, Rod?"

He told me.

62

ROD SAID HE would need a couple of days to find a suitable boat, something secondhand that he could get on the cheap. He'd be shopping for a live-aboard cruiser that could handle the harsh ocean elements of the North Atlantic. I asked him where he was planning to take us, the Arctic Circle? He didn't laugh. I gave Rod the number to one of my three burner phones. He would call me when he secured the vessel.

The next two nights I stayed in a Quincy hotel near the Braintree split, in case the Boston cops came looking for me in Charlestown. I figured that staying in Quincy would make it harder for them to track me down, but I doubted it would if they really wanted to find me. On the third day Rod called. He had found a boat.

"She's a beauty," he said. "A Beneteau 48 with a fifteen foot beam, twin steering stations, and a master bedroom. I practically stole it. Do you sail?"

"Not as a crewman, no, but I've been on sailboats."

"You're about to get an education in seamanship." Rod said, sounding more upbeat. "Don't worry. She's outfitted with an inboard diesel to maneuver in and out of docks."

"You're the captain."

"Meet me tomorrow morning in the Navy Yard at Dry Dock 2, eight o'clock."

"Aye, aye."

I couldn't sleep that night, so I packed my bag and checked out of the hotel, dropping the first of my three burners, the one Rod had called me on, into a trashcan as I exited. From Quincy I drove to Hull Gut and parked at Pemberton Pier across from the windmill, which was spinning like an Evinrude. I stood on the rocking pier and dialed Buck Louis on my second burner.

"Buck, it's me."

"I knew you'd be calling."

"I'm leaving town for awhile." I leaned on the railing and watched the waves slap the pilings and the gusts starching the flags. "I'm not sure how long I'll be away, maybe a few months, maybe longer."

"You got in trouble, didn't you," he said.

"The move is preemptive," I said. "I'm not a fugitive or anything."

"I don't suppose you want to tell me where you're going."

"I don't know where I'm going, and that's the truth. But even if I knew, I probably wouldn't tell you. It's not that I don't trust you, Buck. I trust you like a brother. Hell, I consider you a brother."

"Me, too."

"I want to protect you," I said. "If you don't know where I am, no legal scheming in the world can get it out of you."

"Be careful."

"I will," I said. "Can you handle things at home?"

"You've got nothing to worry about." There was a pause. "You'll be incommunicado."

"Yup, incommunicado."

There was another pause, and then Buck said, "Victor Diaz is out of jail. He was cleared on the murder charge, but he's awaiting trial for the B and E. I'll be defending him and Juan Rico."

"Okay," I said, sensing there was more to come.

"Victor wants to meet with you. I know you're on a timeline, so if you can't meet him, I'll tell him."

"I'm leaving in the morning."

"It'll have to be tonight."

"No, not tonight." I thought for a moment. "Tell him I'll meet him tomorrow morning at seven o'clock in Kormann & Schuhwerk's Deli."

"Kormann & Schuhwerk's in the Navy Yard, seven o'clock," Buck said. "I'll tell him."

We hung up and I tossed burner number two into the water.

I called Harraseeket Kid on the third burner to talk to him about the same issue, my decision to leave the area.

"Yeah?" he answered brusquely.

"It's me, Dermot," I said. "I'm leaving Charlestown for a spell."

"On the lam?"

"That's one way to put it. I'm not sure when I'll be back."

"It's just as well you're leaving," he said. "It'll give me time to restore your apartment."

"Thanks for doing that."

"Ester moved in yesterday," he said. "She said the sound of the sump pump clicking on and off puts her to sleep at night."

"A woman satisfied with a basement apartment? She is something special, Kid."

"You could say I'm moving up."

"I mailed you a check for the renovations."

"I'll fix it up real nice for you," he said. "I'll take care of everything around here. Talk to you later."

Kid hung up before things got sentimental. I threw the burner into the water. I now had no phone, and I found the disconnection liberating. I also found it scary.

I was sitting in Kormann & Schuhwerk's eating a sesame bagel and drinking coffee when Victor Diaz came in and joined me at the table. I signaled the waitress, and Victor ordered an espresso.

"Thanks for meeting me," he said.

"Glad to."

He played with a menu and then he placed it in the holder. "I got mouthy at Nashua Street and I wanted to apologize."

"There's no need."

"You and Buck Louis saved my ass."

"We did our jobs, nothing more."

"Well, thanks."

The waitress came with his espresso. I looked out to the harbor, at the docks and piers and moorings, at the sailboats and yachts, barely rocking on the calm surface. Seagulls and terns dove in graceful sweeps, cawing and shrieking, adding movement to the seaside snapshot.

"The junk is killing me," Victor said, "the heroin, it's eating me up."

"You ever think of going to a meeting?" I asked. "I'm a member of AA."

"I'm not really a drinker. I drink, but I—"

"Most members are dually addicted these days. The alcoholic-only is nearly extinct."

"Were you dually addicted?"

"Yes, whiskey and beer," I said, smiling. "Don't overanalyze it. Ask yourself this simple question: 'Do drugs cause my life to become unmanageable?'"

"I guess the answer is pretty obvious," he said. "I just got out of jail, and I almost went away for life."

"Try a meeting, see if you like it. Maybe Bianca will go with you."

"No." He pushed away his cup. "It's over with Bianca."

I wondered if she told Victor about our romp. "Did something happen?"

"Yeah, something happened." He looked down at the table. "When I was inside I had time to think about her, and something started to bother me. Did I tell you she visited me at Nashua Street?"

"You didn't."

"She visited me there and the next thing I knew I was in a side room getting laid. Can you believe it, getting laid by a woman in jail?"

"A conjugal visit, life can be good, even in jail."

"I found out later that she had to fuck one of the guards so she could have sex with me." Victor paused. "That was the price she paid to be with me."

"Desperate times," I said. "Don't hold it against her."

"The sex with the guard, I didn't like it." He looked into my eyes. "Hey, it is what it is, right? The sex with the guard, but that's not what bothered me."

"Oh?"

"After we had sex, Bianca made a confession." He splayed his fingers on the Formica top and his knuckles turned white. "She told me that she got involved with Nick Avakian. She said that Nick took advantage of her after I got locked up, but I didn't believe her."

"Why not?"

"Nobody takes advantage of Bianca. She takes advantage of them. So when she said that about Nick, I thought it was bullshit." He paused again and flexed blood back into his fingers. "I feel kind of funny talking about Nick. He's dead."

"I'd like to hear what you think."

"According to Bianca, Nick was a complete dolt. The only thing he could do was make deliveries and stock shelves, and even then he screwed it up. He couldn't even figure out how to work the cash register."

"Because he's a dolt."

"Mr. Avakian asked Bianca to train Nick. She showed him how to use the computer and cameras and lottery machine, and they started getting close, because they were working together—that's what she told me. And then she admitted she started drilling him. And I got mad."

"Don't blame you."

"The sex with Nick didn't surprise me, because I know how Bianca is with sex. She uses it to get what she wants. You've seen Bianca. Who could say no to her?"

"No one I know."

"So she visits me in jail, and takes care of me in a side room, and everything is great."

"But?"

"But I got the feeling she wanted me to kill Nick. Here I was in jail, and she's trying to get me to kill Nick. She didn't come right out and say it, not directly, but that's what she wanted. Bianca knew I had friends on the outside I could call."

"But you didn't."

"No way, I'm not a killer."

"You must be angry at Bianca."

"It's over with her, and it's probably just as well. With a girl like Bianca, you never really know what's going on." Victor got up from the table. "Thanks for meeting me, and thanks for getting me another chance at life. Who knows, maybe I'll see you at one of those meetings." He shook my hand. "Whiskey and beer, huh?"

"I staggered in my sleep." A thought came to me. "What about boxing? When I was in Lowell investigating, Barney D'Amico said you had tons of talent."

"Barney said that?"

"He said you had a tremendous right, a lead-pipe right he called it." I stood with him. "Use the talent God gave you, Victor."

"I miss Barney," he said. "Maybe I'll go back to him after I get the legal problems cleaned up. Barney's all right. Gotta go, I'll see you around."

I watched him go out the door.

I now knew the whole story, the sequence of the crime. Bianca Sanchez conspired with Nick Avakian to rob Gertrude Murray of the winning lottery ticket. Bianca was the mastermind, the puppeteer who pulled the strings, and Nick was her puppet. She heard Norm Yorsky's phone message to Mr. Avakian; she searched the surveillance video; she found that Gert had bought the winning ticket; and she manipulated Nick into robbing her. That's why she wanted Nick dead, because he could implicate her in the crime.

Bianca knew that Nick would wilt under interrogation. She knew that if he talked she would go away as an accessory to murder. Bianca couldn't let that happen, so she went to work on Victor in jail, but Victor was too smart and saw through her ploy. Then she went to work on me, and I was too spellbound to see through it. She handled me like a computer mouse. Point, click, a man dies. Although I didn't kill Nick directly, he died because of me, a fact that only highlighted the genius of Bianca's cunning. She played it beautifully. If I were any stupider, I'd owe the world IQ points.

Bianca got away with it, and there was nothing I could do about it. I had no hard evidence that connected her to the murder of Gertrude Murray. I suppose that if I wanted to rationalize it, I could say that Bianca didn't intend for Gert to be murdered, but when you send a screw-up like Nick on a job, you have to expect the worst.

Bianca walks. I walk. Maybe we're not much different.

I thought of Mr. Avakian, tied to an anchor, attempting suicide, and forced to leave the country. I thought of Nick Avakian, gunned down by Bo Murray. And Bo is dead, too. I was linked to Bo's death, because Glooscap intervened on my behalf, saving me from my own idiocy. He put Nick in Bo's crosshairs, and as a result, he put Bo in the crosshairs of the police.

What a mess. And I caused it.

Self will run riot—that's what we call it in AA.

63

AT EIGHT O'CLOCK I was waiting on Dry Dock 2, on the aluminum pier where the commuter boats come in. Smiling yuppies in designer duds walked by me, talking and gesturing, enjoying the day. I found their joy incongruent, out of place, a contentment I couldn't fathom. A large sailboat came into view with the sails furled. It motored gently through the flat water and eased to a stop in front of me. Rod Liveliner leaned out of the cabin and yelled, "All aboard!" He didn't bother to toss a line.

I hopped on the boat.

He steered out of the harbor on a flawless summer day, the sea air warm and salty and smelling fresh, and the breeze at our back easing us along. When we passed Castle Island, Rod unfurled the sails and killed the engine, and we glided out of the harbor under the power of the wind. Rod announced that we had reached the deep anchorages of President Roads and then Nantasket Roads, and soon after that we passed Little Brewster Island, home of Boston Light, flashing white every ten seconds. Before long the seagulls bid us adieu and land was out of sight. I joined Rod at the wheel.

"Was it you, Rod?" I asked. "Did Glooscap tell you to tell Bo about Nick Avakian?"

"Why do you think I'm on the boat?" he said, steering toward the horizon. "Which way do we go, north or south?"

"South," I said.

"Any destination in mind?"

"The Caribbean island of Montserrat," I said. "I have a friend there who can help us out."

"Monserrat, I'll plug it into the GPS." Rod worked the onboard computer and a map came up. "There it is, Montserrat, in the Leeward Islands, part of the Lesser Antilles chain. These gadgets are great, aren't they? I'll chart the course." He punched in the data. "We're all set for the voyage. This friend of yours, can we trust him? Will he keep his mouth shut?"

"He's an exile himself," I said. "His name is Tossy O'Byrne."

"Tossy O'Byrne? That's a funny name."

"He's a former soldier in the Irish Republican Army. Tossy had to get out of Belfast a couple of years ago. We helped each other out, and in helping each other, we learned we were related."

"Irish Republican Army?" Rod chuckled. "He won't talk."

"We'll be safe down there with Tossy." I opened a pack of Effie's Oatcakes and said to Rod, "Want one? They're made from a secret family recipe in Nova Scotia."

"Sure, why not."

Acknowledgements

This book would never have happened without the love and encouragement from my wife, Maribeth. She is my everything. Her instinct for story and expertise in editing put this novel in shape. And her support kept me in shape.

I am deeply indebted to the following story consultants: Dick Murphy, Chris Hobin, and John Malkowski. Each of them offered outstanding suggestions. They commented on dialogue, story logic, scene depiction, and word usage—you name it, and they had something to say about it, all for the betterment of the novel.

To my high school classmate and friend, Heidi Hurley, art director of the Braintree Public School, who designed the book cover.

And, of course, you always need your family. A special thank you to my my mother, Patricia MacDonald, and my uncle, Frank Carney. Their edit corrections (there were many) and their story comments, especially their comments on one aspect of the story that I rewrote at their urging, brought believability to scenes that had run askew.

About the Author

BEST-SELLING AUTHOR TOM MACDONALD has Boston in his blood. Born, raised, and living in the Boston area, Tom knows of what he writes. As Director of Harvest on Vine Food Pantry in Charlestown, he brings his fictional work to the pages of *Murder in the Charlestown Bricks*. This is his fourth novel in the Dermot Sparhawk Series. Tom has a B.A. in sociology from Stonehill College, an MBA from Boston College and an MFA in creative writing from the University of Southern Maine. Tom teaches writing at Boston College.

CPSIA information can be obtained
at www.ICGtesting.com
Printed in the USA
BVHW081326070119
537203BV00011B/1329/P

9 780996 733236